IS IT FISH FOR DINNER?

My Time in Yesterday's Police Force

PART II

James Graham

Copyright © James Graham [2024]

The right of James Graham to be identified as author of this work has been asserted by him in accordance with sections 77 and 78 of the Copyright, Designs and Patents Act 1988.

All rights reserved. No part of this publication may be reproduced, stored in a retrieval system, or transmitted in any form or by any means, electronic, mechanical, photocopying, recording or otherwise, without the author's prior permission.

Any person who commits any unauthorised act in relation to this publication may be liable to criminal prosecution and civil claims for damages.

This book is a work of fiction. Names, characters, places and incidents are either products of the author's imagination or are used fictitiously. Any resemblance to actual events, locations, or persons, living or dead, is entirely coincidental.

First published by James Graham [2024]
ISBN: 9798303747814
https://jimgraham579293579.wordpress.com

PREFACE

I am, or was, Police Constable 776 and, later, Detective James 'Jim' Graham. I served my community for over 32 years as a police officer. Part I of my police career was captured in the book, 'Pushing Doors Marked Pull.' This is Part II of that wonderful journey in a largely forgotten era of policing, the 1980s and 1990s. These are true recollections of those early days, from leaving Sandford Division, Westshire Constabulary and joining the Regional Crime Squad (RCS). The later book will detail my time as a Patrol Sergeant and an investigative supervisor in Oldtown.

My Crime Squad journey began in 1989 and the accounts could be from any police force in the country during that era. The characters are transferable. My story is of human tragedy, humour, police life and, of course, the many unsung heroes. The police forces and names of individuals have been changed for the privacy of all.

CHAPTER ONE

A DIFFERENT LEVEL

The walk to the church was a lonely one. It was cold outside and my denim jacket gave me no protection. I didn't care, nor did I feel the chill. My mind was elsewhere. I glanced over my shoulder to see Eddie and Dave close behind me. It was Thursday afternoon, the 21st of December 1989 and the main street in Priestown was busy with Christmas shoppers. It was very dull as I looked around intently for a police presence. I couldn't see any. The Christmas lights twinkled in the fading afternoon light. I carried my holdall and contents as we headed for the church steps opposite the Building Society. This was our arranged meeting point and escape route. We huddled in the church doorway.

'Here,' said Eddie as he handed me a black balaclava, 'put it on now and give me a gun.'

'Not here, Eddie,' I said through clenched teeth. We need to be closer. We can't walk across High Street wearing balaclavas and holding guns.'

Dave was beginning to put the balaclava over his head.

'Wait, wait,' I said to him, 'wait until we get across the street.'

We were now out of the doorway and in full view of the Building Society on the far side of the High Street.

'Just give me a fucking gun now, I'm going for it,' said Eddie. He bent down for my holdall and tried to unzip it. I had to act and act quickly. I grabbed the bag away from him and put it over my shoulder, rattling the metal contents. Eddie and Dave were under the impression I had brought the shotguns as agreed. Dave looked at both of us, now wearing his black balaclava. I could see the bristle of his moustache and beard sticking through the material. His eyes were like sharks, black and cold.

'I'm ready when you are, let's do it now,' said Dave in his scouse accent, moving towards the steps down to the High Street. The tension was mounting and the adrenaline started to rush around my body. I peered around the corner, again looking for the police. They weren't in place.

'Come on, let's fucking go,' said Eddie, now becoming agitated.

I had no choice, police or no police; I had to go. The robbery at the Building Society was going ahead and happening now! I walked slowly down the steps and looked over my shoulder to see Dave still wearing his balaclava. Eddie was right behind me, grunting as he started to pull on some gloves. I stopped at the bottom of the steps, now on High Street. People were now looking at Dave in the balaclava. Eddie went into his jacket pocket, pulled out his balaclava, then threw me one.

'Gun, gun,' screamed Eddie, 'fucking gun, come one.'

Now was the time. I unbuttoned the Levi jacket and took it off. I opened the holdall, placed it inside, and waited. It seemed an eternity. I looked at Eddie. He looked straight at me. Then, BANG! I saw white, pure white dust before my eyes. The surge of pain was excruciating. It was like being hit full-on with the force of a train. I lost my breath as the force of the impact knocked me forward. My head jolted backwards with a whiplash effect. My legs buckled under the impact. I hit the ground hard, unable to break my fall. For a moment, time stood still. Nothing moved. The pain in my back now rushed through my shoulders; my cheek pressed hard into the cold, wet floor. I could smell the tarmac of the roadway. I tried to lift my head, but there seemed to be a significant clamp on my neck. I couldn't move.

'You're under arrest, pal, for attempt armed robbery. You don't have to say anything unless you wish to do so and what you say may be given in evidence. Barry, Barry, get the holdall mate, where's Col, Col, Col.'

The voice came from behind my head, and I was now conscious that someone was grabbing my arms. Someone was kneeling on my back and I couldn't move. Breathing was difficult. I turned my head to take the pressure off my cheek and looked straight into the eyes of Eddie. The whites stood out in contrast with the dark balaclava. He was on the floor with a uniformed officer sitting on top of him. Blue lights flashed all around us. Time then seemed to speed up, as if someone had pressed fast-forward. It became chaotic, shouting, screaming, revving engines, car doors banging, but Eddie's eyes never left me. I felt the handcuffs snap into place and I was lifted to my feet. It was cold and my tee shirt offered little protection. My arms were grazed and I now felt a surge of pain in my back and shoulders. I looked again at Eddie and he was glaring at me, his eyes never moving from me. He never blinked. The voice from behind me shouted,

'Col, Col, put yours in this first van here.'

I turned around to see Dave being put into the back of a white police van. He didn't look back and was now devoid of his balaclava. I then heard a dog barking and growling and could see a German Shepherd dog on a long leash wandering between us. The leash wrapped around Eddie's legs as he was led to another police van. He was also devoid of his balaclava. He looked over his shoulder, staring at me until he got to the back of the van, eventually disappearing out of sight.

'Not your lucky day pal, is it?' the voice said as I was marched across High Street towards the back of another waiting police van. A uniformed constable opened the doors in front of me and I was pushed in the back from behind and fell forward into the van, unable to break my fall. I hit the van floor and someone grabbed my legs and pushed me further in. One side of the doors closed. I was still lying on my front and looking down when the voice said,

'Merry Christmas, mother fucker,' and I was engulfed in darkness as the other door closed.

***

The drive to Priestown Central wasn't too far. I tried to stand up in the back of the police van, but due to the driver's continual swerving from side to side, I found it impossible. I couldn't see outside but sensed the engine slowing and then eventually heard the handbrake being applied. There were shouts from the outside and then silence. I could see small cracks of light through the doors and then the sudden rush of brightness as they both opened. I squinted at the two figures,

'Come on, pal. Out you come,' said one of them as I began to edge myself to the doors. 'Have you searched this one, Col,' shouted one of the voices across the parking area.

'What's in your pockets, pal?' asked another voice as I felt hands go into my jeans pockets. They were deliberately empty.

I was marched through the back gates of the police station, which then clunked shut behind me. An officer was on either side, holding my arms. The station was a hive of activity inside, and I waited in line behind a woman who had been shoplifting at Boots. When she was processed, I was next.

'Yes, Colin,' said the custody sergeant.

'Just before one o'clock, Sarge, I received a radio message that three men were acting suspiciously outside Priestown Building Society. When I arrived, I saw this man carrying a holdall. He was with two others, one of whom was wearing a balaclava. I'm told that one of the other men had a note demanding money on him. I believe firearms are in the holdall, but that's not confirmed. CID are at the Building Society now. I arrested this man for conspiracy to commit an armed robbery and cautioned him, to which he made no reply.'

I gave the name James Bentley and answered as many questions as I could. I was of no fixed abode, which raised eyebrows with the staff. I was led away and could feel the handcuffs being taken off behind me. I felt the pain as the blood rushed back into my hands and fingers. I was told to remove all my clothes and shoes and stand on a sheet of brown paper, which I did. I thought this would be a good time to use the code word I had been given to effect my release. I didn't want to go in a cell.

'If I was to say Timex to you, do you know what that means?' I asked the officer, who I presumed was Colin. He looked at me, puzzled.

'If I was to say Big Ben to you, would *you know* what that means? Now shut the fuck up and take your jeans off.'

'Do you know DS Mick Stephenson or DI Gordon Roberts?' I asked in desperation.

'Nope, nor do I want to. Take off your jeans as they are being seized for forensic examination.'

'I need to speak to them as a matter of urgency.'

'I don't care what you want to do. Now put this white suit on,' he said as he threw me a white paper suit that we see crime scene examiners wear, 'and follow me.'

Having never been in this position before, I didn't know what to do. Should I declare myself and tell the officer exactly who I was and what I had just done? Or should I stay silent and let things take their course? I chose the latter.

We stopped at the cell door, and I smiled. It reminded me of my early days with Tommy Goodall, who opened bombs in the hatch. I missed Tommy. Always positive and quick to remind me that if I stood to the side, I would only get my arms blown off if it was a bomb. That was reassuring. The keys went into the lock, and the clanking noise was followed by the creaking of the iron door as it slowly opened.

'In here,' said the officer.

'Timex…. Timex,' I said again, 'Speak to DS Stephenson and tell him I said Timex.'

The cell door slammed shut behind me. My venture into the world of undercover policing wasn't going to plan.

The walls were full of graffiti, and the smell was a mixture of disinfectant, urine, and stale beer. A figure was lying on the only bench and covered in a blanket. He was facing away from me, but I could see he had a shaved head, covered in sores and tattoos. Below the bench, on the floor, was a plastic pouch of tobacco and Rizla papers. There was also a rolled-up newspaper, a polystyrene cup and an empty paper plate. I slid down the wall and sat on the floor.

'I told em I want to be alone, so you best fuck off,' came the voice from the bench, 'you hear me.'

I didn't know what to say or do. So, I sat there in silence in my new white paper suit.

'Are you deaf as well as daft?' said the figure as it started to turn over and look towards me. My cellmate was big and had tattoos up his neck and around the back of his head. I didn't fancy my chances with this one. He started to sit up, and I could see his black T-shirt emblazoned with AC/DC, a new group that was hitting the charts.

'Do us both a favour. Press that button on the wall and get them to get *you* out of my cell, or I will batter you! Understand?' he said, glaring at me.

I stood up and pressed the button. A small red light illuminated above.

'Now, when they come, tell them to get you out of this cell for your own safety.'

'I will,' I squeaked.

'I know,' he said, nodding his head towards me.

He reached down for his tobacco pouch, took out a Rizla paper, and began rolling a cigarette. He began to pull the strands of tobacco thinly and placed them into the paper. I pressed the button again, then slid down the wall into my sitting position.

My new friend then lifted the blanket and found his training shoes. He put his hand inside and pulled out a lighter and lit his very thin cigarette. I knew he shouldn't have a lighter in his cell, but I couldn't do anything about it. Far from it! I could feel my mouth starting to dry as I considered my options.

'Click, clang,' the hatch opened, 'What,' came the voice at the opening.

'I'm told my friend here doesn't want me in his cell,' I said as I walked towards the face, 'Timex, Timex,' I said again. The hatch slid up and slammed into place. If I thought the next sound was going to be the keys turning in the door, I was wrong. My AC/DC friend was now glaring at me as he took a long drag on his roll-up and inhaled deeply. As he spoke, the fumes bellowed out of his mouth and nostrils into the middle of the cell, captured by the rays of sunlight from the frosted glass window blocks.

'If you haven't gone by the time I've finished my ciggy, I'm going to fucking kill you.'

He then leaned back against the wall and still staring at me, banged his head against it. Thud! He glared and banged again. Thud! And again, Thud! Thud! Thud!

'You, my friend, Thud! Thud! Thud, are dead.'

This was a different level. My introduction to undercover policing was not going as planned. I was in big trouble. I braced myself for the imminent beating.

CHAPTER TWO

THE ROBBERY

Let me explain the events leading up to the armed robbery and my imminent beating in the cell. How did it all begin? The week before the robbery, I had been introduced to Eddie and Dave in a pub in the back streets of Priestown. I had been in my new post on the Regional Crime Squad for a few months. It was a steep learning curve and I was attempting to settle into new surroundings, new staff, new supervisors, and a new way of working. This was no Sandford.

I was still somewhat disorientated when I was alone in the office at the beginning of December and the direct line telephone rang. This direct number was only used by staff and criminal informants. It was someone wanting to arrange a meeting with a previous member of the office, a detective called Fred. I knew of him, but he had left the department some time ago. The caller explained that he had just been released from prison and had information regarding an upcoming robbery at the Priestown Building Society. It was one of those 'what do I do' moments as there was no one around to assist.

'Where do you want to meet?' I asked the caller.

'The Red Lion on Fulton estate at one o'clock,' he replied.

I knew of the Red Lion but didn't know it too well. This could be a trap and I didn't want to be lured into anything like that.

'I'll be wearing a pink carnation, sat under a clock, with a copy of the Times under my arm,' the caller said as I laughed at his humour.

'What's your name?' I asked.

'Just call me Jason, I'll tell you the rest when we meet. I was a good friend of Fred's; he'll vouch for me.'

'Make it one o'clock in the tap room of the Railway Inn near the station. I'll find you,' I said as I replaced the receiver.

I knew the Railway Inn and had been there several times while awaiting the train. It was a big, spacious pub in the centre of Priestown, not on some estate. I eventually contacted the unit's Detective Inspector, Gordon Roberts and told him about the phone call. He knew of Jason and his relationship with Fred, the lad who had moved on. I got the nod to go and see Jason, but I would need to take someone as backup.

Just before one o'clock, Shaun, a colleague from the office, pulled the car onto the Railway Inn car park. It was quiet, with the odd car here and there. I noted all the numbers and put the note into the glove compartment. Shaun asked if he wanted me to wait for him outside, to which I agreed. He parked in a corner, facing a wall and slid down in the driver's seat.

'Good luck,' he shouted as I closed the car door and walked towards the front of the pub.

My appearance was now different from those CID days at Sandford. I had been allowed to grow my hair long and supported a beard. People commented that I looked like a Colombian drug dealer. My uniform of the day was my trusted and rather tatty Levi's denim jacket, tee shirts, and jeans.

I walked into the pub entrance and turned right into the tap room. Sat alone in the corner was a middle-aged man in a pin-striped suit. He had short, dark and tidy hair and indeed had a copy of the Times on the table. He was wearing a pink tie and did look the part. I noticed he was very thin and although sat down, appeared tall and gangly. He was wearing small round-rimmed glasses, which he had on the end of his nose, as he peered over the top of them in my direction.

'You're early,' he said, raising his hand to shake mine. Jason, Jason Saunders, pleased to meet you.' I shook his hand, and then he continued, '...and you are?'

'Jim, Jim Graham, pleased to meet you, let me get you a drink.' He then pointed to his half-pint glass and said he would get me one. I immediately declined and told him I'd take care of myself. Saunders was very confident, but I was unsure of him or his motives at this time.

For the next hour, I listened to Saunders talk about his past. A former investigative journalist with a tabloid newspaper, he had fallen foul of the law and his fondness for younger men. He had just been released after serving 9 months of an 18-month sentence for indecency, which he claimed was sex between two consenting adults. He claimed to have photographs of several powerful political figures in comprising poses, which he held in a safety deposit box. He also claimed that his life may be in danger because of his knowledge of such things within the 'establishment'.

Saunders was well-spoken, obviously well-educated, and in a different league from the informants I had dealt with at Sandford. He had been released to a hostel in Priestown, and it was a short-term agreement. He said he would move to Cambridge after he had sorted all his issues and found accommodation. It was in the hostel that he had met 'Eddie' and 'Dave'. Two likely lads from Merseyside who had also been detained at Her Majesty's pleasure. Saunders said that the two lads had been watching the Priestown Building Society on High Street in the town and had noticed that cash deliveries were made just before lunchtime on Thursday. They planned to enter the offices just after lunch and rob the place. They really hadn't thought it through but intended to commit the robbery as Christmas was closing quickly. They had planned their escape route, through the church opposite and down the steps at the rear, to their getaway car. There was only one problem, and it was a big problem. They needed a gun.

Saunders gave me his address, and I told him I would be in touch. I didn't know how to take this further. I also needed to do some checks on Saunders as, on closer inspection, the suit was a little jaded, and the shirt collar was tatty. We went our separate ways and I returned to the car in the car park. Shaun was fast asleep. Good backup, that was. As we drove out of the car park, Saunders stood at the entrance and nodded his head as we drove out.

Back in the office, I chatted through the options with the boss, Gordon Roberts, but he seemed as unsure as I was. I did the checks on Saunders and sure enough, he was who he said he was and had a host of previous convictions for fraud, deception and indecency with children. I decided not to make any enquiries myself at the hostel about Eddie and Dave as I didn't want to prejudice the investigation. I spoke to the neighbourhood police officer, who said he would call in one day on his beat and ask for a list of all the occupants. I also spoke with Fred, the detective who had previously dealt with Saunders. He explained that the information that Saunders had provided in the past was accurate, and he ran a successful operation, apprehending two very well-organised drug traffickers on the back of it.

'I wouldn't trust him as far as I could throw him, though,' said Fred before I thanked him and ended the phone conversation.

Later that afternoon, the office phone rang, and the clerk, Julie, handed it to me. 'It's Mr Saunders, and he wants you.'

'Hello, Jim Graham.'

'Both of them will be in the Strand pub on the Strand estate tonight. They have heard a rumour that someone in the pub can supply guns. Just a thought, but you may want to get in there before them.'

It was just a thought, indeed, and one with which Gordon Roberts was comfortable. I didn't know what I was letting myself in for. I wasn't given any instructions other than to go and see if they turned up and try to introduce myself to them. Later, I would learn the legal side of this kind of covert police work, e.g., entrapment, *agent provocateur,* etc., but it was agreed that I would go along with it and see what transpired.

I phoned home and explained that I would be late again, which was now a common occurrence. The children, Louise and Andrew, were still under three Elaine had her hands full with them all day. She deserved a medal and was a great mother to both. It was a catch-22 scenario as we were a young family who needed money, yet to get that money, I had to work long hours and work away from my hometown. A similar story in every police family up and down the country.

Shaun and I drove up to the Strand pub, which had a reputation around Priestown. I asked around the local officers, who all said they wouldn't go in the place. I didn't tell them why I wanted to know. I had asked to use the new Ford Orion that had recently been issued to the unit and wait for it, the one with the newly fitted phone in the car. This was a technological breakthrough indeed. A phone in a car, would you believe? Whatever next. The fact that you could never get a signal was immaterial; a phone was in the car. If I were to get into trouble inside the pub at any point, I could now ring Shaun, sitting somewhere outside. He had the local police radio handset with him.

Saunders had told me that Eddie and Dave would be in there about seven o'clock. He described them so I knew who I would be looking for. Both are bearded, with scouse accents and Eddie is wearing a donkey jacket with a fluorescent orange panel in the back. I sat in the car with Shaun, counting down the minutes. The tension was rising and I took anything that could identify me out of my pockets, leaving just cash. I took off my wedding ring and gold chain and gave them to Shaun. This was it; I was going in and hoping for a better outcome than the first pub I went to a long time ago when the landlord immediately spotted I was a cop. I said my goodbye to Shaun, left the car and started the long walk to the pub. It wasn't that far, but a thousand things were going through my mind.

The pub was quiet and there was no second look from the server. I seemed to fit in with the environment. I sat with my pint in the corner and started to read the local newspaper. This was pre-social media, don't forget, so we had to keep stimulated in other ways. The Priestown Gazette was fine. It was seven o'clock, and the pub was filling, but no one wore a fluorescent donkey jacket. I noticed a young lad at the bar kept looking at me, and after half an hour or so, I went back to the bar to buy another drink. This time, a shandy.

'Who the fuck are you, mate?' asked the young lad, his hands and arms heavily tattooed, 'what's your business in here, mate?'

'I'm meeting a couple of mates, pal, just waiting for them,' swallowing hard before I replied.

'Who's yer mates?'

'Why? What's the problem?' I asked.

'You're the problem, pal. I don't know you,' he responded as he pulled down hard on his self-rolled cigarette, spitting out the small bits of tobacco, 'not seen your face in here before, pal, that's all.'

The temperature gauge was rising and I considered leaving. I was out of my depth and didn't want to start an argument with the locals.

'Got any baccy mate?' the tattooed lad asked.

'I haven't sorry, but do you fancy a pint?'

'Oh, cheers, mate,' as he drank the dregs in his glass and handed it over to the barman, who seemed to know what he wanted.

'What do they call you?' he asked.

'Jim, Jim Bentley.'

'Cheers, Jim,' as he held the newly pulled pint to his lips before taking a swig.

'Terry Mac.'

'All the best, Terry,' I said.

I returned to my seat, unaware of the two new figures at the bar. One of whom was wearing a fluorescent jacket. Both looked like builders and although I couldn't hear their accents, it was undoubtedly Eddie and Dave, the two soon-to-be Building Society robbers. I watched them as they waited at the bar, joined now by my new best friend, Terry Mac. Terry held them in conversation for a while, I'm sure, about the finer things in life before Terry headed over my way.

'Don't get me giro until next week, Jim, any chance mate?'

With that, I stood up, returned to the bar, and stood next to the two bearded would-be robbers. Terry went to his corner, just to my right. I ordered him a pint of Labatt lager and as the barman delivered it, Terry shouted across to the two beards,

'Salt of the earth is Jim, salt of the earth, mate. He'll help you out,' and once again raised his glass before taking a big gulp. I wandered back to my seat, and sure enough, the two beards followed and sat next to me. Fluorescent jacket Eddie then asked in a strong scouse accent,

'This your local then?'

'Not really, just been waiting for some mates, but I think it's a no-show,' I said.

'We're looking for a big lad who comes in here. Does a bit of buying and selling, you know what I mean?' asked Eddie.

'I'm not sure, pal; there's a few like that in here. What are you selling?' I asked.

'No, I'm after buying, mate. I want something special, mate, you know what I mean, something special to help me and this lad on a job.'

'What do you mean, like a motor or something?' I asked.

Eddie moved closer towards me and furtively looked around the bar. I sat there with a quizzical look on my face.

'Your mate at the bar says you're a good lad and you can sort us out.'

'Maybe I can, but what with?'

'A shooter?'

I looked up at the bar, and once again, Terry raised his glass towards me, blowing plumes of blue smoke up into the lighting. My eyebrows raised somewhat.

'A what! Listen, pal, I don't know you, and it's not every day that people ask me for things like that. Are you setting me up?' I asked.

'Honest, no, mate. I have something planned and I just wanted to know if you could help me, that's it, honest. If you can, you can; if you can't, you can't. We've asked about and were told to look for the big lad with long hair.'

'When for?' I asked.

'Next Thursday.'

'I'll ask around and may be able to help you,' I said, 'I'm going to have to push off now, but if you still want me to help, I'll see you at ten o'clock Monday morning in McDonalds, Wallgate precinct.'

'What's your name? How do we contact you?'

'Jim, like I said, ten o'clock, Monday morning in McDonalds.'

I finished my drink and walked towards the exit.

'Jim,' came the shout from behind. I turned around, and Terry was standing at the bar with his glass raised.

'See you, Terry,' I said and waved in his direction.

I walked out of the pub and disappeared into the Strand estate. I made sure I wasn't being followed and went to the phone box and called Shaun. He picked me up, and I told him what had happened. We both agreed that it couldn't have gone any better. I went back to the deserted office and began to write my notes detailing what had just happened. It had been a long night, but 'job on'.

***

After getting clearance from the boss, I set off walking towards McDonalds in Wallgate precinct in the town centre. It was half past nine on Monday morning, and the instructions were simple: to find out what Eddie and Dave wanted and not to commit myself to anything. As a backup, Shaun came with me once again and sat across the road in a coffee shop. As I opened the door to McDonalds, I could see Eddie looking over the shoulder of Dave and looking straight at me. He was wearing the same fluorescent jacket. I nodded and walked up to their table.

'Anyone want anything?' I asked.

'No, you're alright, kiddo. Get yourself,' said Eddie.

I sat down with them both with my cup of coffee and listened intently to their plan to rob Priestown Building Society this coming Thursday, the 14th of December. Dave was the quieter of the two, but the plan was to rob the place at gunpoint, obviously with my help. Cash deliveries were at eleven o'clock on Thursday mornings, which Eddie presumed were for the ATMs. He said he had been watching the Building Society over the last few weeks since his release. He had a car parked on an adjacent street, accessible through the church and out the back door. He was confident no one knew the escape route. Once in the car, the plan was to head south away from Priestown and then north and back towards the Merseyside area, where he had a safe house.

'Why are you asking me for help? Why aren't you asking people from nearer home?' I asked.

Eddie then explained that he wasn't the flavour of the month 'back home' as he had given evidence against some of his co-defendants to get a lesser sentence on his last job. He had also been released on a temporary licence (ROTL) which could be revoked if he was seen in that area. It didn't occur to him that planning an armed robbery may result in something worse than a recall to prison. I listened rather than asked questions and had two further meetings with the pair. The plan was to either get them to agree I went with them or provide the firearm just minutes before the robbery.

Without insulting your intelligence, it was never my intention to provide a firearm, as I think that could have been dangerous and illegal; plus, I didn't have a spare one knocking around. I went with them both to the Building Society, the church, the back steps, and where Eddie's battered old Ford Fiesta would be parked. Eddie and Dave would pick up some balaclavas from the Famous Army and Navy store, and Eddie would write out a demand note. My excuse for not giving them a firearm was that it would be loaned to me and I had to return it. Of course, there would be a fee, but Eddie said we could take that out of the takings. Eddie did most of the talking and asked some very intrusive questions about my background. I tried to keep my story as 'grey' as possible and there is a saying in the covert world, 'never get caught in a lie.' So, everything had to be as close to the truth as possible so I wouldn't forget, nor would I have to remember to lie after lie.

After the robbery and escape, the two likely lads were going to drop me at a nearby railway station and I was to make my way home by train. The money would be divided three ways and a further meeting was planned in the Strand pub a week later. Eddie and Dave were well on board and no doubt very happy, as if the robbery was to ever take place, they would have written me out of any proceeds, never to be seen again. By now, they had involved themselves in a criminal conspiracy, so there was sufficient evidence to arrest them now. The boss, however, wanted to let it run until the day of the robbery. The final meeting was arranged for ten o'clock, the morning of Thursday 21st December, the day of the robbery.

***

The drive to work that Thursday morning was a little different. I hardly slept with things going over and over in my mind. Going back to my younger days when on bonfire guard duty, I made my own contraption of a gun from copper pipes, wood blocks and black tape. As kids, if anyone ever came to 'burn down our bommy', we would put a lit banger in the copper pipe, then place a marble in behind it, point above the would-be raiders and wait for the bang. The marble flew overhead and although extremely dangerous, we never pointed the guns at people. Honest! It was extremely effective and word quickly got around the area not to mess with the Greendyke lads. So, I put my skills to use again and created another copper pipe and tape contraption.

It was a crisp Thursday morning. The wind was blowing, and the streets of Priestown seemed quiet. The Christmas tree blew in the breeze, and the empty cola can danced down the street before me. I donned my uniform of denim jacket and jeans and walked into McDonald's just before ten o'clock. I saw Dave sitting to the right and Eddie walking towards me with two cups.

'Sorry, lad, I didn't have enough for you. It's payday today, so after lunch, I'll be able to buy you a hundred coffees,' laughed Eddie as he squeezed in next to Dave.

'Where is it?' asked Dave.

'Where's what?' I asked.

'Don't be so fucking smart. You know what I mean, where's the gun?'

'Don't worry, I'll have it for one o'clock; I'm hardly going to bring it in here, am I?'

'Good point, good point,' said Dave as he sipped the coffee, then continued, 'been for the bally's, that's sorted, the gloves are sorted, the note is done, the church is open, so Jim, all sorted and good to go.'

I was about to speak when Eddie leaned in.

'If you're setting us up, kid, I'll fucking kill you. Understand?'

I left McDonald's and returned to the office. As always, Shaun had been my backup, and I sat compiling my notes on what had just happened. I was new to this covert policing game and, honestly, was looking for direction. It seemed I wasn't alone; everyone was looking for direction. I was getting the thumbs up from some of the staff and a 'well done' here and there, but this was way out of my comfort zone.

It was nearing eleven o'clock, two hours from the 'job'. Gordon Roberts, the boss, was in his office. I explained what had happened in the meeting and we were good to go at one o'clock for the robbery.

'Have you told CID?' he asked.

'Have I?' I replied inquisitively.

'Well, who's going to arrest them?' asked Roberts.

'No idea. I thought you would deal with that side?' I replied.

'Me? I'll have to speak with someone,' as he picked up the telephone and waved me out.

I left his office bemused. Shaun was in the corridor. I told him what the boss had just said and the expression on Shaun's face told the story.

'You're joking, you're kidding me,' said Shaun, shaking his head, 'nothing has been sorted to lock these two up?'

At quarter to twelve, just over an hour before the robbery, I walked briskly to Yates's wine lodge in Priestown Centre. Today was the Priestown CID Christmas dinner and all the staff were meeting there. Roberts had spoken to the local command and DS Mick Stephenson was unaware I would spoil his afternoon when I walked into the pub. I didn't know Mick, but after my introduction and a brief explanation, the look of incredulity on his face painted a thousand words.

'No chance, mate, call it off, Christmas do,' he said, shaking his head.

'It's come from your bosses, I'm sorry but…..' I was interrupted.

'Of all fucking days and you have to arrange it for today?'

I walked back to Priestown Police Station, deflated. It was now less than an hour away from the robbery and nothing had been organised to arrest Eddie, Dave, or me. When I arrived back, the boss had gone out, and only Shaun, Julie, the clerk and myself were in the office. I had to call it off.

'Hiya, is Jim here?' asked a tall young man who came into the office. I stood up,

'Yeah, I'm Jim.'

'Danny Walmsley from the pro-active unit. What time is the job, Jim? Is it one o'clock? Not long, have we? I've got six lads to cover it.'

The relief in the room was palpable. Shaun made up the seven and the job was back on. A mini briefing in the office concluded with the final instruction being that I would stand between the Church and Priestown Building Society, with two other men, at exactly one o'clock. When I took my trusted Levi jacket off, that was the sign to come and arrest us. We now had fifteen minutes left. There was no time to lose. I grabbed my holdall, containing my bonfire gun and burst out of the police station doors into the December chill. I went to commit my first and last armed robbery.

CHAPTER THREE

IS IT FISH FOR DINNER?

Let's pick up where we left off. Eddie, Dave and I have been arrested for the attempted robbery. I've been handcuffed and taken to Priestown and the agreed code word for my release, 'Timex', doesn't seem to be working. I'm about to be beaten by an AC/DC fan whose cell I am, hopefully, temporarily occupying. The roll-up cigarette is stuck on his bottom lip and the fumes are rising and swirling around his face. He looks to be in attack mode.

There wasn't much of the cig left when the keys rattled in the cell door. My first attempt at playing a bad guy and armed robber wasn't going how I thought it would, having been rugby tackled to the ground by a seventeen-stone prop forward. Also, my face was grazed and a mess, my hands were blue after being denied blood due to handcuffs. They were hurting badly. I was then placed in a cell with someone who wanted to kill me and when I gave the emergency rescue code, the police officer walked away. Not good.

'Rescued in the nick of time, my friend', said my AC/DC cellmate. He smiled at me, showing a mouth consistent with a packet of Liquorice All Sorts. He was still banging his head on the wall.

The cell door opened and a uniformed officer stood there.

'Bentley, come on, you're going for an interview,' he said.

I didn't take much persuasion and I shot out of that cell. In the corridor was Shaun, who explained that the CID wanted me to complete my written statement as soon as possible so that they could interview Eddie and Dave about the attempted robbery at the Building Society. My introduction to undercover work was a painful one.

I did as instructed and a couple of hours after my 'arrest' on the High Street, my written statement was complete and Eddie and Dave were being interviewed. Both were refusing to answer questions and by now, would have possibly realised the role that I was playing. I walked into the office and didn't know what I expected, but it was empty. Not a sole. No one to say 'well done' or anything. Apart from Shaun, they had all left. I set off for the long drive home. Eddie and Dave were later charged and kept in custody to appear before the Magistrates court in the morning. When I arrived home, the children had waited for me to read their bedtime stories, Meg and Mog. I was tired and sore, but at least I'd made it home. My first armed robbery.

***

The red neon light on the alarm clock illuminated 02.14. The phone stopped ringing, and I knew my wife was talking to someone. My body ached from the previous day's rugby tackle and arrest at the hands of Priestown's finest.

'Yeah, he's here now. Just hang on. I'll pass you over,' said my wife as she stretched the wires for the phone to my side of the bed.

'Hello, is that DC Graham?' said a male voice on the other end.

'It is, yeah.'

'Sorry to bother you at such an early hour, but this is PC Humphreys from Priestown Police Station. I have Jason Saunders at the front desk. There's been an incident tonight at his room involving the discharge of a firearm and someone has sprayed the word 'grass' on his door'

'Right,' I said, 'firearm, anyone hurt?'

'No, they just shot at his door. He's here at the front desk with his belongings. What do you want us to do with him?'

'Erm, erm, I've no idea,' I replied, and genuinely, at that time in the morning, I didn't. When I started to recover my senses, I asked the officer if the night shift would kindly take him to a local hotel. I would visit him in the morning and pay his bill at check-out.

I was up early for the drive over to Priestown and I arrived at the office just after seven-thirty. It was the Friday before Christmas. Usually, it is the busiest day on the calendar for the police. I was the first in and immediately went to find out what had happened to Jason Saunders during the night. Seemingly, someone had discharged a shotgun at the door of his room and sprayed the word 'grass' over it. Officers had attended, but no suspects had been located. Saunders had been interviewed and stated that he heard a loud bang, which woke him. He looked out of his bedroom window but didn't see anyone running away. He told the officers he was too frightened to stay at the hostel and this was retribution for the assistance he had given the police in catching two armed robbers. That was Eddie and Dave, who were still in the cells.

I waited for the boss, DI Roberts, to arrive and told him about the good result from the previous day and the dilemma we now faced with Saunders. It was obvious that friends of Eddie and Dave had somehow found out that Saunders had told the police about the planned robbery. It was agreed to collect Saunders from the hotel and bring him back to the police station while we figured out what to do. The journey to the Avon Hotel wasn't long and Saunders was ready and waiting. He was dressed smartly and was carrying his worldly goods in a black plastic bin liner. I sat him at the enquiry desk whilst I started the search for some accommodation for him. It was ten o'clock, Friday morning, the 22nd of December 1989.

'Hello, Northshire Social Services, how can I help?'

'Hello. My name is DC Graham from the Regional Crime Squad. I'm considering rehousing someone after an incident at his apartment last night. He is a potential witness in an upcoming case....

'I'll put you through.'

'Hello, my name is DC Graham from the Regional Crime Squad. I'm looking to re-house someone after an incident at his apartment last night. He is a potential witness in an upcoming case....'

And so it began. On the desk in front of me was a blank desk jotter on which I started to write the telephone numbers that people gave me to try as they couldn't and wouldn't accommodate Saunders. The main stumbling block was his convictions, especially the sexual ones against children. Saunders was a paedophile! The jotter soon started to fill up and time after time, when I was asked if Saunders had previous convictions against children, the request for accommodation for him was refused.

It was now after lunch and people in the office were packing up and heading home for the Christmas holidays. I was slowly running out of phone numbers and the ones that I was now calling answered with the following recorded message,

'This is Barnthorpe Social Services. There is no one in the office until after the Christmas holidays. Wishing you all the best for the festive period,' before the phone line disconnected.

I was at my wits' end and didn't know what to do. The officer at the front enquiry desk had rung our office a couple of times, saying that Saunders was becoming restless and wanted to know what was happening. Shaun asked if he could help, but he couldn't unless he knew somewhere to house Saunders, at least over Christmas.

People were now wishing everyone 'all the best' as they left offices to go home for Christmas. Some were carrying presents, others flowers. As they left, I saw DI Roberts walk around to his office. I was now devoid of ideas regarding Saunders, so I sought his advice and the next rung of the managerial ladder. I pushed his door open.

'I'm sorry to trouble you, Sir, but I'm getting nowhere with Jason Saunders. Everyone is packing up for Christmas now, and he's still sitting at the front desk. No one will give him accommodation as he has sexual convictions against children. What do you suggest I do?'

I sat down on the chair in front of his desk as he rubbed his chin and pondered on his answer.

'What day is it today?' he asked.

'Friday, Sir,' I replied.

'Is it fish for dinner in the canteen, do you think?' he asked as he brushed past me.

'I've no idea,' I answered, turning my head to watch as he disappeared out of the door.

I sat patiently for about fifteen minutes, waiting for him to return with hopefully a successful outcome for Saunders. I decided to go and see who was left in the office, as it was now around two o'clock. Shaun was still sat there writing away.

'What did the boss suggest, Jim, regarding Saunders?' Shaun asked.

'He asked me if it was fish for dinner in the canteen,' I replied.

'What? No, come on, what did he say?'

I was still a little perplexed at this point.

'He's gone somewhere to sort it out, I think, Shaun. I'm just waiting for him to come back,' I said.

'You'll be waiting a long time. He's gone home for Christmas. He popped his head in here a while ago and wished me all the best and said he was going home,' added Shaun.

'He hasn't, I'm waiting for him,' I exclaimed.

'I'm telling you he has gone home,' said Shaun, 'I watched him drive off the car park. I'm sorry, Jim, he's gone home.'

I was gobsmacked. I rang the new, 'state-of-the-art' mobile phone that had recently been fitted in his car.

'I'm sorry, but this mobile phone has been switched off.'

The office phone then rang and Shaun answered. He placed his hand over the mouthpiece,

'It's the PC on the front desk. He wants to know what's happening with Saunders'

It was now three o'clock in the afternoon of the Friday before Christmas. Most were heading home to be with their loved ones for Christmas while Shaun and I sat in the office desperately ringing for anyone who could help house Saunders. Shaun then apologised as he pulled on his jacket, 'I'm going out with the missus tonight, mate, or I would have stayed to help. What are you going to do?' he asked. I didn't know and the thought did cross my mind of taking Saunders, a convicted paedophile, home for Christmas I was that desperate. I also just considered going home and leaving him sat at the enquiry desk as DI Roberts had left me, but I just couldn't do that. Saunders had helped with the robbery suspects, and I am not the type to leave my mess for someone else.

As desperation set in, my last phone call was to another social services department. The phone was answered, at least, but they refused to help. They suggested that the Seamans Mission in Fleetworth may be worth a call. They had heard that the warden wasn't too bothered about the resident's past, just so long as they paid.

'What happens, son, is that he will stay here for five weeks rent and food free on the proviso that when his giro arrives in week five, he will pay me what he owes. But they never do. They skip town and go and do it again in another town. That's how it works. So, unless you can pay me upfront for five weeks, I'm sorry, there is no place for him here.' said the warden.

'What if I guarantee you will be paid in week five?' I added.

'Well, if you guarantee that in writing on letterhead paper, then he can come and stay here.'

The afternoon was closing in, the light fading fast as I ran down the steps to the front desk. I can honestly say I two-finger typed that letter of guarantee in a nanosecond. I even officially stamped it and if Saunders did a bunk after the five weeks, then the Regional Crime Squad would foot the bill. Was I in a position to sign it? Not at all, and I think I did add something like 'officer in charge' to my name or something similar, which gave the impression to the reader that I was the boss. I gave the envelope to Saunders and a £20 note and ordered him a taxi to the Seamans Mission. His face dropped.

'I'm not staying at a Seamans Mission,' he said as he started to read the letter.

'You are,' I snapped back, 'and give this letter to the warden.'

'But what about a hotel or another apartment or hostel,' he asked.

I explained about his previous convictions and that no one wanted to take him. I also hinted that he was a little ungrateful after my efforts since early that morning. He wasn't pleased, but I didn't care. Problem solved. The relief was incredible and a weight lifted off my shoulders. The taxi arrived soon after and a rather disgruntled Saunders got into the back seat before the vehicle set off for the port of Fleetworth. Phew! I stood and watched it disappear into the Christmas traffic.

It had been a day from hell. So, what did I do? I decided to rid myself of the stress of the day with my very best friend, alcohol. By the early hours, I was dancing and singing without a care. Saunders was just an afterthought. It was a great feeling, and I didn't have to worry about it until we reconvened in early January.

Merry Christmas, everyone.

***

The first office briefing of 1990 was short, and we all shared our Christmas stories. A common theme was, 'No, we had a quiet one this year.' Then, we listened to each other as we explained what was happening with our investigations. I explained the situation with Saunders and asked the boss, if I could see him in his office about it.

'I'll be honest with you, Mr Roberts. On that Friday before Christmas, I came to see you for help, as I didn't know what to do with Jason Saunders. I wanted some help and guidance and you left me alone and went home,' I said as I sat in the same chair I had done that Friday.

'How old are you?' Roberts replied.

'I'm 32 years old.'

'Have you passed your promotion exam?'

'Yes, I have.'

'You're married, aren't you?'

'Yes, I am married with two children.'

'That is a lot of responsibility. Married, two children, mortgage,' he added.

'I suppose so,' I answered, not grasping his point.

'How much do you get paid every month?' he asked.

'Just over a grand.'

'What happened to Saunders in the end?' he enquired.

'As I've said, he went to the Seamans Mission.'

'So, you sorted it out?'

'Yes.'

'Well, in this department, we also give you responsibility and pay you well for exactly that, sorting it out. That's *your* job to sort it out, not mine. Now, was there anything else?'

It felt like I'd been punched. I sat there in silence for a while.

'Is that it? You want me to sort things out?' I said.

'That's why we pay you, yes,' he replied.

I walked from his office and down the corridor to the main office. Shaun was waiting for me and asked what Roberts had said,

'He told me to sort things out.'

***

Edwin Boff and David Dearden had been remanded in custody to appear before the Crown Court on a future date. They were both charged with conspiracy to commit armed robbery and going equipped to steal, meaning they were equipped with all the material needed to carry it out. e.g., the balaclava, the note and my homemade firework gun. Jason Saunders wasn't happy but was now a resident at the Seamans Mission in Fleetworth, eleven miles away. I called to see him and he seemed to be settling into his new accommodation. The warden, however, wasn't happy with Saunders and suspected that he would disappear as soon as his giro cheque appeared. The cheque included the money to pay the Mission for his food and lodging. The warden waved my letter at me that clearly stated if he did disappear without paying, the Regional Crime Squad would pick up the bill. Something I failed to mention to DI Roberts. The Building Society had made an interim reward payment to Saunders, so he had enough money for the time being. It was possible that if Boff & Dearden were convicted, Saunders could net a five or six-figure sum of cash.

 The weeks passed, and the evidence file for the two would-be robbers was completed and forwarded to the prosecutors. It wasn't complex as the main witness was me and I heard a trial date was set for the summer. Week five arrived and I purposely travelled to Fleetworth and the Seamans Mission to meet Saunders. I had warned him of the consequences of leaving without paying for his accommodation and was relieved to find him waiting for me. It was just a matter of time now and wait for the court case.

CHAPTER FOUR

PUSHING THROUGH DOORS

'On the 14^{th of} January, DC 776 J. Graham will be transferred to the Regional Crime Squad (RCS) in Northshire until further notice'.

It was December 1988 when the above lines were printed on Divisional Order 43/1988. Let me take you back to my final days in Sandford CID before moving to the Regional Crime Squad. You may remember my mental health was suffering and I was struggling to cope with the daily workload and family life. I wasn't well and had to declare it to someone. I couldn't go on much longer.

I could see the doctor's waiting area was busy. It was cold outside as the winter wind whipped the plastic bags into a frenzy around the car park. It was dark as the automatic door slid open, producing a gust of warm air against my face. The queue for the receptionist was long and I looked around the room, conscious that everyone was looking at me. 'They all know about me', I told myself, 'they can all see it in me. They know I'm mentally unwell, don't they?'

By now, the anxiety, anguish and worry had taken a stronghold. I was no longer in control and lived, at times, from hour to hour. I had practised what to say to the doctor over and over in my head a thousand times. The pressure at work hadn't receded and now I had made what I thought was an error of judgement by taking the previous Superintendent's advice and moving away. I was stepping out into the big wide world. I had a week left in the CID in Sandford before I transferred to the Regional Crime Squad, situated in Priestown, a town some forty-four miles away. For me, it was a massive jump. Born and bred in 'the village', I was now to join the country's elite in tackling international drug trafficking and organised crime gangs.

'Name please', asked the doctor's receptionist.

'Who me?' I asked as I looked around. Her facial expression said it all.

'Yes, please, you.'

'It's James Graham, I'm here to see Doctor.... Doctor....'. I had forgotten my own doctor's name; such was my emotional and mental condition.

I sat with the coughing and sniffing masses and waited for my name to be called. Doctor Armitage was a lovely man and had been the family doctor for generations. He called me in and I sat in the small chair opposite his desk. He looked at me as I sat in silence. Eventually, I explained my symptoms and he said it was a classic case of 'burn out', or stress and anxiety. Today, we would call it mental health, and mine wasn't good. After a good chat with Doctor Armitage, I felt better, but the worry and anxiety weren't going to lift that easily. Emotionally, I was damaged, and it was going to take time to get back to myself, but I knew I would. I was determined.

'Jim,' the doctor looked straight at me, 'I can give you a list of chemicals that may help you in the short term. But you are no different from thousands of other men your age who come in my surgery and sit in that seat. A young family, a stressful job and the pressures of everyday life. Life would be boring if we didn't have these ups and downs and sometimes, Jim, we must make our own sunshine when it's raining outside. Do you want the chemicals?'

It was a tough call for someone who wasn't thinking clearly. I pondered for a while, then put my head in my hands as I didn't know what to do. I had a prescription in my hand for sleeping tablets and tranquilisers. Uppers and downers. I closed the door behind me and walked out into the cold night air.

I was extremely fortunate to have a good friend in Sandford CID Office. Greg Jones was an extremely competent detective. I looked up to him as he took everything in his stride, nothing seemed to bother him. He got on with the job and did it well. Over a pint or two in the police bar, Greg asked me how I was as he'd noticed a decline in my work and behaviour. He said the prankster and jovial character had disappeared and had been replaced by a 'grey' man who looked disinterested in life. He was, of course, correct and could easily see it. I didn't want to share how I felt within the office for obvious reasons, but the game changed when Greg told me he knew how I felt, as he had the same feelings. I thought it was just me. It was the start of the self-healing process and with the help of Greg, my wife and family and my pre-internet research, I decided to tackle my worry, anxiety, stress or whatever I was suffering from head-on. I threw the prescription away.

My first purchase was a pair of Nike running shoes, and yes, Run Forest Run! I had read about the chemicals in the brain and how unbalanced they become, such as endorphins, dopamine, noradrenaline, etc. So, I ran and ran and swam and swam. I tried to cut down on the drinking and started listening to music and relaxation tapes. Add this to the chats with Greg and I could see light at the end of the tunnel, albeit the tunnel was long!

After some annual leave, I said farewell to my colleagues at Sandford CID and walked the long corridor where McAvoy had once berated me. I pushed the swing doors marked push. I didn't look back.

***

The start time in the morning at the Regional Crime Squad in Priestown was nine o'clock. Travelling from Sandford would be a long journey for me every morning on a congested motorway. I decided to leave very early on my first morning and arrived in Priestown, a busy market town, around a quarter to eight. There was no parking at Priestown nick, so it was street parking. It was then a half-mile walk into town and the police station. The area was all new to me and after negotiating the front desk entrance and explaining who I was, I climbed the stairs to the third floor and the Regional Crime Squad office. It was dark and deserted.

The first to arrive was one of the three Detective Sergeants in the unit, Ray Ingham. He was small for a police officer, around 5ft 8ins tall, thin build, with dark, long swept back hair. He wore a green wax jacket, which was all the rage then. Several complaints had been made that the wax off the jackets would stain the car seats and, in turn, your clothing. They eventually got banned from the CID office. Whilst I waited for all the other staff to arrive, Ray made me a cup of tea and handed me a large file.

'This is what you will be working on, Operation Empathy. It involves a family from Blackton who are importing cannabis and other drugs on an industrial scale. Have a read-through before we have the office briefing.'

The file was thick and in no semblance of order. As I started to wade through it, other members of staff came into the office as the start time neared. The Detective Inspector in charge of the unit was Gordon Roberts. He was a tall, thick-set man but very quiet and unassuming. The morning briefing commenced and I listened to my new colleagues as they explained the progress, or not, of their investigations. The main investigation was Operation Empathy, the international trafficking of drugs by the organised crime family, the Mooneys from Blackton.

Julie was the office clerk. She was lovely and took me through all the form filling that I had to complete. She explained all the office protocols, which were different, as not only was I now in a different police station but also a new police force. This was Northshire Constabulary and they did things differently. Julie had just taken delivery of an office computer. It was huge and no one knew how to work it. Windows 95 was still years away. Computers were the future. Julie showed me around the police station, and on the 5th floor, there was a gymnasium and showers. The 6th floor was the canteen; even at ten o'clock on a Monday morning, it was a hive of activity with patrol officers coming in for breakfast.

Being somewhere new, in a different police force and station, I now had to be serious and grown up so the pranks would have to wait. This was a new era and I tried my hardest to fight maturity, which lasted less than an hour. I had to call into Priestown centre for cash, and Julie helped direct me to the nearest bank. As I left the police station, I noticed the wet and soapy patches on the flagstones. Just around the corner were two young men having a quick ciggy. They stood in a window cleaner cradle and donned all the equipment that led me to believe that they were, in fact, window cleaners. After a quick chat, I went into the cradle, and slowly, we started climbing the outside walls of Priestown Police Station. May I suggest that if you have a fear of heights, as I have, I wouldn't recommend this. Slowly, we passed the first and second floors as the ground moved further and further away. It was a long way down. To make matters worse, the cradle began to sway in the wind and I gripped the rails as though my life depended on it. It did. The cradle then banged against the wall as we neared the third floor and the window that Julie looked out from.

It was a lovely view of Priestown, but now my legs were like jelly and I was feeling quite dizzy. I took the window wiper from the cradle and began to wipe the window. Julie was working on her new computer and hadn't looked out yet. Here I was 200 feet up the side of the police station when Mr. Roberts, the Detective Inspector, walked into the office. He looked once, twice and then the third time mouthed, 'What the……..,' as he looked out of the window. Julie then followed suit and screamed out loud when she saw me, putting both hands over her mouth. She looked extremely shocked as I continued to clean the windows, unperturbed about what was happening in the office. I kept a poker face and continued to clean the windows from the outside. I could see the numbers mount, peering out at me from the inside, as I whistled away and continued my task. There was a mixture of shock and incredulity that the new boy in the office was outside 200 feet up and cleaning the police station windows.

It was meant to be a funny introduction for my colleagues, but unfortunately, things didn't work out as they had done in my mind. As we started our descent from the third floor, the cables became snagged, and the machine, lowering us, abruptly stopped. The cradle swung from side to side in the wind and I honestly thought the thing was going to crash to the floor. The real window cleaner, who was beside me, told me not to worry as 'this happens all the time' and the worst-case scenario was that we would have to call the fire brigade. What a great start to the next chapter of my career.

I eventually got down to terra firma after half an hour or so and collected my cash from the bank. The reception in the office when I walked back in was mixed. Julie pleaded with me never to do that again, as her blood pressure had gone through the roof and she had to take her medication. Others in the office laughed, and I heard the odd comment like 'crackpot', and my new Detective Inspector just smirked, shook his head and walked off. Ray Ingham, the Detective Sergeant, brought play time to a close when he asked me if I lived near Sandford Airport. I didn't really, but the airport was closer to my home address than Priestown police station.

At seven o'clock the next morning, I set off from home to Sandford Airport. To put my new role in some perspective, intelligence had been received that the two Mooney brothers, Michael and David, were travelling to Amsterdam for a meeting with other drug barons over their next consignment. My job was to 'look like a traveller' and hang around the KLM desk to see if they checked in, who they were with, how they were dressed, etc. At that time, there was no agreement with the Dutch authorities to assist us with our investigations and to be honest, if we had asked them to help with drug dealers visiting Amsterdam, I think there would have been a very long queue before us.

I went to the airport's international terminal, carrying an empty suitcase and wearing my old but colourful Hawaiian shirt. I wanted to be in holiday mode, but on reflection, I maybe could have dressed down a little as I shouldn't have been the one to stand out in a crowd. I should have been the one no one noticed. I was learning. It was difficult explaining to my wife Elaine just exactly what I was doing.

My black, zip-up £9.99 Woolworths suitcase was ideal, though. I saw hundreds of them, some with big rainbow ribbons and others strapped with belts, making them identifiable in the masses. I pulled it along behind me, and sure enough, Michael and David Mooney, together with an older man, joined the small queue at the KLM desk. The two brothers were immaculately dressed in suits and suede shoes. I later found out the shoes were the finest Italian, priced around £500 a pair, which, for 1989, was good going. The suits were, similarly, refreshingly expensive. They were travelling light and I didn't see any suitcases. Both brothers walked through and down towards passport control, then the older man walked towards the exit. I went to the public payphone to call the office, as instructed. I then caught the lift to the car park and when I was on the seventh floor, the doors opened. Who should be standing there? It was the older man with the two Mooney brothers. He looked directly at me as he walked into the lift,

'Forget my head if it was loose, wouldn't I?' he said to me as he walked in, 'been anywhere nice, love the shirt.'

I just smiled and hadn't prepared myself or planned what to say. I couldn't say I was going somewhere as I was heading to the car park.

'Hawaii then,' he asked as we both left the lift on the ninth floor.

'I wish,' I said and parted company with the old man at the first line of cars in the car park. I stopped before my car and watched him get into a large red Mercedes estate. I tried to get the number but couldn't. I'm not sure my surveillance skills were the best, but I knew, I had a lot to learn.

I reported my findings back in the office, and it transpired the older man was, in fact, the father and figurehead of the organisation, Anthony Mooney. The red Mercedes was on record and after completing my notes, I was asked if I could travel to Birmingham airport the day after, as enquiries revealed that the two brothers were flying back from Amsterdam to the airport there. Not long after, one of the brothers left the country via the Hull to Rotterdam ferry and later came back via Heathrow airport from Spain. Two days later, the other brother left for Spain via Manchester Airport and returned to the country via Glasgow Airport. This was indeed an eye-opener for me. Two weeks ago, I was dealing with thefts and burglaries in Sandford and now I was travelling up and down the country watching international drug dealers go about their business.

In the second week of my new role, I was asked if I could prepare an overnight bag and travel to a small Scottish village called Lochgoilhead, not too far from Faslane and northwest of Glasgow. The two brothers had booked into a 5-star hotel nearby. Such is the life of a drugs trafficker.

On my way to Scotland, I was partnered with a younger officer who had recently joined the unit. Mark had also transferred in from another rural shire constabulary and I couldn't resist when we stopped at the motorway services for refreshments. Mark was still in the toilets when I returned to the car park. As I passed the rubbish bins, sat on top was a huge hot dog, untouched except for a small bite out of one end. What a waste of money, I thought. It was smothered in onions and tomato ketchup and seeing that it was February, it was freezing cold. I took my new hot dog friend back to the car and waited for Mark. I put the hot dog on the dashboard and as soon as Mark got in the car, his eyes shot straight towards the submarine-style object.

'Oh wow, that looks good. Where did you get that?' he asked.
I told him the kiosk inside and by now the cold food was giving off quite a nice aroma.

'Two quid, mind you, but it's a bit too spicy for me,' I said as I picked it up. I opened the driver's door and started to get out. Mark touched me on the shoulder.

'Wait, what are you doing, where you are going with that?' he enquired.

'The bin, I'm throwing it.'

'Like hell you are,' and with that, he leaned across and snatched it from my hand with the stealth of an eagle. Before I could mutter a word, three-quarters of the ten-inch cold tube-shaped object was rammed firmly into his mouth. I looked across and saw his eyes bulge and watched in amazement at the speed at which the cold and stale hot dog made its exit. He clawed at the contents of his mouth, spewing them all over the interior, shouting, 'It's cold, you bastard, you bastard Graham.' The dashboard was now full of sausage, bread and ketchup as Mark coughed and spluttered away. He sulked all the way to Scotland. I just couldn't resist. The angel stood no chance. The demon won in the end.

CHAPTER FIVE

TRAINING

It wasn't long before Mark and I were paired up again on the 'Regional Drugs Course' at Northshire Constabulary Headquarters. The course had international recognition and I sat in the class horseshoe with twenty other delegates from around the globe. Mark was still upset with me, so I sat across from him on the other side as he now didn't trust me. Who would? It was just before nine o'clock on the first morning of the course and we sat there as strangers, waiting for the course trainers to arrive.

I suppose it's at this point I should tell you about my very first interaction with members of Her Majesty's Constabulary. As I outlined in Part I of my police journey, 'Pushing doors Marked Pull', I was born in a little town called Portclay, just on the outskirts of Sandford. There wasn't much happening in Portclay, to be honest and residents from the town were usually classed as 'hillbillies'. Some unusual people were knocking around in the town, but for me, it was home. We lived in a small shop opposite rows of terraced housing, the mill workers' homes. When the manufacturing industries collapsed, so did the mills and the workers. They moved on. Mum and Dad's shop soon closed and we had some hard times. The houses opposite were due to be demolished and as a young six-year-old, my inquisitiveness was to get me into trouble more than once. The demolition contractors had left the diggers and cranes on site and like any other six-year-old would do, I started a dumper truck engine and set off driving around the demolished buildings. We were quick learners in Portclay! Oh, it was fun until I parked the dumper truck and was climbing down the side when my momentum stopped. I looked down and saw the black boots and looked up to see the fast-approaching black gloves. Bang! Across the back of my head, Sgt Strickland's shovel-sized hands struck firmly against my small skull. Bang! And again and again. Three times, he 'cracked' me and then pulled me off the truck by my collar and off I was carried back home, legs dangling. I looked like a kitten in its mother's mouth as my arms and legs were swinging. Once home, the violence was repeated. It was more than three 'cracks' off Mum and then to bed. I was side-lined to my room for a week.

For weeks after, Sgt Strickland was ever-present at our house. As a six-year-old, I couldn't fathom why the state would be so interested in monitoring the activities of a youngster like me when there was so much trouble in the world. It wasn't until much later in life, when I had a quiet moment with my Dad, that he educated me on the Sergeant's real motivation and continual house visits. Mum was a very attractive lady. There you have it. Dad explained that it put a massive strain on the family at the time and that there wasn't any real help dealing with the village Sergeant's unwanted affection. In the end, Mum fronted him up, I think and threatened to report him after he let his hands wander.

So, back to the course and the connection with my first interaction with law enforcement. As usual on all courses, the first exercise is always the 'ice breaker', the introductions and listening to others as they explain their favourite music or claim to fame. Are we really interested, are we?

'Good morning, everyone, and welcome to the regional drugs course. I'm your course trainer. Let me start with the introductions. My name is Richard Turner and I joined Northshire Constabulary in 1964. I was posted to a small town and if England was to ever have an arse hole, it would be firmly planted in this town. People went around holding their hands up, shouting, 'Give me six', residents had webbed feet, their sister was their mother and their father was their brother. They were all interbred and the only entertainment was to watch the traffic lights on a Saturday night. The town is called *Portclay* and it's a shit hole. There are 10,000 inhabitants in Portclay and only two surnames in the phone book,' concluded Turner to a round of laughter from the nervous audience. He then invited the first person in the horseshoe of delegates to continue with their introduction. The first person to lead? Yes, you've guessed it. Me, of course.

'Thanks, Richard. Yes, good morning, everyone, my name is Jim Graham from Sandford Police, but originally born and bred in a lovely quaint town that Richard has just graphically described called *Portclay…*'
Before I could carry on, trainer Turner burst into laughter,
'There are always two jokers in a pack, and I think we have our first one here,' he exclaimed, 'Go on, carry on, Jim.'
'Ok, thanks. Before I was interrupted, I said I am from Portclay, where people do not have six fingers, as suggested.'
Turner interrupted again, 'No, let's move on from your joke, Jim, where are you from?' he asked seriously.
'I'm born and bred in Portclay, where we had a Police Sergeant called Strickland,' I continued.
Boom! The atmosphere changed. Turner wasn't laughing or even smiling now. His face became extremely serious in an instant. He was trying to work this one out.
'How do you know my sergeant was called Strickland,' he asked.
'Because Strickland caught me driving a dumper truck when I was six years old and was trying to get into my Mum's knickers, but her webbed feet put him off,' I replied. The class burst into laughter.
'Oh, I'm afraid you can't say things like that these days as some people may find it offensive,' Turner came back with. The irony of what he had just said about Portclay was lost on him.

'I was born and lived in the off-licence opposite Glen Mill on Market Street. My family are all from Portclay,' I explained. This latter piece was a lie, but I thought I would go for the jugular now. Turner was turning pale and stuttering as he tried to explain he was only joking and I shouldn't read anything into it. I didn't, as he was right in a lot of respects. Portclay was and still is a very weird place. Remember Portclay Pete from Book I, with the tattoos and the shitting monkey? The delegates didn't know whether to laugh or be serious now as it became quite embarrassing. Turner decided to move on quickly and went to the next person who droned on about their police career. Sadly, I didn't listen as I was still reliving the dumper truck and Strickland's hand whacking me across the back of my head. It hurt.

The introductions carried on, and by the time they had reached the other side of the horseshoe and delegate twenty, I had lost the will to live. Interestingly though, there was an Inspector from Malta in the delegation. Victor was a smart chap dressed in a blazer, chinos, collar and tie. He was from Valetta, which was a place I had visited on the holiday where my hair was bleached in the sun. I was disciplined off Himmler when I returned to work for dying it. Eventually, the introductions came to an end, thank goodness and I couldn't remember anything about anyone, only Victor and my colleague Mark. At coffee time, trainer Turner headed straight for me and apologised profusely about what he had said about Portclay and its residents. He then went on to tell me about the antics of 'shagger' Strickland. I'm sure he kept looking at my fingers to count them as he enlightened me with tales of Strickland's many victims. Most of them, I knew.

The first speaker of the course was excellent and I can still remember the input to this day. Doctor Mills was from Widnes and had developed a strategy to deal with the new drug wave that was sweeping the country, diamorphine, better known as heroin. He first explained what the drug did to the body and how the addiction grew. I was fascinated and found the subject matter interesting. He explained that to curb the illegal supply yet support those addicted, he devised a strategy whereby addicts called into his surgery twice a day, once in the morning, the other before the surgery closed. They could choose between smoking a cigarette with a very thin trace of diamorphine on the cigarette paper or a sugar lump, again laced with the drug in sufficient quantities to keep the user 'normal'. Doctor Mills claimed it was extremely successful and that around fifty or so registered addicts were in his control, and with each visit, the dose of heroin would get less and less until, eventually, the user would be drug-free. It sounded good, but I noticed a 'bum twitching' reaction from the trainers at the front of the class and a few groans from the audience. The Doctor also explained that the war on drugs was futile and compared it with an air bed. He produced facts and figures from his area to show that crime was down and drug dealers no longer frequented that part of the country because there was no demand.

'Step down hard in one area,' he said, 'and another area immediately pops up behind you,' as he brought his speech to an end. It was common sense and I liked it. He claimed that if heroin wasn't given out in measured quantities by medical practitioners in a controlled environment, then we would incur major problems. For example, more importations from Pakistan and Afghanistan, gangland killings, turf wars, child drug dealers, more addictions and a strain on the NHS like never before.

The room was silent as the Doctor packed up his belongings and headed for the door. When he left, the course trainers apologised, stating that the powers that be had included Doctor Mills in the curriculum and that they could do nothing about it. I looked around the room at the others for a response but saw blank faces.

'Giving free drugs away, whatever next, eh,' said trainer Turner as he moved his chair to the centre of the horseshoe, 'nice bloke and all that, but honestly, should we give burglars the keys to our houses?'

Most of the class dismissed the doctor's input, so I remained silent and we moved on. Doctor Mills, I doubt very much that you will ever read this book, but if there is the slightest chance you do, I was with you that day. If only they had listened.

By Wednesday of the course, every drug had been passed around the group. The inputs were all didactic, in other words, they led from the front with an OHP. Remember them? An overhead projector (OHP) with acetates. At the time, OHP's were ground-breaking and, I suppose, the equivalent of today's PowerPoint. Now, if you wanted photographs or slides in your input, you needed a 'carousel', which lifted the slides into the projector and displayed the results on the screen at the front of the class.

Being talked at for eight hours a day was challenging. I wasn't learning, and I couldn't remember all that had been said. It was still winter, so the heating was full on, making everyone drowsy, especially in the afternoons. I was sitting facing Victor from Malta, and I must admit, watching his head roll around and flop as he tried to fight off his fatigue was far better than listening to someone talking at us about the chemical constituents of amphetamine. Victor was literally on a roll.

Ged, one of the trainers, was Yorkshire-born and bred. His accent was broad and deep, and he was as old-fashioned as they came. His favourite saying was, 'Al go turt top of our stairs,' whenever something new was brought up in class. As we were giving our final speaker a good listening to and watching amusingly as Victor tried to keep his eyes open, 'Yarksher Ged' outlined Thursday morning's input for us.

'Reet then, listen up thee lot. In't morning we have Northshire Drugs Squad coming to give thee an input in't workings of a police drugs dog. That alreet?' he announced, 'so get thee sen here early tomorrow people as lads and lassies are gonna bring a dog wee em'

'What kind of dog is it, Ged, a whippet? Are you going to wear your flat cap?' I asked.

The class erupted, and I knew I had crossed the line as soon as I said it. Poor Maltese Victor didn't know why everyone was laughing, nor why he was laughing, but he joined in regardless. There was uproar, but Ged's face never flinched. He looked directly at me and waited for what seemed like an eternity for things to quieten down. I was trying my best to stop giggling, but I couldn't. My shoulders were the giveaway, and once I laughed again, the rest of the group fell in line. I know it wasn't funny and unprofessional of me, but it was hilarious.

'Have thee finished then?' asked a stone-faced Ged, 'have thee?'

I sat there like the naughty schoolboy, mentally arguing with myself to stop laughing at all costs. Laugh now, Jim, and you may get assaulted, I thought.

'If tha's finished please. If tha finds this funny Graham, tha can leave if tha wants. If anyone else finds it funny, tha can leave wee him. People are giving up their time to cum and speak to thee lot, tha nos. Does tha know how many people died from drugs last year lad eh?'

I apologised and sat in silence, looking at the floor. Still, in the far corners of the class, there were titters and laughter as delegates picked their coats off chairs and headed for the exit.

The following day, we discovered the whippet was a cocker spaniel, and Ged had the last laugh. The handler led the dog around the room in an anti-clockwise direction; therefore, I was the last one the dog stopped at. Except it didn't stop at me but ran around me repeatedly. Then barked at me, then jumped up at me, then barked again and again, before jumping on my lap. The class was in uproar. The handler looked bemused, and I could see Ged at the side of the room with a Cheshire cat grin. The handler was concerned as he said the dog was showing a 'positive' result for me and that I may have cannabis on me. How very interesting. The dog and handler were ushered out of the room, and all the class laughed when Ged announced that they had better stay away from me at coffee unless they wanted to get arrested by the drugs squad. As I went towards the door to get some caffeine, Ged leaned in towards me and whispered,

'These fucking whippets are good, aren't they, Graham.'

I was later told that he had smeared cannabis oil on the back of my chair. The class kept their distance from me for the rest of the course, thinking that I was actually on drugs myself. Nice one, Ged.

The lesson before lunch had Victor's head rolling around and the boredom of the input was interrupted as his head tilted backwards and his mouth gaped open. The lad next to him, Pete, was from Thames Valley Police. He started giggling when poor Victor started snoring. As the rasp of his inward breath hit a crescendo, Victor startled himself and now eyes wide open, he attempted to be interested in the input. He wasn't and soon the head started rolling again until it finally came to rest and the mouth opened and once again, the rasp of his snore titillated Peter and the rest of the class. Victor woke again and the cycle continued. It was hilarious to watch and kept me occupied until lunch.

Northshire Police Headquarters had a licensed bar above the canteen, or restaurant, as they were later called, before they all disappeared from police buildings. And yes, if you wanted a pint at lunch, you could have one. Those were the days. There were consequences if you had a drink and went back to work. I called in, not for a pint, but for a packet of peanuts. Back to the classroom after lunch for a presentation on the Misuse of Drugs Act 1971. Riveting stuff.

The first acetate went onto the machine about legislation and it didn't take long for Victor's head to begin rolling away. Eventually, the neck vertebrae locked into place, the head fell backwards, the mouth opened, and the snoring began. Thames Valley Pete started to giggle, as did some of the others around him. Out came the peanuts, and with the precision of darts player Jocky Wilson, the peanuts began hitting Victor about the head and face. I had to be careful as the course trainer was now aware that he didn't have the full attention of the group. Victor would wake momentarily, then the head would roll and off we went again until the snoring began. What happened next surprised us all and I didn't plan for it. If I could put this in some perspective by explaining that as a youngster, I remember reading a book on the German battleship, the Bismarck. Named after a German general, this giant of a vessel spread fear through the British Navy as it scoured the North Atlantic in World War II. The Bismarck was responsible for sinking many British and American ships, but one, The Hood, stuck in my mind. My Great Uncle Tom was a stoker onboard the Hood when a shell from the German battle cruiser supposedly hit one of the Hood's turrets and went down into the ammunition store, where it detonated. The explosion ripped the Hood apart and it sank in 3 minutes with the loss of 1400 souls. Please forgive me if you think I am trivialising such a tragedy. It best describes how my last peanut travelled across the room and went straight down the turret of Victor's throat, where it lodged. First came the scream, the red face, the cough, the spluttering and Victor fell to his knees.

    The group's attention focused on Victor and the trainer stopped mid-sentence. People ran towards Victor, bringing him to his feet. Thames Valley Pete got behind him, attempting to render the Heimlich lift.

    'Get him a drink, someone, quickly get him some water, quickly,' came the cry.

    With Pete now looking like he was committing some sort of sex act on Victor, one of the trainers came forward and loosened his tie. The packet of peanuts slipped into my pocket, but I couldn't help noticing several nuts being squashed under the feet of Victor's rescuers.

    After a short while, normal service was resumed and Victor regained the use of his throat and was breathing correctly. It caused a ripple of laughter in the class but also a hint from the group that it was a childish stunt and immature of me. I agreed and it didn't take long for him to set off again in his cycle of head rolling and snoring. I pulled out the bag of peanuts and the eyebrows raised on the other side of the room. I took a handful and placed them into my mouth and to the relief of my colleagues, placed the bag back in my pocket.

On the final night of the course, delegates went into Priestown for the nightlife and ended up in Spires nightclub in the centre. Young Mark was proudly sporting a young lady on his arm as I left in the early hours. He called me over, advising me that he might be late for morning class as he was going to be busy when he got back to the accommodation block at Police Headquarters. Wink, wink, know what I mean. Sadly, it wasn't to be for Mark as before he got back to his room, someone had emptied it. Every single item, and I mean everything. Bed, cabinet, carpet, clothes, chair, toiletries and so on. Whoever did it had the decency to leave him a towel, which, by all accounts, he used to cover himself as he shivered on his floor. What a shame. Poor Mark.

***

The final training for my new role was the surveillance course. It was held in a small town called Ripley in Derbyshire, which had striking similarities to Portclay. I looked for the six fingers and webbed feet but saw none. The four weeks went quickly and involved driving around the country at breakneck speeds to covertly follow the course instructors. I loved it and learnt new advanced driving techniques that I still use to this day. I met new friends and colleagues from around the country and the odd challenging character or two. We spent just a week on foot surveillance in cities, using public transport and the only downside was that despite all our best efforts, we always needed to be better for the course instructors. The daily debriefs and feedback sessions could have been better. Very negative and constant criticism of our best efforts rather than encouragement and development. I did, however, warm to the instructors when one of them said that he didn't want to spoil our last night's party, but there was a one-hour exam on the final morning of the course. We all laughed at him and went to a local pub for our farewell drink and buffet. We were confident there wouldn't be an exam.

At nine o'clock the following and final morning of the month's course, the delegates assembled bleary-eyed outside the main hall to be met with a sign that read,

'COURSE EXAM. DELEGATES TO WAIT UNTIL
9.30 AM THEN TAKE A SEAT IN THE HALL'

Eyebrows in the congregation raised an inch or two and people tried to peep through the doors to see what was happening in the hall. I hadn't revised anything and I wasn't alone. There was quite a lot of theory in the course, but most of the month was spent applying the knowledge gained in the classroom. An hour's exam, this was very concerning. At nine-thirty, the hall doors opened, and the head of the surveillance training unit stood there, inviting people to go inside. There were rows and rows of desks and another instructor was sat at the front. This was sobering up time.

'Come in, sit down and please remain silent. You will be given an exam paper shortly. This is a pass-or-fail paper. You will need a pen,' he said.

This was serious. I sat at one of the desks and patiently waited as another course trainer came around with the exam papers, instructing me *NOT* to turn them over. I looked around at some very serious faces, and it was now sinking in that this was for real. The head came to the front.

'Ladies and gentlemen, when I tell you, please turn over your paper. You have one hour to complete it and it is pass or fail. When you finish the exam, you are free to go back to your police forces. We will notify you of the results in due course. Drive safely and please turn over your papers. One hour.'

As I turned over the paper, a lump stuck in my throat. All that hard work over the last month came down to an hour-long exam on the last day. I started to read the paper but then had to go back and read it repeatedly.

*Thank you for your participation on the National Surveillance Course. You have worked extremely hard and we wish you a safe journey back to your force. THIS IS NOT AN EXAM. However, over the last month, Jeremy from the green syndicate has been an absolute pain in the arse. He has complained about the food, the accommodation and about every aspect of the course. In short, he has been very challenging. Jeremy has received a **real** police promotion exam paper regarding surveillance and the questions are extremely demanding. We have sat Jeremy at the front nearest the stage. Do not laugh or talk amongst yourselves, but please sit there quietly for at least 10 minutes and then one at a time, please come to the front and hand in the blank sheets of paper and say goodbye. Once again, thanks for all your hard work and all the very best for the future.*

Brilliant. Ten minutes passed, and the first person stood up and reached the front to hand in their paper. I looked at the front and Jeremy was sat there in his green cardigan. You couldn't miss him as he was a big lad. He had indeed been one of the challenging characters on the course and if your dog had four legs, his had five. If you went to Tenerife for your holiday, he went to Elevenarife. Jeremy lifted his head in amazement as the first person handed in their paper. Then the second, the third, the fourth and so it went on. Jeremy's head was still down and he was busy completing his exam paper. I got up after 15 or so minutes and walked to the front. I looked down and there he was, ticking the boxes on his multi-answer exam paper. He was constantly looking around, looking at the dozen or so sheets in front of him and trying to answer the questions. He looked stressed out.

I had already packed the car with my cases and thirty minutes or so had passed since the start of the exam. Jeremy was still in there. I was saying my goodbyes to people outside in the car park. A delegation gathered at the hall window and were laughing out loud when Jeremy burst through the entrance doors,

'Bastards, go on fuck off the lot of you. Bastards, absolute bastards,' as he walked towards the car park.

'Take care, Jeremy,' I said as he neared me.

'Oh, you can fuck off as well,' he shouted as he walked away.

CHAPTER SIX

THE DUTCH MANX MAN

The trial date for Eddie and Dave for the Building Society robbery was fast approaching. I regularly met with Saunders, who was still resident at the Seaman's Mission in Fleetworth. We went for breakfast nearby and he told me a Dutch drug trafficker was travelling to the Isle of Man soon and was looking for a route into the UK for his drug consignments. One route was Amsterdam to the Isle of Man and then either Liverpool, Marsham or N. Ireland. He said his contacts in the Isle of Man could arrange for the Dutchman to travel to Fleetworth and meet with Saunders to discuss the deal. It sounded like a plan, so I agreed that Saunders should open himself up to his contacts and agree to be the deal-maker on this side of the Irish Sea.

With what seemed like daily visits to Fleetworth and Saunders, a plan was put in place to monitor the meeting with the Dutch trafficker. Shaun had acquired a black cab taxi from a friend. After chatting with my peers, I booked Saunders into the best hotel in Fleetworth. I decided to mount a surveillance on the pair when the Dutchman arrived. I didn't tell Saunders my plans.

The meeting was set for a Wednesday morning in February. The arrival time of the Manxman ferry was eleven o'clock in the morning. Shaun was ready with the black cab and a surveillance team was plotted around the ferry terminal in Marsham for the arrival of the Dutchman. We only had a first name at this point, as Saunders's contacts had been unable to provide full details. 'Henryk' was described as white-skinned, 5ft 10' tall, with slim build and dark collar-length hair. I had given Saunders extra cash to buy a decent suit, shirt and tie and as he stood outside the arrival area in the ferry port, he looked quite the businessman I wanted.

Saunders had given his description to his contacts, and to keep the tradition, I thought of the pink carnation in the lapel for him but decided on a specific place to stand. There was a sign just outside the arrival hall from the Government about the dangers of drugs, with the logo 'Drugs don't work'. Saunders was told to stand next to the sign.

'Standby standby standby, white male, dark hair walking towards arrivals. He's carrying a dark holdall and a black and white baseball jacket. He's alone, could be our man,' crackled over the radio.

'Baseball jacket now approaching the friendly. Now shaking hands. Trumpton, are you in a position to take over?.'

'Trumpton, yes, yes.'

Each officer or operative, as we were sometimes called, had a radio nickname. This made it easier for in-car communication, was more informal and didn't mean much if some of the criminals were scanning the police radio channels, which they often did. Shaun had picked the name Trumpton for whatever reason. He started the black cab and pulled around the front of the arrivals hall. Saunders was aware that I was arranging the taxi pick-up but not aware that Shaun was the driver. Shaun was wearing a covert radio, as were all the surveillance team and when he pulled up in front of Saunders and the Dutchman, Shaun opened up his microphone so all the team could hear.

'Where we off to gents?' asked Shaun.

'Grand Hotel, Fleetworth, please,' replied Saunders as Shaun selected first gear and pulled away.

The journey to Fleetworth was mundane. Shaun was trying to engage his passengers in conversation, but only Saunders was doing the talking and keeping it short. The surveillance team followed on behind and commentated to each other on the black cabs movements. It wasn't long before it pulled into the large driveway of the seafront hotel, the Grand. Saunders paid the fare and tip, which Shaun readily accepted as it was police money in any case. Both men walked up the stairs to the Grand reception and the commentary concluded.

'Subject is in, in, in the Grand Hotel, Fleetworth. Did you receive that Preacher?'

'Yes, yes, Preacher received, stand-down teams, stand-down,' I replied.

I suppose you have guessed the origin of my radio nickname or 'handle'? Given the American gospel preacher the Reverend Jim Graham, my peers duly awarded me the radio name 'Preacher'. I'm afraid as soon as I left Sunday school and was free of the clutches of the clergy, I quit religion.

Over the next couple of days, Saunders and Henryk's movements were monitored, and enquiries with the ferry company revealed that no one named Henryk had travelled on the ferry the morning of his travel. The plan was for Saunders to front these initial meetings with Henryk and for him to later introduce 'his man', who would have the money and may be the actual dealer. This would be an undercover police officer.

However, something wasn't right for me, and I had a gut feeling that Saunders was possibly playing us. He had, in the past, provided first-class information that had led to arrests and the recovery of substantial amounts of drugs. Saunders was a clever man, but after raising my concerns with the team and DI Roberts, it was business as usual and carry on. I did have sight of the travel manifest for that morning's ferry and there was a total of thirty-nine foot passengers and seventeen of those travelled alone. Henryk, or whatever he was called, should be one of those.

The surveillance team reported that Saunders and Henryk were in a local pub having lunch, so I decided to visit the hotel and speak to the manager. Arrangements had previously been made with the same manager to book the rooms. We had taken him into our confidence about the situation with Saunders and the mysterious Dutch drug dealer. As the police were paying the bill for the two rooms, I didn't see a problem with being allowed access to them for a short while to see if there was anything that would assist the enquiry. I made DI Roberts aware of what I was doing and carried on. The manager greeted me in reception and I explained the situation as best I could without going into too much detail. Initially hesitant, he agreed to give me the keys to the two rooms but told me that 'this never happened'. I agreed and quickly headed up to the fourth floor, where the two rooms were situated.

Room 43 was the first room I entered. It looked out over Fleetworth Bay. There was a damp smell about the room, but it was clean and tidy and the bed was made up. It didn't look slept in. This was Henryk's room. I looked in the wardrobe to see the baseball jacket he arrived in, some shirts hanging up and a pair of shoes in the wardrobe. The shoes were a cheap pair of black brogues and not those befitting a Dutch narcotics dealer. I checked the bedside table, but nothing. The dressing table, nothing. The covert radio crackled into life.

'It's out, out, out of the Flying Horse and a right, right, right back towards the Grand Hotel.'

They were coming back! I checked the bathroom, and again, there was nothing except a bar of soap here and there. There was no passport, cash, or personal belongings other than a few clothes. I left the room and entered room 47. This was Saunders's room. This room had a different feel. It was scruffy, the bed was not made, and clothes were on the floor.

'They are now at the Grand Hotel and it's in, in, in to the main entrance,' was the announcement over the radio. They were here. I quickly looked through the wardrobe and apart from a couple of hanging shirts, there was nothing. Then I noticed the holdall Henryk was carrying when he came off the ferry. It was in the bottom of the wardrobe in Saunders' room. Inside were some socks and underwear and some paperwork. I took it out and started to read it. It was from the Isle of Man ferry company and it was a return ticket in the name of 'Michael Johnson'.

I activated my radio, 'Preacher to any of the team. What is their location, please?'

'They're in the elevator on their way to the fourth floor, Preacher.'

I threw the ticket into the holdall and put it back in the wardrobe. I went to the door and listened for noises in the corridor. It seemed to be quiet. I opened it slightly and looked outside. I couldn't see the lift from where I was, but I had to leave quickly. I stepped into the corridor and quietly closed the door behind me and then I heard the voices. It was Saunders; he was here on the fourth floor with Henryk and they were just around the corner heading my way. I looked to my right and noticed a door open. There was a cleaner in one of the rooms.

'Can I help you?' said the middle-aged lady who was stood by the window.

'Oh yes, sorry. I checked out of this room earlier, and I think I left my keys in here,' I replied, trying to keep out of sight of the corridor. In the pause, before she spoke again, I heard Saunders behind me, and then the room door swung open and closed with a click. The voices fell silent.

'In this room? I thought it was a young couple in this room, let me check,' said the woman as she walked towards me and the cleaning trolley near the door.

'It's okay,' I said. I'll return to reception and make sure it was this room.'

'Well, I can check that on the roster. Here, let me check for you.'

I turned around and walked back out onto the corridor. I didn't want to catch the lift and looked around for the stairs or fire exit. The cleaner appeared at the door,

'What name was it, by the way?' she asked.

'Johnson,' I replied, 'and where are the stairs please?'

'There, love, right in front of you. Can't see for looking, eh? Johnson, Johnson, I don't have a Johnson listed.'

I opened the stairs door and quickly headed down. I made my apologies to the manager at reception and told him to keep this between us. I also mentioned the cleaner on the fourth floor and she may ask some questions about me and he assured me he would deal with it.

I made my way back to the office in Priestown and spoke with D.I. Roberts. Some of the jigsaw pieces didn't fit the puzzle correctly for me. My judgment was swayed as Saunders had previously supplied information which had led to the arrest and conviction of international drug traffickers and the recovery of a substantial amount of drugs. So, we decided to make all the enquiries we could about 'Henryk' and 'Michael Johnson' before our next steps. Don't forget this was pre-9/11 and the internet, so things didn't happen quickly in those days. There was no Bluetooth nor emails and fax machines were state of the art.

The surveillance on Saunders and the 'Dutch drug dealer' continued until the next morning when Saunders rang the office asking for me. As I was with the team in Fleetworth, he said he would call back in an hour, which he did.

'He's going back this afternoon,' said Saunders, 'his full name is Henryk Peters and he is from the Rotterdam area of Holland. He is going back to Holland at the weekend via Manchester.'

I thanked Saunders and planned to meet him later in the afternoon in a café in Fleetworth. We followed 'Henryk Peters' or whoever he was, back to the ferry port and made sure he caught the ferry back to Douglas.

The ferry company was investigating Peter's and Johnson's travel manifests for the dates in question. I also spoke with our Manx Police colleagues.

The next meeting with Saunders took place at the café on Market Street in Fleetworth, next to the Royal Bank of Scotland. Saunders was jovial but stated that he was now becoming tired of the Seamans Mission and could we assist by supporting him to rent an apartment. He also said he had an embarrassing moment when 'Peters' asked about his address, and he was embarrassed to give the Seamans Mission, as it didn't match his profile. He did have a point. He said he came out with some bullshit story about keeping this visit neutral and would divulge more to 'Peters' as their relationship grew. I told him I would look into the apartment later but was more interested in the visitor from the Isle of Man. Once again, Saunders told me who he was and where he was from but told me he was travelling under a false name. He also had several false passports and different aliases he used. The trip was also a reconnaissance of this side of the Irish Sea and the opportunities available for the consignments to be shipped over. Peters was looking for someone to oversee the project and was checking out ports such as Marsham, Fleetworth and others on the west coast of England. He had access to a fleet of fishing vessels in Holland and that's how the cannabis resin would be transported. Saunders stated he didn't divulge much more but would be in touch. Peters had a pager, the number he had given to Saunders and had said when he wanted to contact Saunders again, he would do so through his contacts in the Isle of Man. It all sounded very credible.

I returned to the office and began working on the different names and intelligence. Enquiries with the international desk at the National Drugs Intelligence Unit (NDIU) revealed that Henryk Peters was known to the authorities in Holland and was actively involved in drug trafficking, having been recently arrested there. The pager number was a Dutch number and again enquiries by the authorities were being made to establish the owners. The Dutch were very interested. Enquiries with the ferry company revealed that the name Michael Johnson was also used for the return journey to Douglas, and the police on the island were searching their indices for the name Johnson. Don't forget, no databases or Microsoft yet!

It was decided that Saunders should be moved to more suitable accommodation nearby in Blackton. With some financial assistance and visits to second-hand shops, we equipped his new apartment with a washer, TV, and other modern conveniences to make Saunders a little more comfortable. The latest news was that the Dutchman wanted another meeting, this time in London.

The Manx authorities came back to us, and they had sixteen Michael Johnsons on record and could eliminate four of them due to their age. As we were told Peters was using false details and an alias, this part of the enquiry was on the back burner as we awaited a photo of Peters from the NDIU.

A couple of weeks passed, and my attention was directed to the incidents happening on the long-running enquiry, Operation Empathy. I had been to see Saunders on a couple of occasions and he was settling into his new accommodation. He had already started to give information about criminals in Blackton. He rang the office one Friday afternoon. Julie was just packing up and ready to go home and Back to Life by Soul II Soul was playing on the radio. After some more money, Saunders asked if I could go across to Blackton to see him. Unfortunately, it was late, but I told Saunders that I might see him early in the week as the trial of the two armed robbers, Eddie Boff and David Dearden was listed for trial at Priestown Crown Court the following Monday. Don't forget Saunders gave the information about the armed robbers and was waiting for a reward. As the court case was next week, he said he could wait.

Monday morning came quickly and I dressed in my suit and tie for court. I arrived at the office at my usual early time. I had completed my five-mile run in record time, showered and sat in the empty office waiting for the others to arrive. I read over my written statement about the events of Thursday, 21st December 1989, the day of the Building Society robbery. I still had a few aches and pains from my arrest. DI Roberts, DS Ingham and I walked the short distance to Priestown Crown Court, arriving shortly before ten o'clock. The court was a hive of activity, with police officers, witnesses, clerks and barristers rushing around, all searching for something. Checking the register revealed that Boff and Dearden were listed for trial in Court Three and it was decided to wait outside that court for the prosecuting counsel. Time ticked by and the atmosphere was like the ubiquitous dentist waiting room. Two barristers chatted intently to my left and Roberts and Ingham stood to my right. One of the barristers broke away and headed our way with his cloak trailing in the wind behind him.

'Are you the officers in the case of Boff and Dearden?' he asked.

'Indeed we are,' added Ingham.

'Well, the two are pleading not guilty and are putting forward a rather bizarre defence, in that they believe they have been set up by someone,' the barrister said. 'Does the name Jason Saunders mean anything to you? I doubt it will,' he went on to add. My eyes dashed between the Detective Inspector and Ingham. There was a deafening silence.

'Apparently, this Saunders chappie said he could claim £250,000 reward money from an attempted robbery at the Building Society. He supposedly convinced Boff and Davies to go ahead with it as they would be arrested before any offence would be committed. Their sentence would be a light one and when they came out, he would ensure they had £100,000 each waiting for them. But they are saying they haven't heard from this Saunders since. Apparently, Saunders has contacts in the police. Rather far-fetched if you don't mind me saying,' added counsel.

I looked at Roberts and Ingham. The Inspector closed his eyes and rubbed his chin. I looked at Ingham and said, 'I think we need to speak in private, don't you?' before asking the barrister to allow us some time to think this one over.

'Shit, shit, shit, shit,' said Ingham. 'Get your arse over to Blackton now and get to his apartment and bring Saunders into the office immediately. Leave the case to me and the boss.'

I ran across Crown Square and down towards the police station. Danny Chadwick was in the office and asked how the case was going. I couldn't speak. Eventually, I got my breath, and Julie stood beside Danny.

'I expect this to be the photo you were waiting for from the NDIU. You know your Dutchman,' she said as she handed over a brown envelope marked confidential. Indeed, on the reverse side was the NDIU logo. Danny was pushing me about the case, and I kept saying, 'Just hang on a minute, just hang on.' I ripped open the envelope and lifted the report and many press clippings. A paper clip held a small black and white photograph in the top right-hand corner of who I presumed was 'Henryk Peters' from Holland. I froze. The photo of Henryk Peters was *not* the person Saunders met from the Isle of Man!

The car journey over to Blackton was interesting. There was a lot of swearing and promises of what I would do with Saunders. The apartment we helped him to obtain was down towards the south of the seaside town. He lived upstairs in the building and other occupants rented downstairs. I remembered the location as we had previously carried washing machines, microwaves and furniture up the stairs when we helped him move in. I parked a distance away from the apartment and walked as near to the gardens and buildings as I could. Danny walked quietly behind me. I was fuming.

The garden gate was open. Just one path led down to the building, which then branched off to front and side doors. Saunders was the side door and the stairs were directly behind the door. I opened the letterbox and just had a gut feeling he would not be at home. I banged loudly on the door and some dogs in the adjacent garden started barking. Danny went around the back and looked up to the windows. He was shaking his head as he looked back towards me. I banged again and the dog barking followed.

'Who y'after,' said the voice to my left-hand side. A young woman with a baby on her hip looked towards me. Danny came back and stood beside me.

'You dibble?' she asked, which was a street reference for the police.

'No love, on the contrary,' I said, 'I'm looking for Jason.'

'He's gone down south, moved out last week. I hope they don't move any scum in here now,' she said as she disappeared around the corner.

I looked at Danny and he gave a smirk and cocked his head to one side, 'Looks like he's done you here, Jim. Bastard.'

It took a while to arrange a spare key from the estate agents before Danny and I returned to the property. The woman from the downstairs flat was standing in her window, once again with the baby resting on her hip and rocking from side to side. We both walked down the garden path to the side door and as soon as I inserted the key into the door, I sensed the inevitable. At least the stairs carpet was still there but I sensed little else as I climbed the last stair. The view across to the kitchen confirmed my fears as Danny and I had struggled up those stairs only a few weeks before with the appliances.

Danny and I stood there, looking into every room. Everything had gone: the TV, cooker, fridge, the lot. I walked into the bedroom, and he had the decency to leave the mattress, but the bed frame had gone.

'Bloody hell,' said Danny, 'he's wiped it out, hasn't he? What are we going to do?'

The first thing was to get to a call box and ring the office to let the boss and DS Ray Ingham know what we had discovered. They were still at Priestown Crown Court, 'holding the fort,' so to speak. As we opened the door to leave, the woman from the downstairs flat was waiting at the door, child on hip, sucking a huge sugar dummy.

'If you do find him, will you tell him I want my £200 back, as I can't afford to lend money out like that. He said he would give it me back before he went, but he hasn't.'

We stopped at the first call box and spoke with Julie in the office telling her to get a message to DS Ingham or the boss. They were both back from court and in the office. The prosecution had requested that the case be put back until after lunch and the court agreed. I told Ingham what we had found and there was total silence from the other end of the line.

'Just make your way back to the office and we will have a scrum down over lunch. You've got a message to ring the manager at the Royal Bank of Scotland in Fleetworth,' added Ingham, 'He rang on the direct line.'

Again, it didn't take long to drive back to Priestown and the office. Time was of the essence as it was now after twelve noon and the court would reconvene around quarter past two.
'A message from the Manager of the RBS in Fleetworth, ' Ingham had said, but I had no connection with the bank. What would the manager want from me? I had no idea but was soon to find out.

Danny and I dashed up the stairs to the office, where Julie waited for me with her hand on the phone's mouthpiece.

'It's someone from Fleetworth Library for you.'

I took the receiver from her, 'Hello, DC Graham. How can I help you?' I asked.

'Oh, hello, it's Jean Titchmarch from the library in Fleetworth. It's a courtesy call, as we don't want you racking up too much in fines for your books. But they are four weeks overdue now,' she added.

'But I haven't got any books out. I've never been to Fleetworth Library,' I replied.

'Well, if I'm talking to Mr. James Graham, courtesy of Priestown Police Station, you have been to the library. You have two books out. One is 'How to claim your benefits', and the other is 'Consumer rights explained' by B. Taylor.'

'Mrs Titchmarch, I must come and see you as I haven't been to the library. Let me take your number and I'll get back to you.'

I slumped in the chair, and Julie asked if everything was alright. It wasn't. DS Ingham and the boss, Mr Roberts, walked in and sat opposite me. I explained the library phone call and told them about a bank manager who expected me to return his call. At this point, I assumed the reason why.

'Yes, Mr Graham. Thanks for calling. This is about your bank account and the overdraft facility. You haven't made any payments yet,' said Mr Bruce, the RBS manager.

'Mr Bruce, I don't have an account with you. I'm sorry, but I know who has used my details to obtain one. I will come and see you very shortly.' Oh dear!

The meeting with Roberts and Ingham about what to do with the court case didn't last long. The prosecution in the Building Society robbery case was willing to accept guilty pleas to lesser charges of 'going equipped' to steal from Boff and Dearden, which would, in effect, allow their immediate release from custody. After the morning I had, this was indeed good news. The two pleaded guilty and were released, joining the queue of those trying to locate Jason Saunders.

Over the next couple of weeks, letters from finance companies, store cards and furniture stores started to arrive at the police station in the name of 'James Graham', seemingly for the loans I hadn't paid back and the furniture I hadn't paid for. As I was so involved with Saunders, it was decided that the enquiry should be given to the local Priestown team. I was relieved and we tried our best to keep it 'within the office' as it was an embarrassing episode. It was a steep learning curve indeed. The authorities in the Isle of Man confirmed that Michael Johnson, one of the 12 they had left to eliminate, was a convicted sex offender on the island and matched the photographs of our Dutch drug dealer. One had to give Saunders credit. He's been consistent throughout.

Saunders was now circulated as a 'wanted person' and all 43 police forces were alerted. Nothing had been heard of him for over three months when Julie passed me a stickie note with the name DCI McFarlane, Cambridge and the police station number. I called him and we had a long chat about a man named James Graham who had recently been appointed a caretaker at a boys school in Cambridge. The DCI had somehow linked it to possibly being Saunders and then to me. Once again, we had to wait for Royal Mail and the photographs to be sent out. It was a long shot, but James Graham and Jason Saunders could be the same person. There was also an urgency about the case now because if it was Saunders, he was a convicted paedophile and should not be anywhere near a boys school. I asked to drive to Cambridge to assist, but the boss told me to stay out of it and leave it to the local team of investigators. The week came to an end. I had been busy working on Operation Empathy, which helped me take my mind off things. However, the Saunders case had taken its toll on me and knocked my confidence. I was trying to convince myself that one day, I would look back at the audacity of Saunders and laugh about it.

Well, with the help of alcohol, that day may even arrive sooner than I thought. Sadly, it didn't.

I took the children to the park on a beautiful Sunday morning. They were growing fast, and I felt guilty for being away from home so much.

'You've got to ring a DS Ingham immediately,' my wife announced as she greeted me carrying in the pedal cycles, 'it seemed urgent,' she added. The phone number was written on the notepaper at the side of his phone. It was his home number.

'Hi Ray, it's Jim Graham, you wanted me?' I enquired.

'You seen this morning's papers?' he asked animatedly.

'I haven't, Ray, no, I've been with the kids in the park; what is it?' I asked.

'It's your man Saunders. He's all over the front pages, Sunday People, News of the World and Sunday Mirror. Looks like they've traced him to a boys' school in Cambridge. Can you believe they've given him a job at a boys' school with his record,' said Ray, 'Cambridge Police have been onto the boss as well, as they were making enquiries into the caretaker, but it seems the press got there first. They must have had a tip-off.'

'Oh, right. Do I need to do anything?' I enquired.

'No, not really; I just thought I'd let you know. It's certainly hit the fan in Cambridge as questions are now being asked how he got the job at a boys' school in the first place.'

Jason Saunders was wanted for a host of different offences nationwide. Being a former investigative journalist, his work eventually made the front pages, but for all the wrong reasons. Cambridge Police never found out who had tipped off the press, making Saunders public enemy number one. I later heard he pleaded guilty to numerous offences at Cambridge Crown Court, including the Priestown Building Society robbery conspiracy, and received nine years at Her Majesty's Pleasure. It ended a rather embarrassing and turbulent time for me, but there was one final thing for total closure. Jason, if you happen to read this book, do me a favour, mate, and take those library books back. The fines are mounting up.

***

The story of Jason Saunders was later converted into a three-week national police training course for covert operatives on how to handle or maybe how *not* to handle criminal informants.

CHAPTER SEVEN

THE WHISTLER

Frank Whitehead was a character, an enigma. He was a Detective Sergeant in the unit and couldn't be faulted for his work ethic, passion and love of the job. He had his own vocabulary and sayings and did not suffer fools. He was black and white. It was, or it wasn't. He didn't do the grey bits; usually, it was violence or the threat of it. There were rumours that he had fallen out with a supervisor earlier in his career and ended the argument by whacking said supervisor around the head with his truncheon. Looking at Frank, it was believable. He was a stocky man with a long, curly 'Robert Plant' hairstyle and a little goatee beard. He sometimes wore a black leather waistcoat with a silver chain linking the front two sides. It was always open and the chain held it in place. He wore denim jeans with a big black belt and a very bright silver buckle shaped like an eagle. Underneath his leather waistcoat was a thick denim shirt and if not for his dark curly hair, had the appearance of a stocky Meat Loaf. It was difficult to grasp what he said as he spoke fast and in an accent I found difficult to place. It was northern but maybe with an Irish or Gaelic twang. He spoke in riddles, winks, whistles and nods and reminded me of a character that Billy Connolly once described. When we were introduced, he told me to hold out my hand, which I did, fearing the consequences of not doing so. He then wiped the sweat off his brow with his hand and flicked the sweat onto my hand.

'That's with grafting son. If you're coming to work here, that's what I expect from you: sweat from grafting,' he said as he turned and walked away.

'What did you just say,' he said as he spun on his feet and looked me straight in the eye.

'I didn't say a word, Frank,' I said.

'Good, that's how I like it, eh Julie, that's how I like it, eh Shaun, that's how I like it,' as he looked around the room at the others for recognition.

I looked at Julie and Shaun and they were rolling their eyes as they both answered, 'Yes Frank,' as if it was too much trouble.

Later that day, several of us were in the office when the door clattered open. Frank, carrying bags, thudded down on his desk and looked at me.

'Found the doctor, pal, that's all. He's been with the chef all day and he's cooking chowder. It's looking more and more like a drugs triangle.'

We all nodded, and there were murmurs of 'Oh right, Frank' as people carried on with what they were doing.

'Good news that, eh, Preacher,' he said, looking directly at me. I'll say again, good news, Preacher.'

'Yeah, great news, Frank,' I replied, but I didn't understand why a doctor would be making chowder with a chef.

'Manchester, Sheffield, Liverpool and Stoke,' added Frank as he scoured the office, 'there's your drugs triangle, right there,' which raised an eyebrow or two. 'Chefs cooking chowder up in Snotland.'

'You mean Scotland, Frank,' some brave soul shouted, eager to correct him.

'No, Snotland, I said S-N-O-T land or Phlegmland, you know, over the pond,' said Frank with a look that said we should all know what he was talking about.

'Over the pond? You mean America, Frank,' another potential victim shouted up.

'Where the hell do you get American from?' he asked as we all looked bewildered. 'Snot, phlegm… phlegm land… phlegmish. The doctor is from phlegm land….. Belgium.'

There was a joint, 'Oh right,' from the nodding heads in the office, who, like me, didn't know what Frank was talking about.

'Yeah, they're dropping the clicks off in Stoke and taking the whizz up to Manchester where they pick up the sheckles,' he added before dialling a number on the telephone. He held his hand up to everyone, indicating that they should shut up, and he started speaking into the phone. Welcome to Frank's world.

***

For a while, we had been surveilling the organised drugs network headed by the Mooney family from Blackton. This was code-named Operation Empathy, and our journey had taken us north and near Sandford. Somehow, I ended up in Frank's car, as I had been out on foot at some point. Each office member was paired up with someone else and allocated a covert car. We all had covert radios and earpieces with the transmit button secreted somewhere on our body, usually near the wrist or hand. The microphone was pinned inside your jacket, out of sight, up near your mouth. When you wanted to talk to the other team members, you pressed the transmit button and talked. When you finished your message, you let go and listened to the response in your earpiece. Nowadays, with the advancements in technology, such as earplugs, pods, and the like, no one gives a second look when someone walks past them and appears to be talking to themselves. Back in the day, it was very different. You stood out if you began chatting with yourself, so you had to be very careful. It was 1989 and the mobile phone had yet to break through.

The surveillance team usually had five cars, each containing a driver and passenger who became a 'foot operative'. Back then, we called them 'footmen' as the unit consisted of 99% male officers. Also in the surveillance team, weather permitting was a motorcyclist who could get to where a vehicle couldn't much quicker. If the subject you were following got out of their vehicle and started walking, then foot 'men' would be deployed from the surveillance vehicles to follow on foot. When the subject returned to their vehicle, the footman jumped in any passing surveillance car to ensure they didn't get left behind. Hence, I ended up in Frank's car.

We had to drive near where I lived in Sandford to return to the unit, so I asked Frank nicely if it would be possible to call in at home and kiss the children good night before bed. I hadn't seen them all week. He agreed, and as I walked in through the front door, there were shouts of 'Daddy, Daddy' as the kids ran towards me. They hugged onto my legs and I tried walking down the hallway with them hanging on. Frank came in behind me and young Andrew broke free from my leg and ran into the lounge. He was now three years old and just too young for nursery. Louise was older and, I think, had just started at nursery that year, but the house was busy with toys and boxes everywhere.

Andrew went to his toy box and lifted out Trojan the Turtle. Some friends had been to the Caribbean and brought the cuddly toy back for Andrew. He looked up at me and hugged Trojan tightly to his chest. Frank pushed forward.

'What have you got there, son?' Frank asked.

Andrew was shy and tucked his chin into his chest. He looked up from the top of his eyes, and when Frank held his hand out and said, 'Let me look then,' little Andrew passed Trojan across to him. What happened next will stay with the whole family forever. Frank stood upright, then let go of Trojan and drop-kicked the cuddly toy better than any rugby league star. Poor Trojan shot across the lounge in mid-air before crumpling into the far wall. The poor thing slid down the wall before flopping onto the carpet. The room was silent. The expressions on the children's faces were that of sheer horror. Poor Trojan. My wife Elaine was motionless, mouth wide open, not knowing what to do. Did she go to little Andrew, who was about to burst into tears or go and rescue poor Trojan. Before she could move, Frank leaned forward, finger-wagging and looking at the two children. They were now clinging ever so tightly to my legs,

'That's what your Daddy does to bad men,' he said to them before standing upright again and looking at my wife, 'Alright love, how do you put up with him, eh?' pointing at me. 'Come on Jim, let's get back to the unit.'

I had to prise the kids off my legs and do my best to calm them down before leaving the house. There were shrieks and screams as I got to the front door. Elaine was saying, 'Just go, go, please go.' By this time, Frank was down the drive and getting into the Vauxhall Cavalier. He looked towards me, 'Kids, eh? Who'd have em.'

The forty-five-minute drive back to the unit was different. I listened to Frank talk about job after job. As soon as we got in the office, I called home and the conversation was obviously about Frank. The kids were still loud in the background and should have been in bed by now, but Trojan's injuries still had to be treated. Elaine said there were bandages around Trojan's head and arms and the treatment was far from over.

Both kids had gone to bed when I arrived home just after eight o'clock. They were waiting for their bedtime stories and although it was very late, I agreed, as young Andrew was still traumatised by the Trojan incident. Sure enough, the little turtle was tucked up in bed, all bandaged up.

'Daddy, that man won't be coming back, will he?' Andrew whimpered as his eyes drew heavier and heavier. I was only two pages into 'Burglar Bill' before his eyes fell shut and off he went into a deep sleep, hopefully to forget about the night's trauma. Louise was still waiting for me when I went into her bedroom and she too asked if that naughty man was ever going to come back. I got to page four of Meg and Mog before she too slipped away into a deep sleep.

More than 30 years after the Trojan incident, the trauma lives on in the Graham household. Frank was never invited back.

Many surveillance exercises were mounted during Operation Empathy, which I will detail later. The Mooney network was large and the Father and two sons rarely got their hands dirty, leaving the day-to-day work to many lieutenants and foot soldiers. I spent a lot of time in Blackton, where the gang operated from and spent many an hour either driving along the seafront or walking down the promenade waiting for the 'off, off, off' command from the surveillance team. Some days, some weeks, the boredom was hard to deal with. We spent days and nights, week after week, waiting for one of the gangs' vans to move as we had received intelligence it was en route to Scotland to be filled with drugs. Then, from dozing in a car or lying down somewhere, you heard the radio crackle and 'off, off, off' and went from zero concentration to 110%. It was a world away from the CID in Sandford.

It was a dull day in Blackton, and once again, I waited with the others for the 'lift-off'. One of the lieutenants had been assigned the task of moving some cannabis resin from a 'lock up' somewhere.

'Standby, standby, standby subject Tulip is on foot, and it's left, left, left into Victoria Street towards the seafront. Description to follow.'

This was it. We were off and running and would now follow one of the team we had nicknamed Tulip to see if he would lead us to the gang's lockup. Tulip walked quite a distance, then doubled back on himself and carried out some anti-surveillance manoeuvres. Just in case he was being followed. By this time, I had jumped out of the car I was a passenger in.

'It's a right, right, right into Fennel St. 'Preacher', are you in a position to take him,' the radio crackled in my ear. I pressed the transmit button, 'yes, yes,' I replied as Tulip came into view. I had seen him many times before. His real name was Carl Toolan, a well-known and convicted drug dealer. He was walking on the opposite side of Fennel Street to me and after completing half its length, he stopped and lit a cigarette. He started to look around, so the best tactic for foot operatives was to find some 'cover' and disappear from view. I stepped inside a shop and looked outside through the front window to see Tulip leaning against a wall. I then noticed a telephone box beside him that I had missed before. I continued my commentary into the receiver as quietly as possible to paint the picture for my surveillance colleagues. I looked around me and then realised I was in a joke shop.

'Can I help you?' asked a small, scruffy man behind the counter.

'I'm just looking, pal, if that's okay?' I asked.

'What in particular are you looking for?' he asked.

As he did so, Tulip threw down the cigarette and entered the phone box. I had to communicate this to the surveillance team outside, but the storekeeper was looking at me.

'What are these here?' I asked, pointing to some metal devices under the glass counter.

'One is an exhaust whistler and the others are detonators. You put them under telephones and the like and when people pick them up they explode. The whistler goes in the exhaust of a car and would you believe, it whistles as it drives,' added the shopkeeper.

'Give me two of each, please,' I asked, and as the shopkeeper was busy, I transmitted to the team that Tulip was in the telephone box.

'Were you talking to me, son?' asked the shopkeeper as he stood by the till.

'No, I was just talking to myself as I have a few things on my mind and have a list of things to pick up. I've had my instructions off the missus, you see,' I said as I tried to convince him.

'Some missus if she wants car whistlers and detonators,' he said laughingly.

I joined in with his laughter, explaining that they weren't for her and, at the same time, looking at where I could go next. Tulip was still in the phone box and I noticed a bus stop with a queue on my side of the street, which was just lower than the phone box. That's where I was heading. I put a £10 note on the glass top, which protected vampire teeth, a nail through a finger, blue sweets and a host of other tricks and japes.

'You're missing something obvious, aren't you?' my scruffy friend added. I didn't know what he meant. Was he referring to me watching Tulip? 'Caps, you'll need caps.'

'I'm not with you, what do you mean?' I asked.

'Caps for your detonators,'

'Of course, silly me, throw us a couple of those in as well,' I said, noticing the door of the telephone box opening. It was Tulip he was coming out. At the same time, a white Mercedes sports car pulled up at the side of the phone box and Tulip headed over that way. I collected my change, and the shopkeeper mumbled something about having fun, but my focus was now 100% on that car. I left the shop and headed for the bus queue. The Mercedes had the engine running but was stationary. I couldn't see who was driving but continued my commentary to the surveillance team. I heard the call sign 'Jethro' in the radio chatter and I knew this was Frank's radio nickname. He was close by. The Mercedes started to move off, driving down Fennel Street towards the seafront. I continued commentary until I heard in my earpiece,

'Jethro to the teams, the vehicle is approaching a junction. Nearside indication and a left, left, left onto the promenade. Vehicle is traveling at 25 mph and it's a stop, stop, stop near to the phone box and post office on the promenade.'

Fearing they may be being listened to, the gang often used different phone boxes in the Blackton area. They had numbered them all so they wouldn't mention street names or locations in conversations, just numbers. Tulip may have made a call from one and then travelled to the other to receive a call. The surveillance team now had to regroup and after looking in the phone box on Fennel Street and dialling 123 to get the speaking clock. I then moved away from the promenade to 'go again'. The speaking clock marked the phone call with 123, so when an application was made for the phone data from that particular number, we knew that the call before 123 was the one Tulip received or made. It was all state-of-the-art stuff.

I doubled back on myself in the next street and was walking towards the promenade parallel to Fennel St. I saw a familiar blue Vauxhall Cavalier parked and unattended and realised that Frank, aka 'Jethro,' must also be out on foot. A thought crossed my mind regarding my recent purchases!

Not long after, Danny Chadwick picked me up and at speed, we joined the surveillance team as Tulip had come out of the second phone box and the white Mercedes was heading south. It had been confirmed that Michael Mooney was the driver and the vehicle was registered to a 'shell company' the Mooney family owned. Tulip was dropped off near his home address and the Mercedes headed for home. It was time to stand down. No drugs had been moved, but there was some good evidence of association and we had to follow up the phone calls with BT, so we were happy with the day's work. The whole picture, however, was still a long way off completion.

As we drove back to the unit in Priestown, there was some 'in car' radio chit-chat about the day's events and some 'banter' as we called it, where people just usually took the piss out of everyone else. We arrived at the garage not long after and as people were parking their vehicles, I told them to wait for Frank; on no account must they say anything when he arrived. People looked at me quizzically, and I explained that everything would be revealed. It was!

'Vvvvvvrrrrzzzzzzzzzzzzzzzzzzzzzzzz,' was the sound echoing around the garage as the Vauxhall pulled in. Frank was alone behind the wheel. Everyone turned round as he drove towards us.

'What the bloody hell is that noise?' asked Danny. I told him to be quiet, 'Please don't say anything,' I added.
As Frank manoeuvred for a parking space, he placed the car in reverse,

'Vvvvvvrrrzzzzzzzzzzzzzzzzzzz,' came the loud noise from the car's exhaust. People were smirking, and some started laughing as

Frank finished parking and alighted from his vehicle. His audience was staring at him, some smirking, others smiling and some laughing out loud.

'You think something's funny, do you?' he growled to the crowd as he started to get his bag out of the car. 'What's so fucking funny then, eh?' His poker face now peering at his audience, who slowly drifted away, 'Nothing, Frank, nothing.'

'Been out grafting all day for my clicks, and you lot take the piss,' he said as he closed the car door. 'You behind this, Graham, eh? What are you laughing at, pal?'

'Nothing Frank, I'm sorry for any misunderstandings, but Danny just told a joke and…..' Frank cut me off.

'Laugh with me, big boy, but not at me, or I'll break your legs,' he said as he scuttled past and headed for the lift.

Back in the unit, there was a resemblance to the headmaster's office at school when you were in trouble and about to get the cane, but that nervous laugh or giggle came along. People looked at each other with cheeks puffed out like hamsters, ready to giggle at Frank.

'There something going on here, and it would appear I'm not part of it,' said Frank in a very serious tone, 'come on, what's going on?'

People shrugged their shoulders and just carried on with their work. The atmosphere changed a little and people started to leave or go and work elsewhere. You could hear the laughter as they hit the stairs. Frank looked directly at me. It felt uncomfortable, but I just carried on and picked up the phone.

The next morning, the office tension lifted and Frank was chirpy. He sat diagonally across from me and after his usual morning phone calls and cup of tea, he reached for his bag and took the car keys from the board. As he walked out of the door, the office emptied and followed him. As he waited at the lift doors, people discreetly filed down the stairs to the ground floor. I, too, followed on. When I arrived at the enquiry desk, there was a mass of bodies and one by one they went outside in the morning sunshine. They waited patiently until the inevitable happened.

'Vvvvvrrrrrrrzzzzzzzzzzzzzzzzzzzz,' the loud sound came before the sight and then Frank driving the Vauxhall pulled into view. Totally oblivious, he indicated to turn right and pass in front of the police station, where now some twenty or thirty people had gathered to watch and listen.

'Vvvvvrrrrrrrzzzzzzzzzzzzzzzzzz', the noise rising as the car accelerated and whistled past us. Heads on both sides of the street turned to investigate the noise. Frank took a cursory look to his right and then did a double take at all the people lined up laughing as he pushed through the gears. As the car disappeared, the whistling noise continued for a while, and people started filing back into the building, giggling as they went. I went back inside and carried on with my enquiries, tittering to myself as I did so.

It was late afternoon and the office was shutting down. People were packing their bags and closing their drawers when the office door burst open. Holding it open with his right arm, Frank stood there with an angry look on his face. His bag was over his shoulder and he was wearing his black leather waistcoat over his denim shirt. His long hair fell over his face and he cleared it with a puff of upward breath from his mouth.

'You think it was fucking funny, do you?' he said as he panned the room. There was silence. Nobody moved.

'So, I've been driving around doing surveillance on an international drug trafficking operation and all the people in the world have lined the streets listening to me as I drive past. You think it's funny, Graham, do you?' and with that, he threw the metal whistler at me. I ducked and Julie took it full on the chest.

'Aaargh,' shouted Julie as the mechanism dropped to the floor.

'Blame him, blame Graham, for that Julie. Warped he is, warped,' said Frank, pointing at me as he sat down. He reached across the desk for the phone and 'BANG', the detonator went off, causing Frank to throw the handset away as he pushed back in his chair.

'What the fuck,' he screeched as the handset landed on the desk, 'what the bloody hell was that.'

The smirks started to appear on people's faces, and some rushed for the door.

'This you again, Graham, eh? This you again? You're a crackpot lad, crackpot.'

I tried to keep a poker face, but it wasn't easy, like being in front of the headmaster with that nervous laugh. Life in the office was difficult for the next few weeks as Frank accused everyone and took a while to settle down from the whistling exercise. I'm sure underneath, he may have seen the funny side of things. Then again, maybe not.

CHAPTER EIGHT

TOMORROW IS NEVER PROMISED

We were all summoned to an office meeting and told we needed an overnight bag. It was 'job' on! The boss was sat up at the front of the office with Frank and as people came into the office, questions were already being asked about what the 'job' was. Operation Empathy was still running and we knew the Mooney gang were bringing fishing boats into Scotland, so that looked like where we might end up. However, DS Ray Ingham was the main man for Operation Empathy and Frank was sat at the top of the table with the boss, so we were all intrigued about where we were going. We soon found out it was Birmingham.

The instructions were brief, but in Frank's drug triangle of Manchester, Sheffield, Liverpool and Stoke, it appeared he had missed off Birmingham. It later transpired that he also missed Leeds. It's more a drug hexagon than a triangle. Word on the street was that a cocaine deal was going to take place just south of Birmingham in the Cotswolds. Full details would be given to us at a further briefing in Birmingham at some stage tomorrow. The plan tonight was to travel up to Tally Ho Police Centre in Birmingham, where we had accommodation booked for the night and to be ready for a further briefing at eight o'clock the following morning at Bourneville Police Station. I was teamed up with a new but very experienced lad who had recently joined the office, John Topham. John was a good detective and had an arid sense of humour.

We started to load up the cars in the garage with equipment and our bags, checking the fuel, etc. when Frank walked past us, leather waistcoat and all, carrying his bags and his new toy, a Vodaphone. It was incredible that you could take a phone and walk outside without any wires? Unbelievable, really, but Frank had one under his arm. It was huge but a state-of-the-art beige Motorola with a large protruding black aerial. You couldn't miss it. As Frank started loading up his trusted Cavalier, John, Mark, Shaun and another lad new to the office, Paul McDonald, assembled for our little pre-trip briefing. As Frank was good for a laugh, well maybe not, we discussed how to make the journey to Birmingham a more interesting one. Engines started, no whistling this time, indicators checked, dipped headlights flashed and it was thumbs up as the convoy pulled out of the garage.

In each surveillance vehicle was an in-car radio system that allowed you to communicate with each car in the surveillance team, car to car. You used your allocated radio call sign or nickname to identify each other quickly. Unfortunately, the in-car radio frequency was on an open channel, so lots of criminal gangs acquired radio scanners and were able to monitor what we said. There was also another radio in the vehicle; this was a national police radio system, and there were codes to tap in to connect to the channel of the particular police force you were travelling in. While travelling to Birmingham, we would pass through numerous police force areas. We needed to tap into their local codes to speak with the radio operators in Shropshire, West Mercia Police, etc. Our national call sign was CS 215. (Crime Squad)

We also had pagers, or bleepers, as they were called. You dialled into a central number and gave the call taker the pager number you wanted to contact and the call taker would type in your message. You were only allowed a certain number of characters, so messages were brief, as in 'Call the office'. Another way to communicate was obviously via the new mobile phones. Before the personal phones hit the markets, the supervisors' cars were fitted with 'in car' phones. Usually, they were built into the central console or on the passenger side. The handset still had wires which went to a central unit. Hands-free calls were still a thing of the future. Finally, add to the communication list the personal mobile phone, which in some cases were like huge beige bricks with an aerial. Others had giant battery packs you had to carry in a shoulder bag.

What happened next was silly, stupid and dangerous and I had to be talked into being a part of it. I objected straight away, but with a little persuasion, I was talked into partaking. We were travelling in convoy on the motorway and Frank (radio nickname Jethro) was the lead car in his sparkling Blue Cavalier. I was driving a Ford Orion and new lad, John Topham, was in the passenger seat. I'm not sure if John was fully in tune with what was going to happen, but at exactly four o'clock, Paul McDonald (radio nickname Juice) called over the in-car radio for the attention of 'Jethro'.

'Juice to Jethro receiving, Juice to Jethro.'

(In normal language Paul to Frank)

'Jethro to Juice, go ahead', replied Frank. Paul had left the microphone open so everyone could hear.

'Jethro, go ahead,' replied Frank, 'just wait, my bleeper is going off as well. Oh, bloody hell, Juice, the in-car mobile phone is ringing now.'

I was two car lengths behind Frank and could see the car wavering from side to side as he jostled with his gadgets. He was wanted on the in-car radio, his pager was bleeping and his in-car mobile phone was ringing, all at the same time.

The national police radio erupted into life: 'CD to CS 213 receiving, CS 213 receiving.' It, too, demanded Frank's attention. Frank's national call sign was CS213. CD was the call sign of the police area we travelled through, and Crime Squad 213 (CS 213) was Frank's car on the national police radio.

'CD to CS213, CD to CS213 receiving.' The police force we were passing through wanted to speak with Frank.

'CS213, can you please wait one minute? My pager is bleeping, my phone is ringing, and I'm wanted on the in-car radio,' replied a frustrated Frank to the police national radio operator.

Then, the in-car radio crackled into life. It was just chaotic.

'Juice to Jethro receiving, Juice to Jethro receiving.'

'Yeah, just wait one Juice will you, it's all going off in here, bloody phones going off, radios, bleepers, what the bloody hell now? Oh Jesus, my mobile phone is ringing now.'

It's a good job traffic was light as the blue Cavalier straddled the middle and slow lanes as Frank grappled with radio receivers, mobile phones and pagers, which somehow all seemed to go off simultaneously. Then, to cap it off, the in-car radio,

'Jethro to Juice, just wait one Juice,…. BANG! What the hell…' and a scream came over the radio from Frank's car.

The Cavalier pulled to the left, then to the right before correcting itself and slowing to 40mph in the slow lane. The radios went quiet. John, my passenger, was looking at Frank's car and then at me, 'What the hell is going on?' he asked. Again, I said I didn't know but it appeared at exactly four o'clock, Frank was in great demand. The 'bang', I suspected, was a strategically placed detonator, which I must admit was a very stupid and risky thing to do, and it wasn't funny despite the many giggling heads in cars behind me. Before you all start jumping to conclusions, no, I did not put a detonator in Frank's car.

The rest of the journey to Birmingham was uneventful and as we pulled into Tally Ho Police Training School car park, the headlights picked up a figure standing between the gates. I recognised the waistcoat immediately. Hands-on hips and looking directly at the queue of oncoming surveillance cars was Frank. This looked serious, so the giggles and laughter were brought to a sudden halt. I was second in line behind Mark's car. Frank waved Mark down and a conversation took place at the driver's window. Frank initially was leaning in but then straightened himself up and the finger-wagging began. Slowly, Mark pulled away and I manoeuvred towards the gates and Frank. He waved me down, so I lowered the new invention, the electric window.

'Are you fucking stupid, son? Eh? Are you? Just stupid lad, aren't you, just stupid.'

'Frank, Frank, what are you talking about?' keeping the best poker face I could.

'All the bloody phones going off, then the bleeper, then the radio and who put that bloody banger in the sun visor?'

Sun visor. Now, that was silly. Trying to suppress the laughter was hurting me by this time. I held it so tightly that I thought I would break wind. It was painful. Then John chirped in,

'Frank, I can vouch for Jim. He had nothing to do with it whatsoever. I sat with him all the way, Frank, and I would tell you. Honest Frank, it had nothing to do with this car, I swear.'

Maybe John was right. Maybe he didn't know.

'It'll be that fucking new lad McDonald won't it. Well, if I don't get him on the roundabout, I'll get him on the slide. See you in the bar in a minute,' and with that, Frank waved us through and stopped the next car containing Paul McDonald. Roundabout and slide? Yet another Frankism.

After a few beers, Frank was laughing with the rest of us and reliving the journey down. He was jovial and told the people at a nearby table that he was a supervisor as we were all offenders and had just been released from prison on temporary licence. It had the desired effect as everyone got up and left, which was disappointing for Mark as I'm sure a young lady was attracted to him. I got up from my chair to visit the bar and noticed that my coat was missing. Paul McDonald said his was missing too and so was John's and yes, you've guessed it, Frank was sitting there with a rather large grin.

'All I'm saying is if you dance with the devil, you may get your fingers burnt,' said Frank gleefully as he sipped his pint.

'If you play with fire, Frank, is the saying,' added Mark.

'Not in my book pal, not in my book, play with the devil,' as the grin broadened.

'It's dance with the devil as well, Frank,' added Mark.

Frank just sat there smugly.

The rest of the evening was spent trying to find the various items of clothing that Frank had hidden. I was still without my jacket when most of the team were retiring to bed. I was hungry and when Paul McDonald suggested we go for a late-night curry, I jumped at the suggestion. One of the best curries I had ever tasted was whilst I was carrying out enquiries into the sneak-in burglar called Hardaker. Remember him from Book I. He completely took the old lady's window frame out as she watched Crimewatch UK, then laughed at what he had done. Our enquiries into Hardaker had also led us to Handsworth, an area of Birmingham with high poverty and crime but great curry houses. It was an area we shouldn't have gone to, but the curries were worth the risk. It was my first introduction to the Balti. It was superb at the time, so we went again.

The front doors were locked when we arrived back at Tally Ho training centre in the early hours. A light was on in a small side office, and soon enough, a small, old, oriental-looking man came out to greet us. We showed our warrant cards, and when I got to the reception area, I started to pat my jeans and then search my jacket pockets. Paul wondered what I was doing.

'I'm so sorry,' I said to the night watchman, 'I think I've left my key in my room. Do you have a spare and I'll bring it back down? Room 75.'

Paul's head spun round and before he uttered a word, I put my fingers to my lips. He bent in close to me and whispered,

'Your room is opposite mine; you're not in 75.'

'I know,' I replied, 'Frank is.'

Like two young children, we hovered around room 75, whispering to each other. If the layout of the rooms were the same, the bed would be to my left of the door and the desk area to the right. Don't forget this was pre-en-suite bedrooms, so the toilet and shower rooms were in the corridor. The corridor light was bright, so I turned it off, which pitched us into darkness. If the light had shone into the room, it could have woke Frank. But then again, he could be awake and waiting for me behind the door. My breathing was becoming shallower as I placed the key slowly into the lock and gently slid it forward. A turn to the right and a push down on the handle and the door moved inwards an inch. I could just see the outline of Paul but could hear him start to snigger. If only he would grow up, I thought. The door opened further and soon it was wide enough for me to get into the room. I stood perfectly still and listened to Frank's breathing. He was fast asleep. I tip-toed into the room and looked to my right. It was very dark, but I could see the outline of a chair. The desk was further behind the door and the bed was to my left. Frank was on his side facing the wall. I felt for the chair and Frank had folded his jeans over the top of it. Job done, let me get out of here, I thought. I slowly retreated towards the door with his jeans tucked under my arm. The key was still in the lock and I turned it very slowly. Paul was trying to feel what I had recovered as it was still dark in the corridor. We made our way to the staircase, whispering and giggling as we went. I went back down to the ground floor and returned the spare key for room 75 to the night watchman and thanked him. Heaven knows what the outcome of this was going to be, but knowing Frank, there could be violence.

    Paul and I said goodnight and agreed to knock on for each other for breakfast in the morning. The canteen, we had been told, was open at six o'clock and we still had to drive to Bourneville after that. We set a time of half past six for breakfast. It was now three in the morning.

    I was first aware of the light coming through the cheap curtains and then heard the low drone of the alarm. It was time to get up already. It seemed I had just got into bed, which was about right. After a quick shower in the communal bathroom, I knocked on for Paul and we both headed down for breakfast. I had my overnight bag with me, which, of course, contained Frank's jeans. As we headed for the stairs, I heard a bleeping noise from my bag. Frank's pager must be in his pocket. We both got to the reception and handed in our keys and I explained to the young receptionist that I had found a pair of jeans on the stairs and could she look after them until the owner reclaimed them. She looked surprised but agreed.

The canteen, or restaurant if you prefer, was pretty close and was busy for the time of morning. Some of our group from Priestown were sat at the far side, in the corner. I walked over and placed my bag on an empty table and Paul placed his bag on the seat opposite me. There were still giggles in the group after the japes of the previous evening and the journey to Tally Ho. It was nothing compared to what was to come. I went to the kitchen area and ordered my bacon sandwich and coffee and returned to the table. Paul sat down opposite me and had the full view of the canteen and the double-door entrance. We called this the master seat, giving you a full view of people entering and leaving. Paul gave me a running commentary on what he could see as I tucked into my sandwich. We awaited Frank's entrance with trepidation.

'Standby, someone approaching the door. The door opens and it is……. Not Frank, relax,' relayed Paul.

'Oh, here we go. Man walking towards doors and……. It's not Frank,' again he relayed.

Paul's commentary went on for ten minutes or so and by that time, I had finished my sandwich. Others from Priestown had also started to join us and then,

'Oh, my lord. Oh, Jesus Christ,' said Paul.

'What, what, what's happening?' I asked impatiently, 'what, come on, tell me'.

'Whatever you do, please, whatever you do, DO NOT look around. Frank's here, in the middle of both doors, holding them open. Honestly, Jim, it's a pity you can't see this.'

The canteen fell quiet. People were gazing over my shoulder in amazement. The odd smirk and smile evident.

'He is dressed in a Hawaiian shirt tucked into a pair of red boxer shorts pulled up to his midriff. He's wearing his black Chelsea boots and black ankle socks. He has no pants on. Just his hairy legs.

Everyone Jim, everyone is looking at him,' added Paul, 'He's scouring the room looking for….. you Jim and he's seen you and he's coming.'

With my back to him, I depended on Paul's commentary and the picture he was painting was that Frank was not impressed. Frank seemed extremely angry as he marched towards our table. I could see Paul looking over my head, so I knew Frank was close to me now. I looked down at the floor. Then I saw the hairy legs first to my right side. Then, the black ankle socks and red Asda boxer shorts. I still hadn't turned around. I daren't. I then noticed his breath and odour on my left side where he stood. I couldn't see the Hawaiian shirt, but his pale, hairy legs were a picture. His voice was measured and menacing,

'Do not open your mouth. I do not want to hear you speak one single word. You need to listen to me very carefully, my friend. I don't know how the fuck you have done it, nor do I care. But if my jeans are not in my room in five minutes, I'll fucking neck you. I'll snap both your fucking legs. Do you understand?'

'But Frank,' he immediately cut me off.

'Five minutes, five minutes, or I'll snap your legs.'

With that, he did an about-turn and marched back to the exit, people giggling as he passed. I quickly turned around and I couldn't help but laugh. The sight of the shirt and the boxer shorts will never leave me. Others in the canteen laughed as Frank barged through the swing doors, his long hair swaying as he went. Others started to look my way and I gestured with a shrug of the shoulders as if I didn't know what was happening. John and Mark from Priestown came over to our table and asked what was happening and without saying who was responsible, I told them that someone had pinched Frank's trousers from his room in the middle of the night. This caused a ripple effect of laughter as the story was passed on from table to table. I did mention to Mark that someone may have handed them into reception and he took the bait and went to ask.

The laughter and hilarity were calming as we left the canteen, and John and I headed for our car. Frank and Mark were out in the car park and the conversation looked heated. Frank was now wearing his jeans and was finger-wagging again. Mark was holding his arms out wide and I assumed he was pleading his innocence after maybe telling Frank, his jeans were at reception. It didn't look good. As John and I walked by, Frank looked directly at me and said,

'Not wired up right, you lad, you've a switch loose, you're one can short of a picnic, one slate short of a roof.'

I continued walking past him and said, 'Bourneville Nick, then? Where is the briefing?'

***

The briefing was held in a gymnasium and several other officers from different regions were present. The crux of it was that a team of drug traffickers were travelling down from Leeds to meet a team from the south and to do a deal near the picturesque village of Bidford-on-Avon. The village was in the northern Cotswolds and had a fire station, petrol station and curry house. Next to the river Avon and the lovely Roman bridge was a large recreational area where the drug deal was supposed to take place. The Leeds contingent was headed by a well-known convicted drug dealer called Peter Hargreaves. They were a tasty team and there was a suggestion that they could be armed. They had 2 kilos of cocaine to sell. There was also a contingent of armed officers in the gym who were going to play a background role as it was too dangerous to deploy them. Too dangerous for the public, that is. The bosses didn't want armed officers making any arrests or being in public view. They would be on standby if shots were fired and we needed them. It seemed a little odd to me that unarmed officers were being deployed to face possibly armed criminals and the only time we could bring the armed officers into play was if they shot us. Really?

Frank was still sulking, but we were all paying attention as the briefing became more complicated. It was being delivered by a West

Midlands Police Detective Chief Inspector and I was trying my best to keep up.

'If the target car comes from the direction of Stratford on the B439, the Priestown vehicles 215 and 216 will join with the West Midlands vehicles 79 and 80 and take up a position on the south side of the river to cover the possibility they leave via the B4085 towards Honeybourne. If, however, they approach from the A46 and then onto the B439, then the Priestown vehicles will join the East Midlands vehicles 134 and 142 and cover the B439 heading towards Stratford. However, should the target car approach from the south, the Priestown vehicles 213 & 214 will team up with the Priestown vehicles 215 & 216 and cover the reverse route towards Alcester on the A46. However.......'

Stop, please. I'm lost here, I thought to myself. I did not have a clue who was doing what or who was supposed to be where. The Chief Inspector continued for over an hour with different options and plans B, C, D, and E. People were looking around with blank expressions on their faces and miming to each other 'What' and shrugging their shoulders.

'If they split up and leave the area in different vehicles, then we need to block roads, so can Priestown vehicles 215 and 216....'

It was too much, far too much, and just after nine o'clock, the briefing came to an end when the Chief Inspector asked if there were any questions. Faces were pale and blank and I hoped someone else would pick up what was happening. Frank came over to the Priestown team and said, 'Pretty straightforward, that. Good luck.'

I looked at John and him at me, then Paul, then Mark. No one had any real idea what was happening apart from the fact a grey-coloured Ford Cosworth, registered number J887 LRJ, with three, possibly four armed men on board, was travelling to the quaint village of Bidford-on-Avon to sell £40,000 worth of cocaine to a team from the south somewhere, who were possibly armed. Now, the team from the south, 'if they approach on the B439 then......'

It seemed all very complicated, but I gathered that when the meeting commenced on the recreational area, south of the river, the police teams were to pounce. I think?

John and I headed for our vehicle and then set off for the quaint village of Bidford on Avon. Our call sign was CS 215 and the Orion handled the journey well. When we arrived, we found the single-track Roman bridge over the river Avon, and down to the right was a small car park with a fantastic view of the larger car park and recreational area on the far bank. I pulled into the car park and stopped in a bay alongside other cars. John got out and walked down the riverside. It was a lovely setting. We knew that other West Midlands Crime Squad cars were covering the meeting place on the far bank where 'the deal' was going down. The police radios were quiet as I watched John trying his best to skim stones across the river. It was a lovely day, the sun shining and a clear blue sky. The setting was tranquil. The quiet was interrupted by the sound of tyres on the gravel car park. John was still by the river as a car drove slowly in front of ours and parked in a bay, maybe four or five cars down. I looked at the operational order we were given and checked the number of the car the Leeds gang were driving. A Ford Cosworth, registered number J887 LRJ. I waved through our car window at John and he headed back towards me and the driver's window. I asked him to check the number of the new arrival on the car park and come back.

'J887 LRJ,' said John, 'and there are three heavies in it.'

I quietly advised John to get into the passenger seat as soon as he could, as it appeared I had parked in the car park where the drug deal was to take place. Oops!

'CS 78 to all patrols, all quiet, no change, no change. No sign of the Cosworth,' crackled through the radio. This was one of the West Midlands cars that was transmitting, which was parked on the other river bank. There was no sign of the car on that side of the river for the simple reason it was parked four cars away from me on my side of the river. John got into the passenger side and I started whispering to him that the target vehicle was parked near to us.

'What are you whispering for? They can hardly hear us,' he said calmly, which I thought was a valid point. 'We best get the fuck out of here then, hadn't we,' he added.

I slowly started to reverse the car out of its bay and noticed a rather large figure leaning on the back of the Ford Cosworth, lighting a cigarette. He looked directly at me and nodded. Instinctively, I nodded back and carried on with my manoeuvre. He was roughly six feet tall, with a shaved head and wearing a blue shell suit, all the fashion at the time. I slowly pulled out of the car park and turned away from the bridge, heading in the direction of a village called Honeybourne. Phew, that was close.

'CS 215 to all patrols, the subject vehicle is parked in a small car park on the far bank of the river and NOT in the recreational area. There are at least three males on board,' I transmitted over the radio. Other Crime Squad vehicles then joined in with the radio traffic and the confusion in the briefing room was now being repeated over the radio.

'Approach with caution teams as this lot could armed,' the Det Chief Inspector (DCI) reminded us. He then went on to explain plans B, C, D, E, F and G.

I approached a crossroads and decided to leave the main road. I had no idea where I was but knew that the Avon River was to my left or nearside in surveillance speak. I was looking for somewhere to park when the car radio burst into life,

'CS 65, it's an off, off, off. The subject vehicle is right, right, right onto Honeybourne Lane. Three on board. We are in pursuit.' Once again, the DCI used his talent to confuse us all with his plans.

'CS 65, speed of nine zero, nine zero (90 mph) as we approach the crossroads at Honeybourne Lane.'

'Keep the commentary coming, CS65,' replied the DCI, who once again took up valuable airtime by explaining plans H, I, J, and K.

It then occurred to me that I had just turned left at that crossroads, but don't forget that this was before Sat Navs or GPS.

'CS65, speeds now in excess of 120mph, that's 120mph teams. We are losing the Cosworth,' came from the radio, 'it's a left, left, left at the Seagrave Arms. Back up, are you in a position?'
This was a term used to see if the backup vehicle behind the lead car was ready to take over the lead. There was silence over the radio. The Cosworth had disappeared,

'CS65, it's a total loss teams, total loss near the Seagrave Arms.' John and I looked at each other thinking that didn't last long did it?

The Leeds dealers had obviously seen something after we left that car park that had 'spooked' them. A car I knew could do more than 160 mph would be long gone. John opened the red hard-backed map book and found the page with the Cotswolds so that we could find our way back to civilisation. We were lost somewhere near Honeybourne, heading down high-edged country lanes. The car radios had been quiet and there was no sighting of the Cosworth since it was lost near the Seagrave Arms.

'Take the next left,' said John, 'that should take us back towards the river and the bridge.'

I did as instructed and turned into a farm track with just enough room for one vehicle. It was a twisty turny lane and the car scraped the blackberry bushes as it drove through. We hit a sharp left-hand bend over the crest of a hill and on clearing the bend, my attention was immediately drawn to the yellow flashing lights. The size of the combine harvester, or whatever farm vehicle was before us, was huge. I could see high up, nearly in the trees, the driver, perched on a platform with a huge steering wheel. He was looking down and then up at our approaching vehicle.

Dwarfed beneath the green giant of the farm vehicle was a grey car, and as we got nearer, I could clearly see the number plate: J887 LRJ. It was the Cosworth. The rear passenger was looking out of the back window as we slowly approached. The Cosworth was trapped between us.

John immediately grabbed the radio, 'CS216, contact, contact, contact, subject vehicle and occupants held on a road.......'
He let go of the microphone. 'Where the fuck are we?' he asked, a question I couldn't answer.

The Cosworth doors opened and the occupants managed to get out. It seemed like slow motion as the doors would hardly open due to the lack of space. I kept my eyes on the driver, who was stuck with nowhere to go. The farm vehicle had taken up all the room and the only escape route for the three heavies was a ten-foot wall on the passenger side. The side of a farm building blocked the driver's escape route. There was no way through, certainly not for the driver. John ran down the passenger side and I could see two figures trying to clamber up the wall. The driver looked back at me as he stood in the narrow gap between the Cosworth and the wall. It was Mr. Shell Suit from earlier and he watched his two friends clambering up the wall. He kept looking back at me as I was fast approaching him. He was thinking of what to do. He climbed up onto the bonnet and started to slide across to the passenger side. The farmer was now looking down with great interest at what was unfolding below him. Mr Shell Suit cleared the bonnet and dropped down into the small space on the passenger side. He turned in an attempt to climb the wall the other two were near the top of. I was now opposite him, across the bonnet, when the Cosworth slowly rolled forward. It veered to the left and the gap on my side of the lane grew larger. Mr Shell Suit let out an almighty scream as the rolling Cosworth pinned him against the wall.

'My legs, my legs, get the fucking car off my legs,' he yelled.

He then faced me across the bonnet and fell forward, face down on the vehicle. I considered climbing over, but there was nowhere to go on the other side. The gap between the Cosworth and the wall had gone, locking Mr Shell Suit firmly in place. He calmly lifted his body off the bonnet and looked directly at me. He reached down by his side and then lifted his right arm and pointed it directly at me. He joined his left and right hands together and cupped them.

I then saw him very slowly take aim at my head. I looked into his eyes and could see rage. His right thumb reached out and pulled back the hammer and his right forefinger pulled around the trigger. I stood perfectly still and stared at him as he closed one eye. They say time slows down at times like this, but it didn't. Everything became very focused and I felt my mouth drying. This could be my last few moments on the planet, in some small leafy Cotswolds lane, miles from anywhere and a long way from home and my loved ones. I saw Mr Shell Suit gently squeeze and then pull the trigger. He smiled and looked directly at me. I felt nothing. I stared back, unable to move in the moment. He blew the smoke away from the end of his pointed fingers and said, 'Bang, you're dead.'

***

Peter Hargreaves and two others were arrested for their part in supplying controlled drugs, namely cocaine. A kilo of the drug was found in the passenger footwell and at the time of the debrief, no one was saying anything. Hargreaves was staying stum. Frank was beaming. He was calling all the Crime Squad bosses as the arrest of Hargreaves was the start of a bigger operation. Armed units were on standby up north in Leeds and also down south to execute warrants at various other addresses.

'Yes sir, oh yes, a great arrest, Sir. I know Sir, thank you, Sir, thank you, yes a cracking job I know Sir,' said Frank into his new mobile phone, as the smile on his face stretched across the room. He was jubilant and everyone shook his hand as we entered the debriefing room. The confusing DCI wanted to debrief the operation and give Frank the success he deserved. The room was packed with conversations about the speed of the Cosworth and the cocaine, but no one seemed to bother that John and I, both unarmed and without today's personal protective equipment, had successfully arrested Hargreaves and his pals. Frank was mopping it all up.

The phone rang, 'Hello Boss, yes this is DS Frank Whitehead. Oh, thank you Sir, yes it was a great job, thanks Sir..... and you have now gone to arrest the others, have you Sir? Wonderful news. Yes, I'll keep you posted, Sir. Thanks once again.' Frank placed the new mobile phone back on top of the battery pack, which took three to carry.

'That was the Assistant Chief of Northshire Constabulary lads, they're effecting the arrest of all the others on the back of the recovery of this cocaine,' Frank announced to us as we all sat around waiting to be confused in the debrief. The room was filling up with long-haired, bearded and look-alike drug-dealing cops. There was an announcement from DCI Confuser,

'Ladies and gentlemen, we won't be long before the debrief starts, but what I'm being told from a quick analysis of the drugs recovered this morning is that we have recovered a kilo of baking powder.'

The whole room gasped. Frank's colour drained from his face and open-mouthed, he just turned around, 'What did he say, what did he just fucking say?'

'He said the drugs that Jim and John recovered this morning from Hargreaves are a bag of baking powder,' came a voice from one of the Priestown crew.

'Baking powder, baking powder, I've just told Chief Constables up and down the country to go and search and arrest all the rest of the bloody drugs gang. Baking powder, baking powder, Oh Jesus,' said Frank and he buried his face in his hands.

Expressionless, Frank reached down for the telephone and battery pack and heaved it towards himself. Slowly, he prized the handset off the top, took a small booklet out of his waistcoat and started to dial.

'Hello, Sir. This is DS Frank Whitehead again. Yes, sorry to disturb you, but have you set the wheels in motion to arrest all the other members of the gang? You have.... Ah, well, we may have a problem. Would you be in a position to recall the officers, Sir?.... Ah, I see, it's too late, is it? The problem, Sir? What's the problem? Erm, I'm being told that the drugs we've recovered aren't cocaine but baking powder.'

As though someone had asked Frank to suck on a lemon, his face screwed up into a tight knot as the voice bellowed down the phone from whichever Chief Officer he had just rung. With the palm of his left hand across his forehead, he fielded the abuse with the occasional, 'I know boss, I know.' Frank closed his eyes and slowly replaced the phone receiver of the battery pack. He then dialled another number and went through the same grimacing procedure. He looked beaten as DCI Confuser got to his feet.

'Ladies and gentlemen, can we please have some quiet? It's my mistake, but the kilo we recovered this morning is, in fact, 66% cocaine! We thought it was baking powder for a moment.'

Frank's head turned towards me slowly and measuredly, like the opening of a canal lock gate. His eyes looked straight ahead. His stature was robot-like and when his eyes met mine, he locked on his missile system. Here they came. Again, expressionless, his gaze never left me.

'You.... You are just warped, lad. You're not wired up right.'

I went to speak and calmly, he raised his hand, which I knew was for me to stop. In the circumstances, I thought I'd better. Frank continued, 'Again, I don't know how you've done this... Shush,' as I tried to speak again, 'but when I find out you are behind this, I will thrash you. Do you understand? I need a yes or no answer.'

'But Frank......'

'Shush.... Yes or no answer.'

'Yes, Frank, I understand.'

'You, my boy, are driving back to Priestown with me when we leave.'

I was now more worried about the return journey with Frank than when I was stuck in the lane with the three drug dealers.

'I've just made a fool of myself ringing up all the Chiefs saying the drugs were baking powder. Do you understand that, lad? Do you?' he shouted.

I remained quiet and again felt like the naughty schoolboy. I lowered my eyes to the floor.

'Warped lad, fucking warped.'

The debrief commenced and DCI Confuser described the sequence of events that led to the arrest of Hargreaves and his heavies. We were told the operation went like clockwork and it was obvious that everyone had listened to the various options at the briefing. Sadly, it was more like Keystone Cops meets good luck, but the job got done and Hargreaves and his crew met their fate.

I walked out of the briefing room, trying to avoid Frank at all costs. I couldn't see him anywhere and all the other Priestown officers kept asking me who had told the DCI that the drugs recovered were baking powder. I told them I had no idea, but to be fair to DCI Confuser, he played a good game.

Frank was waiting by his Cavalier in the car park and waved for me to go over to him. As I got near him, all he kept saying was,

'Warped, warped son, just warped.'

He opened the boot and said, 'Get in.'

'But Frank, I have no idea what......'

'Get in.'

So, for the next couple of hours and a hundred or so miles, I lay down in the boot of a Cavalier as it travelled at high speed along our lovely motorways. Frank listened and sang to his favourite ZZ Top C90 cassette tape all the way. When we reached Priestown, he calmly opened the boot and I climbed out. He never spoke as I calmly lifted my overnight bag and walked towards my car in the now dark and empty car park.

Peter Hargreaves and crew elected Crown Court trial where some months later, he admitted attempting to sell drugs that day but not cocaine. He claimed he had a kilo of amphetamine sulphate. He claimed that I had switched the amphetamine for a kilo of cocaine, which drew a lesser sentence as it was a different class of drugs. Please stop before you start thinking about how I pulled that one off as well. The jury didn't believe Hargreaves and he was sentenced to ten years imprisonment along with similar sentences for his fellow gang members. Firearms were found at the addresses in Leeds, but there was no evidence, at the time, linking Hargreaves with them.

Call it immature, stupid, unprofessional, whatever you like. It was how we got through the day. It was work hard and play hard. It wouldn't happen today as the operation would be risk assessed and armed officers would have intercepted the gang beforehand. Added to that would be all the issues and allegations of 'bullying in the workplace' and 'misconduct' and of course carrying passengers in a dangerous manner.

Yesterday was different; we gave what we got. We were deployed unarmed that day without any personal protection. No vests, no guns, no taser, nothing. They say tomorrow is never promised. Hargreaves may have had a real gun that day and not used his fingers. You are reading this book by virtue of that. I was very lucky. Many times, an officer has said goodbye to his family and gone to work, never to return home. They weren't lucky enough to get stuffed in the boot of a car for a ride home.

'Bang, you're dead.'

CHAPTER NINE

THE FAT LASS

The nights were drawing in and the mornings darker as I made my trek across country to Priestown. I had a long journey to work and I couldn't start any earlier than nine o'clock. To beat the traffic, I had to leave home just after six o'clock, which meant I arrived at work just after seven-thirty. I had asked nicely if I could start at eight with my clerical duties, but alas, I was told that the hours of work were nine to five.

My mental health and emotional state were on the mend, but every day was a battle. Initially, I lived in small time compartments, from the start of the day to lunch, from lunch until tea-time and so on. That was it. If there was an issue that affected me any time after lunch, then I wouldn't engage. Let me deal with what's in front of me now was my mantra. It seemed to work and when I bought some self-help books, I started feeling better. Any mention of any of this to anyone outside a chosen close-knit set of friends would have meant losing my job. It was difficult working so far away from home in a job where you didn't know what was going to happen next or where in the country you were going to end up. It was really tough for Elaine, who had two pre-nursery kids to look after. We needed the money. So, off to work I went.

I never realised the significance of the phrase 'run, Forrest run', but the inspirational movie Forrest Gump gave me an idea of how to fill my time from arriving at Priestown until the start of the working day at nine o'clock. I would start running. It was a game-changer. I became fitter and stronger and had time to think things over. Each run provided me with a sense of achievement and purpose. I went a little further and a little faster each day.

I had also been researching the theory side of mental health issues, so I knew that running produced all the nice chemicals in the brain that we need for survival: noradrenaline, dopamine and others. It gave me a buzz. I also read up on the benefits of cold showers and so the road to my mental and emotional recovery began. However, it is a journey that never ends as I still practice some of the techniques today that I learnt in those early days.

The cool air hit my face as I left the headquarters changing rooms that Thursday morning and drove the short journey to the office. I had run five miles and ended with my cold shower and felt alive. I had run five miles every day that week.

'Have you got your overnight bag?' was the greeting as I entered the office. The boss, DI Roberts, was also on the phone when he asked me the question. I went to reply, but he held up his hand as he began to speak on the telephone.

'Yes sir, I'll get as many as I can. We will have at least three or four cars with you as soon as possible,' and then he replaced the receiver. 'Get your car and when Danny comes in, make your way to London and we will keep you posted on the way. There's a job come in.'

I did as requested and when Danny arrived at the office, we jumped into a car and headed to London. Danny lived en route, so he called in at home and explained to his wife what was happening and said goodbye to his kids. I never got that opportunity. From the in-car radio traffic, I was aware of some of the other car units joining the convoy and the message came through to head for the motorway services at Farthing Corner on the M2 in Kent. That was a long way.

I noticed Frank was with us and was paired up with Shaun from the office. I could also hear Mark Smithies and Ray Ingham on the radio. That meant we had at least four cars heading south and we knew where we were going but didn't know why.

The journey down was uneventful. Danny was a good lad. A very good investigator and had come into the unit from another force. Sometimes a serious individual, he paid attention to detail and hardly missed a trick. He was the very sensible one of the partnership. What about me? Well, you can make your own mind up on that one.

I worked with Danny for a while and we had a good working relationship, although we were poles apart. He was exactly what I needed, though, someone to reign me in. He was definitely the adult. I must confess I made life hard for him with all the pranks and japes. Call them what you will, but he sometimes got the blame. He, too, had a story to tell about his past police career and how it affected his mental health, but like all of us at that time, we kept it close to our chests for fear of losing our jobs.

It was early afternoon when we arrived at the M2 service station, and we were told to assemble in the coffee area for an update. The boss and Ray Ingham had arrived, so whatever the job was, it seemed important. We were hardly recognisable as police officers as we had a diverse group of characters. Frank with his Meat Loaf appearance and black leather waistcoat, me with long hair and a beard, Danny with his sensible look but a little untidy and certainly not your stereotypical cop look. Ray Ingham was small in stature and always smoking rollups in his wax fishing jacket and long hair. The only one that did look something like a police officer was Mark Smithies. He was a good-looking lad with neatly cut blonde hair and a tidy appearance. His family had a history in the military and he spoke very well, so people would probably pass on him as a member of a law enforcement team.

We had been sitting around for a while and rumours mounted about what job we were being deployed on. Mark announced he was hungry and made his way to the Burger King counter. I was hungry and whenever you worked away from your normal place of work for a set number of hours, you could claim expenses. It wasn't a lot of money and just covered what you spent. The echo of the Chief Inspector's speech when I first joined always rang true, 'You will never be rich, you will never be poor.' I decided to give the burger a miss and hopefully catch up on some liquid refreshment at some stage.

When Mark left his table, a young couple sat down and occupied his seat. Our conversations became muted and we waited for the boss to direct us further. I watched Mark in the burger queue and when he returned, he realised his seat had been taken. He scoured the restaurant area and picked a window seat on the far side. He didn't sit down though, but placed the Burger King brown paper bag on the seat and covered it with his jacket. He then looked up again like a meerkat, searching the horizon until his eyes locked on the toilet sign. Off he went to do his duty.

Again, I know it was a childish thing to do, but I did it. Please don't ask me where these impulses came from, but they came. I walked over to Mark's seat and opened his paper bag. I looked back at the table containing everyone else from Priestown, Danny, Frank, Ray, Shaun and the boss and their attention was on each other and not me. I opened up the cardboard 'Whopper' container and plunged my open jaws into the sesame seed bun. Delicious. I quickly replaced the burger, minus the bite, in its box, replaced the box in the paper bag and sauntered back to my seat with no one batting an eyelid. I continued to talk with the others about the continued speculation of why we were sat on the M2 in Kent.

After a couple of minutes, I saw Mark on the far side of the restaurant. He was heading back to his seat near the window and his lovely Burger King Whopper, minus the bite. I thought it best not to watch him at this stage as it may point the finger of suspicion my way. So, I joined in the conversation about what we were doing. I was expecting a pair of hands to come around my throat or a slap across the back of the head and the word 'bastard' being shouted in my ear. But neither came. Curious about why not, I saw that Mark was no longer in his seat near the window. Where was he? I scoured the restaurant, looked towards the toilets and Mark was nowhere to be seen. What a mystery, I thought. Perhaps he was outside? I looked all around and decided to get up and check. Was he planning an attack on me? Had he worked out what I had done?

As I walked the few paces to the exit, I heard a commotion and shouting coming from my right. I looked across, and yes, you're right, it was from the Burger King counter. There was Mark in full swing, fingers pointing and shouting at someone, presumably about the appearance of his Whopper and the fact it was missing a sizeable chunk. When I returned to the table, the team's gaze was now on Mark and his continuing argument and near-fist fight with, presumably, the Burger King manager.

After a short while, Mark returned to our table extremely flustered, agitated and angry. He explained to the rest of the staff what had happened and that they had served him a Whopper burger with a bite taken out. There were gasps from the audience and comments such as, 'bloody sue the buggers,' and 'hope they compensated you.' They gave him a new burger and his money back and sincerely apologised after they had accused him of trying it on.

The boss became very interested in Mark's plight and I thought that the best course of action in the circumstances was for me to remain silent. However, Frank had become very observant and noticed that I had been quiet. He continually stared at me and inquisitively lowered one eye. The poker face remained in place.

Back on the travels and no doubt Mark enjoyed his 'Whopper' as we zoomed down the M2 towards Dover. We had a mini briefing on the car park by the boss that there was a large consignment of drugs heading to our region. The world of intelligence is full of misinformation and 'cloaks and mirrors', as Frank would say and we were being fed enough information to allow us to do our job. The drugs were contained in an articulated lorry, which had been parked up at some motorway services in Belgium. This was an authorised stop to allow the drivers to rest or swap due to the hours they had travelled. The origin of the drugs wasn't known to us, but no doubt those higher up the chain knew everything. Whilst the lorry was in the services, we gleaned that there would be a switch of some sort or possibly an extra load of drugs put onto the lorry. Our job was to sit tight at Dover and wait for the truck and load to cross the channel.

As this involved importing drugs into the United Kingdom, the boss had to notify Her Majesty's Customs and Excise, or 'cuzzies' as they became known. Customs had its own investigation department, and we worked alongside them on some cases, especially those involving importing drugs into the UK. Customs was the only law enforcement agency that could investigate importations, aided where necessary by the police. More information about the operation and why we were so far away from home filtered through. It transpired that another of Frank's many 'informants' was the source of the information.

Criminal informants have been around since the Court of Star Chamber and form an integral part of modern-day policing. In yesteryear, they weren't properly managed and some exploited the situation, as Jason Saunders did in an earlier chapter. In today's police world and learning from mistakes, the management of informants is now very strict and no longer does the tail wag the dog. Information is received in a very sterile process and close tabs are kept on the source of the information. Some informants are highly paid, which always brings a healthy discussion when the police pay a criminal to catch more criminals. Catch a sprat to catch a mackerel.

Recently and shortly before he retired, the Chief Constable of Northumbria Police drew a large amount of negative publicity when it emerged at the trial of some nineteen paedophiles, one of them was a paid police informer, who had also received a large financial reward. Motive and ethics come to mind, and the argument is that nineteen paedophiles were jailed and taken off the streets at minimal cost. Whilst the counter argument is that the State employed and paid a convicted child abuser to enable that. The arguments and discussions will no doubt continue for years to come.

We were told to make our way to the Post House in Dover, and wait for further instructions. Danny and I had been booked into a twin room as, by this time, it was getting late in the day. We were due to hold a briefing at nine o'clock in the conference room with our Customs colleagues with a plan and await the arrival of the lorry and drugs. Danny decided to get an hour of rest whilst a few of the Priestown clan headed for the bar. I joined them, of course. We sat in a corner and the boss and Ray Ingham held court. Sat with them was someone I didn't recognise but was soon informed by Frank it was a 'cuzzy'. I got the distinct feeling that Frank didn't like our Customs colleagues. They were investigators in their own rights, but they weren't cops. They hadn't earned their trade by walking and talking up and down High Streets in full uniform and dealing with life's broken biscuits as we had. Cops were cops and cuzzies were cuzzies and it was deemed never the two shall mix.

Our Customs guest was Mike. He reminded us that Customs held primacy in this investigation as they were the national 'experts' on drug importations by rights. He was very dismissive of the police and came across as quite 'classist'. A well-educated civil servant, he hadn't endured the trials and tribulations of life as we had and looking at his clothing and watch, he wasn't short of a bob or two. When we mustered in the conference room at the Post House, his sanctimonious attitude continued, and I instantly disliked the man. The boss was moved to one side as cuzzy Mike told us how good he and the Customs department were. It was made very clear that we would be assisting the investigation even though Frank was the originator of the information. The night continued with Customs Mike telling us how good he was and we were joined by other Customs officers, who trickled into the bar area.

Danny explained that he was tired and went up to bed. He also gave me some paternal instructions about not being too late. The news was that the lorry was on its way to Calais but we didn't know which ferry it would be on tomorrow. It certainly wasn't on any of the early ones so a lie in was on the cards. The bar area was now busy as there was another social services conference being held in the hotel. I noticed it was coming up to midnight when Customs Mike, in his Van Heusen shirt with a stiff collar and cufflinks, came and sat between myself and a rather large lady who I presumed was either a customs officer or from the social services. I was enjoying giving Frank a good listening too about his travels when Customs Mike placed his Benson & Hedges cigarettes, lighter and room key on the table in front of me and leaned forward. We had a cursory chat about the hotel and that it wasn't up to Mike's standard but he'll 'slum it' for one night. There was absolutely nothing wrong with the Post House. I'd stayed in a lot worse.

'Want a drink, Frank?' I asked as it was my turn to go to the bar.

'Oh, thanks Jim, I'll have a Thomas Titter,' Frank replied.

I had consumed enough beer in my life to know that Thomas Titter was not the name of a beer brew but another of Frank's clicks, cogs, or menagerie uses of the vocabulary.

'Use your grey matter young one, Thomas Titter. Come on, son, you can do it. If brains were dynamite, you wouldn't have enough to blow your cap off,' he said as he burst into laughter with those around him.

I got Frank his pint of bitter and a drink for most of the Priestown team that were left. It was way past midnight and there was still a lot of energy in the room. Frank downed his pint and shook his glass at me.

'I'll get these, Frank. Please let me,' I said as I went to the bar and replenished the tables with drinks.

The ladies from social services were now singing 'I am sailing' as they waved their arms in the air. Mike was getting on really well with the large lady to my right and Frank was keeping his audience riveted with stories galore. I bought the ladies a round of drinks and they carried on their choir practice with a slurred rendition of American Pie.

Before he left for bed, Mike put me in my place once again by telling me that his rank in Customs was that of a Chief

Superintendent in the police. He was going places and asked why I hadn't climbed the promotion ladder as I had now some fifteen or so years in the police. He advised me to keep plugging away, and one day, I may make a senior officer and be as good as him. He had been in my place once and just 'look at me now'. He was quite pissed as well.

There seemed to be a commotion as he was leaving. I was back at the bar ordering more drinks but didn't realise what was happening. Chairs were being moved and I could see the large lady was all over Customs Mike. It wasn't just a case of the odd touch; they were both on the verge of gently massaging each other. I don't think they were kissing, but not far off. Mike disappeared down the stairs and the large lady sat down, not in her seat, but in the one vacated by Mike. I returned with the drinks and as soon as I sat down, the lady leaned into me and started to ask me what I did for a living. She was intoxicated and explained that she worked for social services in Canterbury and looked at the conference she was attending as a 'play away' conference and did I know what she meant. I think I'd grasped that one. Frank leaned across to her and said,

'Don't be talking to this one, love, he's a serial sex offender and only came out of prison last week.'

'I wouldn't mind some sex offending tonight, to be honest,' came the reply in a broad southern accent. Then she stared directly at me and put her hand on my knee.

Her gaze was broken by Customs Mike, who was back but with a member of staff and once again started moving chairs and looking under tables, etc. He was facially gesturing at me and lifting his arms, but I had no idea what was going on. He was very drunk. I gleaned that Mike had misplaced his room key and had asked for assistance at the front desk. They had supplied a pass key to get him inside in the meantime. This was the final search before he hit the sack. Mike and the hotel porter disappeared down the steps soon after and the party moved on.

'Last orders at the bar please, last orders', came the cry and I was under the impression that there would have been a resident's bar. I asked Frank and Mark about the call and they both said that we were indeed in the resident's bar, as it was nearly three o'clock in the morning. Doesn't time fly when you've had a drink?

The large lady was still chatting away and to be honest, I couldn't make out what she was saying most of the time but just kept agreeing and nodding. I gathered that she was in a stale relationship and looking for some fun, which was interesting. There was a ripple of laughter from those that were left standing and I turned to see what was happening. People were looking at me and laughing and I soon became aware of the reason. In my shirt pocket was a very large prawn looking out over the top. I don't know who or how they had slipped it in but I had a little chuckle myself. As I looked down at the prawn with its dark eyes and spindly legs looking up at me, I heard in a deep female voice, 'I find you extremely attractive,' and turned to see the large lady now by my side and moving very closely into my body. She placed a knee in between my legs.

I looked around to see who was watching as this was becoming embarrassing. Frank, Mark, and the others were dispersing, so I bent down and whispered to the lady, 'Give me five minutes to shower, then come up to my room. Here's the key, just let yourself in, I'm alone,' and I passed her the key and winked. She smiled back at me and then sat down, blowing me a kiss as she did so. She kept staring at me as I walked towards the exit, and I murmured, 'Five minutes,' and held up my hand to her. She puckered her lips and placed room key 35 on the table in front of her.

***

The pain was excruciating. First, I tried the right eye and then the left eye. It was like someone was playing squash in my head with ten partners. Bang, bang, bang! The headache was huge and the dry throat made things worse. I prized one eye open and the shafts of light penetrated deep into the skull.

'Wouldn't go down there if I was you, Jim,' said a voice I instantly recognised as Danny's. 'Something going on with that Mike from Cuzzies. Someone broke into his room in the night or something. Just been down for my breakfast.'

Oh dear. It came flooding back. The large lady, the room key and Mike. I didn't say anything to Danny but attempted to stand and made my way to the bathroom.

'What time did you bloody well come to bed, you dirty stop out?' asked Danny. Frank said it was a good night, and I have to ask you: Are you a 'prawn again Christian' or something? ' I smirked, shut the bathroom door, and started a cold shower.

I skipped breakfast and headed straight for the conference room. I kept my head down as I knew more was to come. Frank and colleagues were laughing at me regarding the prawn in my shirt pocket which was good as it deflected away from the real issue of why the local police were called in the early hours to remove a drunken woman from Customs Mike's room.

The boss and Ray gave Danny and me a local point on the map where we should park up and await further instructions. The lorry from Belgium was booked on the lunchtime ferry and was due in Dover early afternoon. Customs were allowing the importation as we all wanted to know where the drugs were destined for. The importance of the operation was stressed upon us as this was the first time Customs had let a consignment of drugs 'run' into the country. We simply could not lose the lorry. On no account must these drugs get into the dealer's hands. We had to take the drugs and dealer out at the same time.

People were lingering around, but I needed to leave the hotel quickly. Customs Mike was significant because of his absence from the meeting and I certainly didn't want to bump into his large lady lover. I asked Danny to check out and headed for the car park. As I sneaked past reception, I saw Customs Mike having a very heated discussion with who I assumed was the manager. I walked straight on and didn't look sideways. I got into the passenger side of the Cavalier and slid down in the seat. Danny opened the driver's door a few minutes later and climbed in. 'The shit has hit the fan in there,' he said as he manoeuvred in the seat and placed his sunglasses in the tray, 'yeah just overheard that Mike from Customs is arguing like fuck about his bar bill. It seems he got stiffed as everyone put their drinks onto his room bill last night.'

***

We were now deployed in various places, covering all routes from Dover. More information was filtering through about the lorry, which had left a different port earlier in the week empty and was coming back empty, which raised a red flag among our colleagues from Customs. Information was passing from car to car about the shenanigans in the Post House, and rumour had it that Customs Mike had been whacked with a £400 bar bill.

The clock was ticking down and it was confirmed that the 40-ton lorry was on the ferry and the K9 machine had detected drugs. I told Danny it was amazing and an advance in technology that we now had machines that could sniff out drugs. Impressive indeed, until Danny explained that a K9 machine was a dog. Ooops.

'Standby, standby, standby,' those words never leave you. 'Subject vehicle is off, off, off the ferry and it's a left, left, left towards the roundabout, which is signposted the A20. Teams to acknowledge.' All the vehicles then started to acknowledge in sequence over the radio as the white 40-ton lorry steamed through Dover in the general direction of the motorway. Five surveillance cars and a range of Customs vehicles were in the convoy. The lead car began the commentary stating, 'vehicle is nearside lane of two, A20 westbound, speed five zero (50mph)'

We took turns following the lorry from the A20 onto the M20 and then heading for the M25. The speed never increased above 60mph and there was nothing exciting about the surveillance thus far. There was only one driver in the cab and the lorry was registered to a transport company in Nottingham. It was now nearing rush hour as we approached the Dartford Crossing and things started to heat up. Surveillance vehicles were getting stuck in traffic and we didn't know where Mike and his Customs officers were as our radios were on different wavelengths and didn't speak to each other. Frank was close to the lorry and kept the commentary coming, but then he got baulked at the bridge. The lorry went through and then we heard the dreaded phrase, 'Total loss teams, total loss, last sighting of the vehicle was M25 northbound at Thurrock.'

Unfortunately, we couldn't get anyone ahead and check due to traffic congestion. Frank was doing his best to weave in and out of the traffic but wasn't progressing. It was a delicate balance now of trying to make some ground and not showing out that we were the police. The lorry could have its convoy of criminals who were watching the watchers. It was getting tense now in the cars as there had been no sightings of the truck for a few minutes. There was an exit at Thurrock and one of the team came off at that junction. Danny decided to slip up the hard shoulder, but thinking that we were queue jumping, members of the public pulled onto the hard shoulder and blocked our path. This wasn't looking good. Minutes seemed hours as the silence became deafening.

'Contact, contact, contact. Jethro (Frank) to all teams, no deviation, subject vehicle M25 northbound. Nearside lane of three, speed of 50mph. Teams are to acknowledge in sequence,' which we all did. It was a relief to hear Frank. It took a while for the cars to catch up with Frank, but the convoy trundled on, heading for the A1 and M1. The commentary continued, and we trundled along the M25, passing the turn-off for the A1 (North). Not long after, we came to the bigger interchange with the M1 and this time, the commentary went something like, 'nearside lane of four. Speed five zero, three hundred, two hundred, one hundred and it's left, left' left onto the filter lane, which is the M1 Northbound. Teams to acknowledge,' and once again, we all did. The countdown of three hundred, two hundred were the motorway hundred yard markers.

The light started fading as the convoy trundled up the M1 northbound. Danny and I were in the lead position and had the 'eyeball'. The lorry was in the nearside line and crossed the white lines into the slip road for the Newport Pagnell service station.

'Nearside lane of three, three hundred, two hundred, one hundred and it's left, left, left Newport Pagnell service station.'

Silence!

'Preacher to all the teams, left left left, Newport Pagnell Service station,' I screamed into the radio as the lorry trundled forward towards the lorry park. 'Teams to acknowledge.'

Once again, silence. Frank's car came flashing past us, carrying on up the motorway; he had missed the services. Then we saw Mark Smithies fly past in the Orion. They hadn't heard the commentary and once they had passed the exit for the services, there was no doing U-turns on a motorway. Danny and I had to follow the lorry and just hoped the other teams would pick up the radio transmissions. Sometimes shit did happen and the radios went down. It was happening now. We had just received a batch of ex-military and encrypted radios as criminals with scanners used to listen to police frequencies to see if they were being followed. They were state-of-the-art radios, but I'm not sure we knew how to use them properly.

The lorry continued to the car park and turned in a big arc until the cab was facing the services. It was parked in a wide open space and the nearest lorry was some twenty-five metres away. The driver had parked as far away as he could from the gaze of the services and the public. We drove near the perimeter fence of the services and I told Danny to slow down. I opened the passenger door and jumped out, shouting to Danny to pick me up later near the petrol pumps. I climbed the perimeter fence and into the darkness of the fields. I got down onto my front and crawled along the ground for what seemed an eternity. Eventually, I had a perfect view of the 40-ton white lorry, as Frank would say, from Snotland. The lights were still on and the engine was running. I couldn't see the driver, but no other vehicle was near it. I was commentating that there was 'no change', but I'm not sure if anyone could hear me. As I was now out on foot, I had to wear a covert earpiece, which fit snugly into the ear canal. It was silent. The body-worn radios were small and didn't pack a punch when it came to transmissions. They only had a range of a few hundred metres. So there had to be a car nearby that could pick up the transmission from the foot operative and then use the big car radio to 'relay' what the foot operative was transmitting. The car radio boosted the transmissions and could be picked up miles away. I watched and waited, but nothing happened.

Thirty minutes or so passed with nothing happening. I kept up the commentary into the body-worn radio, but nothing returned. I knew that Danny was in our car near the petrol pumps, so if the lorry did set off, I could make it back to the car and we could continue to follow it. It started to get cold lying on the soil, but I couldn't move for fear of someone seeing me. I laid still and every couple of minutes kept transmitting the words, 'no change, no change.'

Then the driver's door opened and holding on to the door and side of the lorry, the driver lowered himself down to the ground. I was too far away to provide a detailed description, but he was tall and stocky. He had a good head of hair and a full beard. I couldn't see his clothing, but he was white-skinned. He lit a cigarette and walked towards the service area and the cafes. I relayed what was happening through the body worn radio, hoping someone would receive it. However, it was very quiet on the airwaves and I couldn't see any of the cars nearby. Danny and I were on our own.

As the driver disappeared into the lights of the services, a large box van travelled up the service road. Again, it was white and I couldn't see a driver or passenger. The lorry was parked alone and stood out, enabling this smaller box van to drive around and circle it. It drove around for a few minutes and then came to a stop at the rear of the lorry. The driver's door opened first, then the passenger door and two dark figures jumped out. They opened the back of the box van and carried items up to the back of the lorry. There was lots of movement and it seemed both figures from the box van were trying to remove one of the spare wheels from the rear of the articulated lorry. Usually, two large spare wheels are fastened at the rear of lorries and this seemed to be where the two figures were working. It wasn't long before one of the wheels dropped to the floor and spun around like a coin until it eventually came to rest. One of the figures then wheeled the spare tyre towards the back of the van and the doors opened. Lifting the wheel inside took a while, most probably due to the weight. Both figures were pushing and lifting until, eventually, it clattered inside. The box van started to move from side to side as the wheel landed.

Both figures then stood at the rear of the lorry and I saw the red glow of cigarettes. They were chatting to each other and I saw one of them throw the cig to the floor and then set off walking towards the perimeter fence and of course, directly towards me. He was slightly to my left and continued walking across the tarmac. Then he rose onto the grass verge and walked directly towards me across the grass. He was now at the perimeter fence and looking into the field. I could smell the cigarette smoke on him. I put my head down into the soil and then held my breath. There was no chance of any radio transmitting as I had my earpiece in, but any slight sound may alert him to my position. I heard liquid hitting the floor and realised he had come over the fence for a pee. It was a relief because I thought he had seen something reflecting from the field. He must have had a few drinks beforehand because he continued peeing for a while, and I caught a whiff of the steam as it drifted my way.

After a while, I heard the jingle and rattle of change and lifted my head ever so slightly to see the figure walking back towards the two vehicles across the grass verge. It wasn't long before he was back with the other figure and the process started again with spare wheel number two. I then saw a third figure and realised the driver of the 40-tonner had returned. It didn't take long before the second spare wheel was in the back of the box van and once again, I saw the red illuminations of cigarettes as all three men stood at the back of the lorry chatting and smoking away.

I was still transmitting and commentating, but I wondered if Danny or any of the team were receiving anything. All three men then shook hands at the back of the lorry. The driver made his way to the cab and the two figures headed back towards the box van. Within seconds, the lights on the vehicle came on and it pulled away and started moving towards the exit. The lorry engine started and a thick, dark plume of diesel smoke bellowed out from the side. The lorry shunted forward slowly before it, too, headed for the exit. I continued the commentary as best I could and climbed the perimeter fence to return to Danny and the car. As I was doing so, my foot slipped, and I soon realised that I was standing in a pool of piss. I waited a while to ensure no one was watching and then jumped onto the grass before running to the petrol station. The Cavalier was parked on the other side and Danny waved at me. I ran across and he drove towards me, leant across and opened the passenger door. With the car moving slowly, I jumped in, shut the door and fell back into the seat.

'Brilliant that, brilliant. Frank (Jethro) is ahead, and Mark Smithies (Smug) is waiting at the next junction. I think the boss is behind us,' Danny explained.

'Could you hear me painting the picture for everyone?' I asked.

'Oh yeah, I could hear you loud and clear. Thought you were a goner when he came over to you for a piss,' added Danny as he burst into a fit of laughter.

Frank then continued the commentary as both vehicles trundled along in the slow lane of the M1, heading north. Danny explained that after I jumped out, there was a frantic exchange of personnel and mobile units trying to get back to the services. The Customs units were with us but were on a different radio frequency. A regional unit at Rugby had also joined us, so things looked much healthier than before.

'Just for the information of the teams, we are approaching Catthorpe Interchange, where the M1 meets the M6,' came a warning from Frank. He continued, 'The subject vehicle box van is in the nearside lane of four signposted for M6 North, the lorry is in the middle lane of four signposted M1 North.'

They were splitting up. Now came a dilemma. The radio exchanges became frantic as one of the Priestown team had now climbed into a Customs Unit so they could listen to our radio commentary. Someone else had also jumped in with the local crime squad for the same reason and one of the customs officers was also with a new team. It seemed like organised chaos and it was, but it seemed to be working. The agreement was for the Customs teams to take the 40-tonner from Snotland and arrest the driver. The rest of us would take the box van and contents and hopefully follow it back to Priestown.

The box van was now travelling north on the M6. It was in the slow lane and travelling around 60mph. The boss and the local Rugby officers were in the convoy with us. The call came over the radio that we would stop the van and arrest the occupants after the next junction. There was also the matter of two spare wheels in the back full of drugs, we hoped.

The next junction was signposted Rugby and Frank gave the countdown: ' Three hundred, two hundred, one hundred, no deviation teams, subject vehicle heading north M6.'

The plan was for Frank to get in front of the van and gradually slow down. Danny and I were to pull alongside the vehicle in the middle lane and slow down to the same speed as Frank. Then, the boss or one of the local cars would come up behind and, yes, box the box van in.

'Jethro (Frank) in position.'

'Chadders (Danny and I) in position.

'Womba now in position. Slow them down, teams,' came the instruction from the boss.

The speed slowly decreased from 60mph to 50mph, then slower, and I looked directly at the box van driver. Maybe he was the one that tried to piss on me. He had signalled to pull out to overtake the Ford Orion that Frank was driving but couldn't as the trusty Cavalier blocked his way. The driver looked directly at me and mouthed something to me. I couldn't tell what it was, but it hadn't registered with him what was happening. Frank put his hazard warning lights on and so did we, as other vehicles were unaware of what was happening. The speed got down to 30mph and then I noticed the look of shock on the driver's face as he realised what was about to happen. What we hadn't catered for was the hard shoulder and that's exactly where he headed. Frank pulled across to stop him and then we pulled across to close the gap. The boss pulled in behind and one of the local cars must have had portable flashing blue lights as they lit up the car's interior. We travelled along the hard shoulder for fifty yards and Frank slowed it right down.

'They're bailing out teams, they're bailing out,' came the shout over the radio.

The passenger door of the box van flew open and a dark figure jumped out into the night. The driver was still behind the wheel as I was looking straight at him. He, too, then jumped over to the passenger side and out of the open door. The box van started to pull out into the slow lane and with no one driving we had no option but to force it back onto the hard shoulder. The crunch of metal from the front of our car sounded expensive. Frank then came to a stop and a crunch and crash followed as pieces of the rear lights fell onto the roadway. Doors opened quickly and bodies jumped from vehicles. Luckily, there was a steep grass bank where we had stopped and Mark Smithies had hold of one of the figures and was coming back down the slope. The other figure was a few paces ahead of me and realised now that his escape attempt was futile. He placed his hands high and slowly made his way down the bank towards me,

'You're under arrest, pal, for conspiring with others to import controlled drugs into the country. You do not have to say anything unless you wish to do so, but what you say may be given in evidence. Do you understand?'

He looked directly at me but through me. What must have been going through his mind at that time? He knew he had been caught, maybe grassed up, but the main thing he knew was that he was going to prison. A couple of the local officers joined us and soon, the passenger and driver were en route to Rugby Police Station, where we would sort everything out. Mark Smithies jumped in the box van and with cars whizzing past us at 70mph, we negotiated our way off the hard shoulder and eventually arrived at Rugby police station.

Steven Taylor and Brent Finnegan, the driver and passenger of the box van, had been booked into custody and now we were awaiting a crime scene examiner to look at the box van and the two spare wheels in the back. Both men were from the north and the van was registered to a company from Cheshire. There was still a little way to go in this investigation yet. The time was getting on by now, and the boss decided to get both men and their haul to Priestown so that we could control everything and not have evidence and suspects in different parts of the country. As I had arrested Taylor, Danny and I were allocated the task of taking him and a holdall that had been found in the front of the box van. It contained bags of white powder and lots of cards that I knew were strips of LSD. Unfortunately, our Cavalier had sustained some damage at the front, and the headlight and sidelight were out. The wing was slightly twisted, but I was prepared to drive it. The boss said no and negotiated with the local team, hoping they could lend us a car to get back to Priestown.

Danny was holding a handcuffed Steven Taylor as we left the custody office. I'd been given the keys of a local Ford Sierra that we were to drive to Priestown and return it when the Cavalier was fixed. I had the holdall full of the powder and LSD and looked on the aluminium key fob at the number of the Sierra. It ended in HND and I scoured the station car park for it. There it was and I couldn't believe my eyes. A Ford Sierra Cosworth 4x4. Wow. They wanted me to get Taylor back as soon as possible then. This was a machine and I'm so glad I volunteered to drive it. I remember Hargreaves from Leeds driving a Cosworth in the previous chapter; it was the criminal's choice of car. It was uncatchable.

Danny was in the back with Taylor handcuffed and there was silence in the car. We had exchanged pleasantries with Taylor but knew not to ask any questions. The Police and Criminal Evidence Act 1984 (PACE) had become law to stop the many miscarriages of justice and police impropriety, so we knew we had to follow the rules. I hit the M6 just before midnight and decided to mimic Nigel Mansell in one of his many Grand Prix. 70, 80, 90mph and still going fast, 110, 120, 130, 140mph and still as smooth as ever. The motorway was very quiet and the milometer was spinning around. 150, 160mph and we would be in Priestown in no time. I had never driven as fast on four wheels before and my previous speed record was racing my motorcycle but this Cosworth seemed to be blowing that away.

I don't know why I checked, but I did. The rearview mirror was as black as could be in the darkness the Cosworth was leaving behind. Except that is for a little blue spec in the bottom left-hand corner of the mirror. I just wonder, I thought to myself as the spec began to get bigger and I slowed the Cosworth down to below the speed of sound. The blue spec became more visible as blue flashing lights rapidly gained on us. It wasn't long before a police Range Rover overtook us. They were chasing someone. I was now down to about 70 mph and was relieved that it wasn't us they were after. Danny and Taylor commented about the Range Rover and then I became aware of a car travelling at the same speed as me in the middle lane. It was parallel to our car and a rather studious character was driving. He was looking directly out of the front windscreen. No other motorist was on the motorway, yet this clown stayed by my side. I did think there are no other motorists on the road and this idiot is by my side. Then, I saw more blue flashing lights behind me. I looked in the rearview mirror and saw the inside lane and middle lane occupied with blue flashing lights.

'They're boxing you in, Jim,' came the shout from Danny. Sure enough, the Range Rover that overtook us was now in front and slowing. Oh dear!

I pulled onto the hard shoulder in the glaze of all the bright lights and immediately exited the vehicle. I had long hair and a beard and even though I may have acted like a cop at times, I certainly didn't look like one. I could see officers jumping out of vehicles, running towards me and reaching for their batons. They'd been chasing me for a while and I had no idea which police force we were in. I could see the red mist had come down with the car driver at the side of us, who now had his car door open and was barking commands at the others.

'Cuff him, cuff him. Don't fucking let them get out. Get him, get him.'

I raised both my hands in the air. I was wearing my trusted but tatty Levi denim jacket. Yes, I did sit in the bath with the jeans on to shrink them. I held my police warrant card high and shouted, 'Police, Police.'

The first officer to get to my side looked up and looked somewhat shocked. It certainly wasn't what he was expecting.

'What, what, what the fuck are you doing driving like that. Here, give me the card.' With that, I handed my warrant card over and then he said, 'Driving licence. What Force?'

The officer barking orders from the car at our side had now joined the other officer with me. He, too, joined in.

'What gives you the need to travel at one hundred and forty-four miles per hour, eh?' he asked angrily as I answered the first cop with my Force details and where I worked. I wanted to correct him with my speed as I'm sure I got the needle up to one sixty, but I thought not the time nor the place. I was thirty-one years of age and still fighting maturity, but I knew if I larked about here, I was in big trouble.

I opened the hatchback, and the two heads of Danny and the drug dealer Taylor looked around to see what was happening. I told Taylor to hold his hands up and show the handcuffs. This appesed Mr. Angry traffic cop somewhat and then he asked again how I could justify the speed. I tried to explain that I had over half a million pounds worth of drugs on board and Taylor was a Category A prisoner, which I doubted he was. I also explained we were in an armed convoy due to the serious nature of the offences and offenders and Mr Angry interrupted me,

'Where is your supervisor then?'

The timing was impeccable. It couldn't have been any better as the headlights grew more prominent in the distance. I looked back and heard the car engine roar as the boss and Ray Ingham flew past in the Toyota at a breakneck speed. The gust of wind that followed rocked all the cars and one of the many cops who surrounded us had to chase his cap, which was rolling down the hard shoulder.

'That's my supervisor there,' I said as the tail lights disappeared in the darkness.

There was another roar as the Orion flew past with Frank at the wheel. He was travelling well over 100 mph. Shaun looked out of the passenger window as he went by but didn't appear to recognise the situation. Vroom and another roar as yet another car went past. I pointed out the convoy of vehicles and came to realise how easy it would be for a criminal if they thought they were being followed. I tried to explain to Mr Angry that the detention clock was ticking and I had to get Taylor back to Priestown because of the PACE Codes, but he knew his law and dismissed that as 'bullshit', which it was. I was floundering.

'I'm going to have to report this matter,' he said as he handed my driving licence back to me. I told him he had to do what he had to and that I would slow down to the maximum speed limit. I wanted to tell him again that I was travelling faster than one hundred and forty-four miles per hour, but once again, the angel on my shoulder won this time and she instructed me to keep quiet, get in the car and drive back to Priestown. Which I did. The devil was vexed!

***

It was late when we arrived back at Priestown and it would be an early start to deal with Taylor and Finnegan. We were all booked into a local hotel and the boss brought a bottle of whisky, which didn't last long between the teams. After three or four hours of sleep, we were back at Priestown and Danny and I had been assigned to deal with Taylor. That meant interviewing, processing and later charging. The box van and the lorry spare wheels were all going to be examined by CSI and the bag of goodies we brought up with the powders and LSD would also be forwarded to the Forensic Laboratories. The laboratories were government-owned back in the day and although there may have been an odd hiccup, they seemed to work fine. The story is different today with change and privatisation. Where there is an opportunity, there is profit.

Taylor wasn't a bad man. He had a couple of previous convictions for minor things and on the record, didn't speak. Well, he did say 'no comment' to all the questions. He had a solicitor by his side to protect him or, in this case, ensure he said nothing. Taylor, off the record, explained that he was just a small cog in a very big wheel and he apologised for not answering questions and hoped we understood his position. The solicitor was not his choice, but his boss's choice, the head of the organised crime group. He wouldn't divulge any more information about that side of things as he said they would quite simply kill him. He was a family man who did some driving for a living to put food on his table.

The powder in the holdall came back as glucose, but the suspected LSD was, in fact, the drug and very powerful by all accounts. The cannabis resin had been extracted from inside the spare tyres and was roughly around 500kg. I had no idea of the street value, but Taylor and Finnegan were looking down the barrel of a long custodial sentence. LSD was a Category A drug and any prison sentence would be more severe. Finnegan followed the same course as Taylor in replying 'no comment' but had not spoken off the record. We heard that the driver of the 40-ton lorry had been arrested and that Customs officers were dealing with that side of the investigation.

Taylor asked to see me and wanted to help himself really but was very conscious that if he gave any information to the police or Customs, then it would get back to his bosses who the source was. He asked if he did provide information, would the police ensure the Judge was aware of what he'd done and how he'd assisted. If you remember, in Book I of my journey, outlining my earlier career, I did explain how that system worked. The information was received from a suspect, processed and then actioned with the results formulated into a 'text' for the Judge to read before sentencing. When I say 'text', I don't mean an SMS message but a formalised report outlining the assistance provided and the results. The issue for Taylor was Finnegan. If the police acted on information that one of the two had supplied, Finnegan knew it wasn't him and would inform the gang boss it was Taylor. Was that a risk worth taking?

Taylor's and Finnegan's houses had been searched, and the box van was registered with a company in Cheshire. That company was a leasing company that had leased the box van to another company on Merseyside. Enquiries to trace that company led
officers to a postal address in Liverpool city centre that was a centre handing calls and collecting mail for hundreds of companies. It seemed that was the end of the line. That was until Finnegan asked to see someone and made a similar request regarding providing useful information to lessen his sentence.

The afternoon was drawing to a close when we were all summoned back to the office for what we thought was a debrief at four o'clock. Taylor and Finnegan were ready to be charged and as I walked into the office, I saw one of the big cheeses sitting at the top of the Office, chatting with Julie. He was Tom Macintosh, a Detective Superintendent who managed about half a dozen regional offices, including Priestown, Blackton, and Burnton. Macintosh had a reputation as someone not to mess with and when he 'went', he did so like a fizzy bottle of pop. He was from the county's Sandford side, so we had something in common. The debrief was, in fact, a new briefing as we were all being asked to stay on duty as there was another operation. I was tired and it was Friday. I just wanted to go home.

We were told that a fuel tanker would deposit some diesel at a farm on the Cheshire, Shropshire border sometime during the night. Along with diesel would be another 400kg of cannabis. It was another joint enterprise with Customs officers as the tanker was again from Belgium (Snotland) and we would all meet at Sandbach Services on the M6. We were all tired as we left the office and it was muted in the briefing that some of us might have to stay up all night carrying out observations on the farm. A CROP officer (Covert, Rural, Observation Post) was to be deployed, whose duty it was to conceal themselves in pig shit if necessary and observe the proceeding from a very close vantage point. John Fordham was a CROP officer who buried himself in the garden of the gangster Kenneth Noye some months earlier. Noye had some rather large Rottweilers that unfortunately found DC Fordham, which alerted Noye to the officer's presence. Noye then continually stabbed DC Fordham with his garden fork, claiming self-defence as the officer was camouflaged. DC Fordham died at the scene and Noye was subsequently acquitted of the officer's murder. Being a CROP officer was very tedious but extremely dangerous.

I slept all the way to Sandbach and was transferred to a Customs Unit to help them with our radio transmissions. A Customs Officer also climbed in with Danny and we were given points on the road near Wombwell Farm to conduct our 'covert' observations. On the drive there, I tried to chat with my new partner, Bob. Let's just say it was difficult. I quickly found out that Bob and I had nothing in common. He liked the quiet life, ballroom dancing and reading. It seemed a lifetime before we reached our observation point, a quiet country lane with a view of the main road. It was anticipated the tanker would come past at some point. Bob managed to park on some raised ground, which gave us a great view but also highlighted our position to everyone. Car headlights lit up the inside of our car. It wasn't very covert. I tried to skirt around the edges, explaining to Bob that we may stand out, but it didn't seem to register. When I went more direct and told him we had to move, he began to sulk. It was going to be a long night.

My eyes were heavy and I could feel myself slipping off into sleep. My head was rolling and I was trying to stay awake. Only a few words passed between Bob and me, but he was making quite a noise with something. First I heard the sound, then the smell of sulphur and I opened one eye to see….. a pipe! He was puffing on a pipe and the fumes quickly filled the car. I gasped for breath before opening the door, which illuminated the inside of the car.

'Shut the door, for goodness sake,' screamed Bob.

'Well, put the bloody pipe out then,' I retorted.

Let's just say it was a very long night and nothing the size of a fuel tanker passed our way. Our CROP Officer with the call sign 'Rabbie' was very quiet. Around four in the morning, someone on the radio asked Rabbie for an update. There was no reply. It was very quiet on all the radios and the first signs of light began to filter through. It was now around six in the morning when the car radio crackled into life,

'Standby, standby, standby, possible subject vehicle approaching the junction, and it's a right, right, right along the A53 towards the M6. Teams to acknowledge.'

As the teams acknowledged the radio, I tried to regain my senses after a night with boring Bob. It suddenly occurred to me that the subject vehicle, possibly the tanker, was leaving the farm but not arriving. Radio operators were now desperately trying to reach Rabbie, the CROP officer, but again, nothing was heard. Womba, the boss car, told us to remain in position as we would soon be moving in on the farm.

As it became lighter and we were ready to move on the farm, there was a crackle on the car radio. It was the whispering sound of Rabbie, who was somewhere on the farm, carrying out those close and dangerous observations.

'No change teams, no change,' came the transmission from Rabbie.

It appeared that Rabbie had somehow missed the lot. It may have been cold in his foxhole, but Rabbie nodded off and missed all the action. The tanker had either been and gone or been there before we arrived, but it had left around six o'clock.

The strike at the farm took place around eight o'clock that morning and Bob took his time driving there. When we arrived at the gates, we were probably last and some of the Priestown teams and others had two more suspects in their custody. Dogs were barking and there was a commotion in the entrance. We were beckoned over to Macintosh, who had surprisingly made an appearance.

'Search the farm from top to bottom. It shouldn't be difficult finding 400kg of cannabis resin, should it?' said Macintosh as a group of us headed wearily for the inside of the farm. I was still playing competitive football and was due to play that afternoon for my beloved Lostow FC, or so I thought.

After five hours of searching and looking high and low, our hands were empty. There was not 400kg of cannabis resin on the farm. All the Priestown crew now assembled in the living quarters of the farmhouse to ascertain what was next on the agenda. Bob and the ballroom dancers were long gone. We weren't there long when Macintosh and our boss came in. He could see that we hadn't found anything and 400kg of anything is big. I was happy where I had searched. I was confident it wasn't there.

'Search again,' said Macintosh. It's here. No one goes home until we find it.' Deep, audible sighs filled the air. With our heads lowered, we trundled off like zombies with our task.

I stood in the kitchen area of the farm and watched the sun setting across the fields. I was exhausted. I could hardly think straight. I've been on the road for 3 days, up all night with boring Bob watching for a tanker and now this. We'd all had enough.

The second search was fruitless as Macintosh stared out of the kitchen window. Others from Priestown gathered in the kitchen, looking at each other with the odd eyebrow raised here and there. We were shattered.

'Why are all those rolls of barbed wire in the middle of that field?' Macintosh asked us. I thought of a flippant answer, but the angel won again. I stayed quiet.

'What are you thinking boss?' chirped Frank and with that, Macintosh set off out of the back door and like the pied piper, led us across the field to the barbed wire. He started to move the rolls to one side and everyone joined in. Underneath the wire was a large piece of new hardboard and when lifted revealed a large safe door, the safe being buried in the earth with the door looking up to the sky. There was some running back and forth to the farm and a set of keys were produced. Voila, lots and lots of cannabis resin.

***

After a day off, we were all back at work and Danny and I were summoned to a meeting with Macintosh and the lead investigator for Customs, our dear friend Mike, from the Dover Post House. The meeting discussed the direction of the investigation and the recovery of the proceeds of crime from the farm holder. Customs Mike then shook Macintosh's bottle, and the top flew off. Macintosh went into an absolute rage at Mike's suggestion that we put Frank's original informant and Taylor and Finnegan into the witness box to give evidence. He wanted to expose the people who had given information. The meeting ended abruptly, to say the least. Putting them in the witness box would be madness and Customs Mike couldn't see how it would place all these individuals at great risk. He didn't seem to care and in his words, could easily 'burn' them. Macintosh was raging. Customs Mike was sent packing, and he felt the full force of Macintosh's anger. I'd never seen anything like it before.

Macintosh told Danny to leave and wait for me in reception. As soon as he left, Macintosh opened a manilla folder and read the contents in silence.

'One hundred, one hundred and forty-four miles per hour. Let me repeat that. One hundred and forty-four miles per hour!' he shouted at me. 'How on earth can you justify that? I know exactly what you've done; you've thought Ford Cosworth, racing car, foot to the floor, and let's see how fast this thing can go, haven't you?'

'No sir, I genuinely wanted to get back as quick as I could due to having Taylor and a lot of drugs on board,' I replied.

'You are double the bloody speed limit, lad.'

'I just wanted to get back quickly, Sir.'

Macintosh stood up and walked to his window. He looked out and left me to sit in the hot seat for a while. His back was towards me. I sat in silence, expecting the worst. He turned and faced me.

'How did you get the fat lass in his room?' he asked, smiling. It confused me and threw me off track.

'How did I what? I don't understand.'

'The fat lass in Dover, how on earth did you get her in Custom Mike's room and then charge all the drinks to his room? Ha ha, hilarious, just fucking hilarious. I wish I could have seen that,' he added with laughter, 'go on, how did you do it?'

I just looked blankly at him.

'In all seriousness, Graham, slow down, will you and get yourself back to Priestown in one piece. I pissed myself when I heard about the fat lass, absolute belter.'

As I turned towards the door, I thought I would push my luck and looked round at him and as the TV detective Columbo said,

'There's just one final thing, boss, it wasn't one hundred and forty-four miles per hour, more like one sixty.'

'What's that? Go on, get out lad, and slow down,' he chuckled.

***

As the weeks went by, I started to reflect on the Dover escapade, the cannabis, the LSD, the lorry drivers and the farmhouse. I had a lot of unanswered questions. We were never told about the outcome of the driver of the 40-ton lorry or the diesel tanker driver. Taylor and Finnegan got five years each, no doubt a reduced sentence with the assistance they had provided. The farm owner got six years and an order that he repay £200,000 or serve another three years in custody. I am told he paid the cash almost immediately.

I assumed that we got to know about the farm through Taylor and Finnegan, but how was it that Macintosh knew to look under the barbed wire in the field? Luck or stage management? Also, no one mentioned how easy it was to find the keys to the safe and find the cannabis. They seemed to be at hand. For the first time, I realised that the world of criminal intelligence was shrouded in secrecy with deceptive tactics and misinformation employed to gather more information. Pawns don't get to know the King's agenda. In those famous words of Lord Tennyson, 'Theirs is not to make reply. Theirs not to reason why. Theirs but to do and die.'

We did as we were told.

CHAPTER TEN

OPERATION EMPATHY

As I have previously explained, when I arrived at Priestown Regional Crime Squad, my first week was spent looking over the edge of a cliff. I had come from the town of Sandford and had been investigating, at times, serious crime. But this was a different world. Highly organised crime groups travelling internationally as they peddled in illegal drugs. It was mind-blowing.

Father Anthony Mooney established his business in the 1950s in Blackton by the Sea. A wheeler-dealer, he opened shops to sell expensive goods at low prices in an auction style.

'Come on ladies, who will give me five pounds for this lovely tea set? Come on, a fiver, and I'll tell you what: I'll throw in some tablecloths, knives, forks and table mats. All for a fiver.'

Remember those types of places? Well, the Mooney family had a monopoly in Blackton. They did it very well and with a very aggressive sales pitch and some audience stooges, they persuaded the public to part with their hard-earned cash for what was cheap rubbish. If you wanted to complain, you were sent to a side door which was never answered, or if it was, the threat of violence made the complaint go away.

Sons Michael and David helped father Anthony build the Mooney empire and before long they were involved in serious and organised crime. The nearby fishing port of Fleetworth saw its fleet diminish with the introduction of the super factory ships and the fishing quotas, enforced by the European Fisheries Commission. When the Mooneys and the idle hands of the fishing fleet met, the importation of large quantities of drugs became the industry of the day.

One of my first assignments on Operation Empathy was to team up with another colleague from the Northshire Police Drugs Squad, Tony Hill. My other partner, Danny Chadwick, had been assigned elsewhere. I am trying to think of words to describe Tony as he was off the wall. People used the word 'crackpot' to describe me, but I was small stuff compared to Tony. He was a knowledgeable individual and not your stereotypical cop. He was ahead of the times, really, as he pumped the weights and regularly visited the gym. He studied 'priesthood' in his spare time and our get to know each other time was the drive across to Blackton by the Sea. We had been tasked with checking to see if some of the cars belonging to the Operation Empathy gang were outside one of the local hostelries, The Royal Oak. This was the Star Wars bar, the scene from Bladerunner and not the place for police officers to visit. We were told it was a 'no go' area and to stay well away. This meant nothing to Tony. I could tell.

It was a glorious summers day and the sun was beaming down. It was busy by the beach and the tide was out, giving a glorious view across the bay. I parked the car and Tony got out and immediately started to undress. I watched as the shirt and the pants came off, revealing a pair of luminous yellow shorts. He had calf-length yellow builders boots on, which looked like they'd just come off a building site.

'What are you doing?' I asked.

'I'm going on the beach and then looking for them cars at that pub,' he said before walking off.

I was fully clothed and started to follow him, running alongside him like 'rain man' as he marched ahead. I tried to talk to him, but he marched towards the sea in his yellow shorts and builders boots like someone from a Monty Python sketch.

'Love the sea,' he said as he started to splash about. I stood and watched from the sands as he walked into the sea. The water covered his boots.

'Come on then, Royal Oak here we come,' and with that he marched out of the sea, across the sands and headed for the promenade.

'And if you think I'm going in any pub with you dressed like that, you need to think again,' he said over his shoulder.

We came off the sands and onto the promenade before marching along the back streets. I followed on walking past the joke shop that sold the detonators and eventually, Tony disappeared into a tee shirt type of shop. I followed him in. He threw a pair of fluorescent chequered knee-length shorts at me with a Bob Marley, red, gold and green 'One Love' tee shirt.

'Come here and try these on and a pair of flip-flops, love, please,' he shouted to a young girl at the front of the shop.

We walked out somewhat different to how we walked in. Picture the scene. Two six-foot men, one with neatly cropped hair and a six-pack body, wearing fluorescent yellow shorts, a string vest, and wet calf-length builders' yellow boots. The other, long hair, beard with a rasta tee shirt, chequered fluorescent shorts and flip flops. It was a sight to be seen. I carried my clothes in carrier bag I got from the shop and it wasn't long before Mr Monty Python, Tony himself, opened the Royal Oak doors and like John Cleese, marched straight inside. I quickly followed and indeed, it was the Star Wars bar. It was wall to wall with Blackton's finest with the two of us stood in the middle. We didn't look out of place, though, and no one batted an eyelid. Life carried on as if two local lads had walked in.

'What are you selling, mate?' asked a voice from my side.

'Just come in for a pint, that's all,' I said as the face at my side pointed to my bag.

'Oh, thought you'd been grafting and was knocking stuff out on the fly,' the face added.

'Just my jeans, mate, got em pissed through earlier.'

'Want some blow, I've got plenty,' he added.

'Gonna stick with my pint, mate,' I said as Tony reached through and passed my pint of shandy. My newly acquired friend disappeared amongst the bodies at the bar.

The two Mooney brothers were holding court in a bay window and I immediately recognised the lad we had nicknamed 'Tulip'. There were some others I didn't recognise in the group. There were six or seven sitting around talking and drinking. Next to them was a fruit machine and we both made our way over to it. I didn't want to do anything to make me stand out or for them to remember me, which was ironic, especially how I dressed. It was bustling in the smoke-filled pub, and sat next to the Mooneys was a fresh-faced young man who they referred to as 'Adam'. They shouted his name as he came up to the bar for drinks. He stood next to us for a while. He was clean cut and there was something odd about him. He looked out of place. Call it sixth sense or a cop's intuition. He returned to the table with drinks and was part of the general conversation and I could only hear snippets about 'in three weeks', 'Scotland' and 'Clive's Van'. It was very loud and I'm unsure if any of this made sense. One thing I learned was that I am no good on fruit machines and spent a fortune while trying to eavesdrop on their conversation.

After an hour of holding court, the two smartly dressed brothers left, leaving Adam, Tulip and two other men. Don't forget this was in the days before mobile phone cameras, so the best we could do was describe them or look at a photograph album when we returned to the police station. We decided to leave after an hour or so to check all the car numbers in the streets outside. When I got to the door, I felt a hand on my shoulder and thought the worst. Someone must have recognised both or one of us as police officers.

'Got some puff if you want some, mate,' said my friend from the bar I met earlier. I thanked him but declined the offer and said, 'Maybe next time, pal,' and winked as I walked out.

We checked the street and walked back, passing the pub door as we headed toward our car. Adam, the fresh-faced lad sitting with the group, came outside and walked toward a Ford Escort XR3. He opened the door, entered, and drove toward the beach area. I repeated the car number over and over in my head until we got back to our car.

I sat in the driver's seat and looked across at Tony. We both laughed at each other. It had been quite an eventful afternoon and evening. We arrived back at Priestown police station and after parking the car in the garage, we walked to the electronic back door.

'Excuse me, excuse me,' came a shout from behind us as a young police officer came towards us both, 'the public area is at the front of the police station. You are not allowed in here. This is police only.'

We both laughed as we rummaged in our clothes for our police warrant cards and the officer was only doing her job. We were a pretty sight, though. Once inside the office, we made our incident log and noted our recollections. We chuckled when we both signed the observations log as Graham / Hill. I checked the Operation Empathy folder, went through intelligence reports and photographs, and recognised one of the gang at the meeting. He sat with Tulip and was called Clive Makinson. He was a former skipper of a trawler based up in Fleetworth. There was a full file on him with all his criminal activities and records.

Tony checked the car numbers, particularly the Ford Escort that 'Adam' had driven off in. The car was registered to Adam Hayes at an address in a nice area on the outskirts of Blackton. We checked Adam Hayes's name in the various files and on the Police National Computer (PNC). There was no trace of Adam.

At the office briefing the following day, we raised some eyebrows when we said we had both been in the Royal Oak. However, interest gained momentum when we told everyone about the conversations we overheard and the people present. It was all good evidence and all the little pieces of information and intelligence fit nicely into a much larger picture. We then mentioned the name Adam Hayes and the Ford Escort. Mary, a Detective from Northshire Police, asked for a description of Adam.

'That sounds like Adam Hayes from Fleetworth,' she said curiously. I explained that we had checked all the files and the PNC, but he wasn't known or certainly wasn't on any of the systems.

'There is a good reason for that,' she said, 'Adam Hayes is a serving police officer.'

***

The weeks went by and slowly we pieced together the small bits of the jig saw. There was indeed another trip to Scotland by Clive Makinson in his white transit van and this time, he based himself in Girvan. Before his trip, we observed his van for two weeks whilst it sat on spare land between Blackton and Fleetworth. We had two teams on twelve-hour day and night shifts. It was painstakingly dull work, but we found a quiet spot nearby at Blackton airport. It was a small private airport, but there were some great places to hide the cars and maybe do a little sunbathing or reading as we waited for the van to move.

The boss and Ray Ingham met with the Professional Standards department to discuss what to do about Police Constable Adam Hayes. It was a delicate issue because if he was questioned about his association with the Mooneys or any gang members, our operation would be over. The Professional Standards Unit monitored PC Hayes and we soon established that his digital footprints were all over the computer records of the gang members. He had been checking everyone on the computers and we just hoped he wasn't aware of our operation.

As luck would have it, a short time later, one afternoon, local police were called to a village pub near where Hayes lived. The landlord had complained that some of the locals had been smoking marijuana in the bar. When the police raided the pub, Adam Hayes was with the regulars smoking, but not marijuana. However, with the information from the licensee and the small amount of cannabis resin that was found at his home address, Hayes was charged with possession of the drug and resigned from the police force. What we didn't know was what he had told the Mooney family.

When we arrived in Girvan, Makinson parked his white van at the quayside and jumped aboard a trawler. Unable to gain entry at the local police station to make a phone call, Frank asked people to stand aside.

'What's the problem?' he asked as a queue of officers formed at the locked station door.

'The door is locked, Frank, and we can't get in,' came the response.

Frank pushed past everyone, removed a small baton from his belt and whacked the window in the door, sending shards of glass flying through the air. Everyone ducked and took cover. Frank reached through the broken window, turned the key and the door opened.

'Doesn't seem to be locked to me,' he said calmly, putting his baton back in his belt.

Frank was a lovely character and if he needed to get into the police station, he was going to get in. His actions caused many problems, but eventually, when we talked them around, the locals assisted. We were allocated the roof space in the local Sheriff's Office on the quayside. It was a significant historical building for the harbour but was now vacant. We had to be careful how we entered and exited the building as 'loose lips sink ships'. An English trawler man arrives in Girvan and at the same time, several English voices are heard in the town and around the docks. It wouldn't take Einstein to work that one out, would it?

I lived in that loft space for a week. By this time, the local officers were aware of Frank's unlawful entry and had resentfully agreed to assist. We based ourselves at a local hotel and the overnight bag had to be replenished with underwear and the like from local stores. We were hoping that the Mooney brothers would show their faces on the quayside, but news came through that David and his family had flown out to Florida for a month's holiday at an exclusive resort near Miami. David was an amateur boxer and rumour had it that he was on the verge of an Olympic call-up, although never corroborated. What opened my eyes even further was the fact that whilst his family were on holiday in Miami, he flew back on Concorde alone to compete in a boxing competition in London. He arrived back in the UK on Tuesday, competed Wednesday and was back in Miami on Thursday. The Mooney family were making a lot of money.

I counted the roof tiles and the spiders, read books, and took many photographs of the trawler Lady Lily and the comings and goings aboard her. Makinson was ever-present and was sleeping on board. It was monotonous watching the same things and one's mind drifted off and started seeing things. Then, in the depths of boredom, action! A red van appeared and two boiler-suited men boarded the Lady Lily. Makinson kept popping up on deck and then, after a few hours, black smoke bellowed out of the trawler's funnel. The two boiler suits left and the smoking ceased. Next to arrive was a local taxi and Makinson popped up and jumped into the back. It was scramble stations as Ray Ingham gave the order to follow the taxi.

Without the chance to say goodbye, everything was thrown in the car boot as we heard Frank commentating on the in-car radio, saying the taxi was heading south towards Newton Stewart and Carlisle. Where was Makinson going? Well, he went home, of course, and after speaking to the taxi driver sometime later, he paid £250 cash from a large wad of notes. That would be in the £1,000's today. This was some racket. Makinson stayed one night at home and carrying a large holdall, was picked up by Tulip, one of the other gang members, the following morning. We were off again and this time we followed them all the way back to.... Girvan. Back to the Sherriff's roof space and all its mod cons.

The next morning, there was activity on the dockside. The boiler suits and plumes of smoke were back. Tulip, Makinson and one other could be seen on board. Then, I recognised another from the Royal Oak and the Operation Empathy folder. Mick Maybell was seen as the gang's lieutenant who reported to the Mooneys. He was Mr Fix it. If he was here, then there would be some action.

Operation Empathy had been running for a year before I joined the team. Slowly but surely, with bits of information and evidence we were gathering, the picture became clearer about what the gang was up to. DI Roberts and Ray Ingham could now go to the senior managers and ask for more resources. This wasn't just a small street dealing enterprise, this was a team importing tons of drugs on a regular basis. A team of financial investigators joined the operation and estimated that in the previous two years, the gang had spent more than £1 million with no real signs of any legitimate income. The financial spike occurred the previous summer when it was suggested that the gang had sailed a trawler into Lochgoilhead in Scotland. The intelligence suggested the haul of cannabis on that trip was in tonnes.

Back in Girvan, with smoke bellowing out of Lady Lily, she headed for open waters. The unknown man stood at the quayside, and Makinson, Tulip, and Maybell stood on deck. Urgent phone calls were made to the coastguard as we hoped the trawler would head out to sea and turn left. The white van belonging to the gang appeared at the quayside and after the unknown member jumped in the passenger side, it also left the dock area. It was scramble time all over again.

The Portpatrick Hotel is a lovely place and an area of the United Kingdom I had never been to before. It is situated on the west coast of Scotland near Stranraer and it seems within touching distance of Northern Ireland. There is a ferry port at nearby Cairnryan where the ships sail the short distance to either Larne or Belfast. The legendary Finn McCool strode across the gap at one time, or so the story goes. Lady Lily and the white van had indeed turned left at Girvan and both were heading south. The trawler was about five miles out to sea, but I was told I could pick her out with some good binoculars. We had been told to concentrate on the trawler and let the white van go. Danny, myself and two others from the office were going to stay in Scotland and monitor Lady Lily if we could. There was also a Coastguard Unit at Portpatrick that we could use if needed.

I sat on a bench looking out into the Irish Sea. There was a crisp breeze as I scoured the horizon for the tiny dot of a trawler. Beneath me were the rocks and cliffs and I just watched and listened as the waves came crashing in. The light was beginning to fade, but if Lady Lily was to sail past our position, as anticipated, we knew she was heading south.

Without warning a gigantic black object broke the surface of the sea yards out from where I was sitting. It was incredible and I looked around to tell someone what was happening, but I was all alone. It was like something out of a movie. More of the object became visible as the surf cascaded into its sides. It didn't take long for the submarine to fully surface and I thought to myself that the powers that be were really pulling out all the stops for this operation. Surely, this wasn't to monitor the trawler. Was it? The submarine sailed a short distance on the surface before disappearing quietly.

Danny and a couple of the others arrived back after a short walk around the golf course. I was the subject of ridicule all evening after my tale of the submarine. No one believed me.

As I said, the port of Cairnryan sits behind Portpatrick in Loch Ryan and is sheltered from the weather. We got the call from the nearby Coastguard Office that Lady Lily was heading towards Cairnryan for the night and wouldn't be coming past our position. After the short trip to Cairnryan and watching the trawler enter port, we returned to the hotel to make the necessary phone calls. It was immediately noticeable how busy the place was. It was packed out and we found out there was a rugby match at Murrayfield the day after. It seemed the whole of Ireland had come across to stay the night with us. There was a great atmosphere in the bar that night and the singing and dancing went on into the wee, small hours. I also received a phone call to say that I had passed the police promotion exam to qualify to the rank of Sergeant. It was a great night. Many a pint of 'heavy' was consumed.

After a few slow days in Cairnryan, the crew and Lady Lily set sail again and headed south. She was to call in at the Isle of Man and then Fleetworth, where she stayed for a few months. Again, thanks to the coastguard, we occupied more roof space and this time armed with cameras and some super lenses, photographed the crew loading up Lady Lily with provisions. Assisting in that operation was the blonde-haired boxer himself, David Mooney. His white

Mercedes convertible, DM 10, was parked beside the trawler. At last, he was getting his hands dirty.

We worked shifts again, watching the trawler, covering it twenty-four hours a day. Family life was once again suffering and although the overtime payments were good, I was often away from home. Only one group knows how much overtime one has worked when one retires: the family.

My drinking to forget, had subsided a little as I was dealing with a different policing issue. The stress was different as it wasn't Sandford CID burnout. I did have a drink or two as I spent much of the time watching and waiting. What did keep me going and helped me tremendously was running. I had my running kit wherever we went and enjoyed a run at some stage. I was running at least five miles a day and on some occasions further. I entered several 10k's and half marathons as I had now determined that running and better mental health went hand in glove. I was getting stronger each day and I kept my mind busy as much as I could. If my mind was busy, then worry, stress and anxiety couldn't get a look in. But as we have seen with my time in Portpatrick, the pull of alcohol was still strong, albeit I wasn't drinking to get me through the day.

We knew Lady Lily was going, but didn't at this point know where to or when. The small pieces of information and more importantly, evidence, were all knitting together nicely. To photograph David Mooney loading up the trawler and his Mercedes parked next to it was gold dust. There were photographs of Tulip, Maybell and Makinson on board at some stage. The white van had reappeared at Fleetworth quayside and the unidentified man was another laid-off Fleetworth fisherman. It was just a matter of time, but the days were monotonous and boring. Even the exciting bits, when people arrived to load up the trawler, became mundane. However, after a few months or so, Lady Lily headed out to open waters and headed for the Bay of Biscay after a brief stop in Southampton. Skippered by Makinson, we believed she was Morrocco bound.

***

As a result of a phone call from the National Drugs Intelligence Unit (NDIU), we learnt that Mick Maybell was with another foot soldier from the gang and was now in Amsterdam. The Dutch authorities had been in touch and Maybell and his partner were meeting Dutch criminals in the capitol to carry out more drug deals. The gang's tentacles were now spreading far and wide. The boss, DI Roberts came into the office and asked Danny and I if we could go to Holland and collect some evidence before it disappeared. We both agreed and after a quick briefing as to who to see and where exactly to go, I started to research how to get there. Firstly, we had to obtain a 'Commission Rogatoire', which in simple terms is a letter of authority agreed by both prosecuting bodies, enabling you to get the evidence. Once we had obtained that, it was pack a small suitcase time and head towards Sheerness. In my footballing days for Sandford Police as well as Lostow FC, I had built up friendships with Dutch players as I had been on tour in Holland. Their teams had also visited the UK. I knew one player well, called Twan Dorens. He lived in Domburg in southern Holland and proved to be a great help in planning the trip. We had to visit a boatyard in a nearby village called Westkapelle. We also had to visit Amsterdam and again, with my links in the International Police Association (IPA) and football, I arranged the journey by bus and all the accommodation. With all the planning and preparation done, Danny and I set off on our travels.

We asked the local police if we could leave the car at Sheerness police station as we weren't insured to drive the police car overseas. We caught the ferry as foot passengers and Twan met us at Vlissingen and took us to our hotel in Westkapelle. The village was deserted, but it seemed that Messrs Maybell and others had been in these parts and purchased inflatable dinghies, later found on the beaches near Felixstowe. At the same time the inflatables were found, financial enquiries revealed that Michael Mooney had booked into a nearby hotel for two nights. The picture was coming together nicely, albeit slowly.

The next morning, we got on with the job and with help from the people at the hotel, caught the bus to the marine yard. The staff there were very helpful and provided all receipts and invoices and we recovered some good evidence. Maybell had given the correct name when purchasing two inflatables, but all had false addresses. The descriptions from staff fitted Maybell and Tulip. The staff at the yard also told us about a boat the two had purchased from a yard in the next village. The next day, off we went again, recovering the evidence and after three days, had amassed some ten evidential witness statements and several other documents which tied Mick Maybell, well and truly into a conspiracy to import drugs into the UK, or so we hoped.

When I called the office in the afternoon, the boss, DI Roberts, answered and asked where we were. I told him exactly where we were, what we had done and the evidence we had collected. He then asked me who had authorised me to take a police car and leave it at Sheerness, who had permitted us to stay three nights in Westkapelle, who had authorised us to travel to Amsterdam, etc. It was all a bit weird, as he had told us to go there and collect the evidence.

The nearest town to us was Middleburg and seeing that there was absolutely nothing to do in Westkapelle, three nights penned in with Danny going to bed early had taken its toll on me. I had to get out. Danny didn't want to venture. He wanted to stay in the hotel again as he said there wouldn't be transport back if we went anywhere. As we got off the bus with our job done in Westkapelle, I asked the bus driver what time the last bus was from Middleburg to Westkapelle. I had in mind a nice last evening in Middleburg before we moved on. It turned out the last bus anywhere was five o'clock and that was from our sleepy village to Middleburg. There was no return bus. None!

'No later buses,' I asked the driver again.

'No Sir, the last one leaves here at five o'clock and the next is nine in the morning,' he replied.

I caught Danny up as he walked the path to the only hotel in the village.

'What did he say?' asked Danny.

'Last bus back is midnight,' I lied.

'How sure are you? I'll probably stay in tonight,' said Danny.

'Listen, it's our last night down here. We haven't seen Middleburg. I've heard it's a great place. Come on, Danny, let's make a memory,' I pleaded.

'Oh, go on then, but I'm not staying out late as we have a distance to travel in the morning,' he replied.

We quickly changed and I constantly wondered when to tell Danny that there wasn't a bus back and that it was eleven miles from the hotel. I thought to myself that no matter how drunk you get, you always seem to find your way home. That was the twisted logic I was applying to the situation.

At five o'clock, the last bus pulled in at the small stop in Westkapelle and we both boarded, paying the two guilders for our thirty-minute journey to Middleburg. Fast forward seven hours, ten beers, a cheap steak dinner and an empty Middleburg bus station.

'There's no buses here,' said Danny. That was pretty obvious and even ten beers in, I could see that. 'Excuse me, excuse me,' as panic set in. Danny approached a couple walking by.

'They've just fucking said there are no buses anywhere until the morning. You absolute bastard,' he shouted at me.

It didn't help when I started laughing, but I'd been in worse situations. We'd had a great laugh. Work hard, play hard, I thought. We started the long walk back, down country and unlit lanes. I saw a rusty old pedal cycle, which I borrowed, that got us a couple of miles further and then things went very dark and quiet in the back lanes. Danny was still cursing me when headlights approached and the good old technique of sticking the thumb out worked again. There was only the male driver in the car and jokingly I said to Danny what a shock it would be if it was one of the Mooneys or Mick Maybell. He didn't see the funny side of it. The driver said Westkapelle was a little out of his way, but he would take us nearer. He seemed a nice guy and spoke good English. He asked what two Englishmen were doing in the unlit country lanes of southern Holland at two o'clock in the morning. I told him we were football players visiting our friend nearby and we were calling at Vlissingen Football Club at some stage. He asked about the teams we played for and I think he was just being inquisitive. He then asked if we were soldiers, which I thought was unusual. It killed the conversation somewhat. To change the subject, he told us that Ruud Gullet lived nearby and when we neared Westkapelle village, he slowed down. I thanked him as the car came to a stop. He told us both to be careful and keep safe, 'Be careful who you accept lifts off in the dark, eh,' he said as his car pulled away into the night. We later found out that recently, the IRA had assassinated a British soldier returning to the ferry port, not far from where we were. A very sobering message.

The morning soon came and Danny sulked the whole time we travelled to Amsterdam by coach to get further evidence against the Mooneys and others. Stood in the Magistrates Court in Amsterdam,

I was shocked to see people of authority wearing jeans, open-necked shirts and jumpers. It was extremely casual. The boat owner that Maybell had purchased in southern Holland lived and worked in Amsterdam. He was a solicitor and knew a thing or two about the law. He was very nice and again provided us with all the information and documents. We then had to visit a couple of hotels to get the login details of Maybell and the team before hitting the Old Sailor pub on the canal side. We had a quiet night as Danny was still a little upset. Again, with my contacts, I had reserved two rooms at the local 'police hotel'.

The journey back home was uneventful. Danny had started to forgive me for the Middleburg crisis and we both agreed that we had done a good job collecting the evidence. However, that opinion wasn't shared by Inspector Roberts. When we handed over the evidence packs, I could sense the unease as he flicked through the paperwork.

'Who authorised you to take a car and leave it at Sheerness?' he asked.

'I didn't think I needed authorisation,' I replied.

'Who gave you authority to stay in that hotel? Who authorised you to travel all that way to Amsterdam by bus and then stay in a hotel there?' he asked further.

I was a little gobsmacked and asked what the problem was.

'I'll tell you what the problem is…' and off he went into a tirade about going off on our own and not letting supervisors know what we were doing and not getting authority for booking travel or hotels.

'Boss, how old am I?' I asked.

'What's that got to do with it?' he replied.

'I'm married with two children and have a mortgage, which is a hell of a responsibility. You said that to me not long ago, remember? I get paid just over £1000 a month and you pay me that to sort things out. Remember saying that? So, I sorted it out. You can't have it both ways. On one hand, you can't tell me to sort things out and then criticise me when I do exactly that.'

Those were the words he said to me after he walked out on me on that Friday in December asking me if it was 'fish for dinner'. He left me to 'sort it out' with Jason Saunders, on my own, without help. The room fell silent. It wasn't lost on him and I could see it hit home, hard. He didn't like it. He got up from behind his desk and walked past me and into the corridor.

***

The weeks and months passed by and the collection of evidence continued, which tied the whole gang into a conspiracy to import drugs into the UK. On another occasion, we followed the white van to London and the driver met up with Mick Maybell who had just arrived at Heathrow from Malaga.

The Lady Lily had been sighted moored off the coast of Morocco and there is no doubt Maybell had been out there or Spain to negotiate its return and load. We were told to head for Trenchard House in the City, where we would regroup and stay the night. There would be a briefing the following morning.

Over breakfast, I read a newspaper article about the summer storms that had hit the South Coast of America. The area near New Orleans had been badly flooded. In particular, an area near the FBI compound was so flooded that some surveillance dolphins breached their pool walls and escaped into the sea. I found it fascinating that the authorities now use dolphins for surveillance.

Before the briefing started, several new and familiar faces entered the room. Our friends from Customs and some more RCS officers from the London area were here. DI Roberts and DS Ingham held court and the objective was to follow Maybell to see if he returned to Blackton or led us elsewhere. Maybell was staying in the Tower Thistle Hotel and had yet to check out.

'Boss, before we finish, and mainly for the benefit of our friends from London and Customs, can I make an important point? '
I got the nod of approval and continued, 'I've read this morning that a number of FBI surveillance dolphins have escaped their pens in the USA due to the recent storms over there.' I now had everyone's attention. People looked at me intently.

'If Maybell or any other subjects go onto the tube and we go with them and if you see a dolphin in the carriage reading a newspaper or wearing sunglasses, please don't approach it. They're possibly on surveillance or even following Maybell,' I said.

Some heads were actually nodding in agreement and it brought the doodling on notepads to an abrupt halt. The boss looked directly at me.

'It's just for everyone's information, really, boss, we don't want to mess anything up for the FBI, do we?'

The boss just sighed and shook his head. There were one or two titters from the Priestown crew as people started to leave the room. Even Frank had a smile on his face.

Comments such as, 'Dolphins on the tube? What did he say, dolphins on the tube reading newspapers?' could be heard as officers filed out of the room.

We followed Maybell around London for a few hours and then to a terraced house in south London near Norwood Junction. The lad had gone to say hello to his Mum before hitting the road back to Blackton, no doubt to report to the Mooneys.

Operation Empathy had now been running for three years and there was a growing impatience on the top floor of the RCS Headquarters that it should be drawn to a close. The plan now was to ensure all the evidence was collected and organised and just hope that Lady Lily would set sail for the UK soon. It was getting time to line the ducks up for the arrest day.

CHAPTER ELEVEN

FRANCISCO TANNER & OTHERS

'There's a vacancy for a temporary Sergeant in Sandford Drugs Squad, I think you should take it,' DI Roberts commented as he looked over the top of a Ken Follet book.

I knew as soon as I said my little speech and that I 'sorted it out' in Holland, he would hold it against me. He did. I asked how long the temporary spell would last, and he didn't know. He guessed it would be at least twelve months. My concern was that if I gave up my position on the Regional Crime Squad, I would never get it back. This Roberts confirmed. Once I left the squad, he didn't want me back. He made it very clear. I made some phone calls and indeed, it would be good experience as a supervisor to go back to Sandford, but all the indicators and my gut feeling was to stay put at Priestown.

'He wants rid of you,' said Macintosh, who I'd phoned for advice. 'He's told me that you're not pulling your weight and haven't brought anything to the table,' Macintosh added. It was like a punch in the stomach and as I went to speak Macintosh cut me off. 'I know what you've done at Priestown, so don't worry, I know. But it seems you've upset him and he wants rid. Keep your head down and sit tight. You're not going anywhere yet until I say so.'

If I'd taken the temporary Sergeant role with Sandford Drug Squad, I would have been returned to my role as a Detective Constable somewhere in the CID. I would have lost my place in the Regional Crime Squad. Why? The temporary sergeant vacancy only lasted two weeks. I knew I'd made the right decision, but there was an uneasy feeling now, knowing what I knew and what had been said about me. DI Roberts wanted me out.

I sometimes played football for the Priestown police team when they were short of players. I became friendly with one of the players who I had previously met whilst working on Operation Empathy at Blackton on Sea. Gary was complaining that all the energy was being directed at the Mooneys, when there were other equally big fish in the town that weren't getting looked at. One man in particular, Francisco 'Frankie' Tanner. He was a Glaswegian Italian and organised all the security for the bars and nightclubs. He was very well connected in Blackton but not with the Mooneys. Tanner was a powders man and still smarting from the comments from the boss I decided to take a closer look at Tanner. With the help of Gary, the footballer, we started the investigation.

Tanner lived with his wife and family in a semi-detached house on the rather leafy outskirts of Blackton. The nightclub security racket was paying well, but I guessed that if he was involved in selling powders, then that's where his income was coming from. He possessed the state-of-the-art BMW, and his right-hand man was Malachy 'Malky' Dawson. Like other operations, you have to start somewhere to build the picture and place the jigsaw pieces in the right place. Initial enquiries on the police systems showed that Tanner and Dawson had been stopped in a different BMW sometime earlier up in Glasgow with £110,000 in a holdall in the car's boot. They came up with a story about house sales, but it appeared that footballing Gary was correct that there were equally big fish in the town.

Intelligence also showed that there was a connection between Tanner and a certain Curtis 'Cocky' Warren, who emanated from up in Merseyside. Warren was, and still is, a well-known international drug dealer who employed the services of Detective Chief Inspector Elmore Davies, amongst others in his circles. Davis was eventually caught, together with the TV Gladiator Hunter, for being involved in corrupt practices in assisting Warren in evading arrest. Davies attempted to derail an attempted murder trial involving one of Warren's henchmen firing a shotgun at a police officer. Both Davies and Hunter were jailed for their involvement.

After weeks of research and enquiries, it was very apparent that Tanner was heavily involved in moving drugs from Merseyside up to his native Glasgow. Intelligence is great, but it is not evidence, which was needed. Proof, not truth.

I was introduced to a criminal informant who knew Malky Dawson. The informant, Dylan, had just been released from HMP Northwood and when inside, had associated with friends and accomplices of Dawson. When the informant was released, Dawson and another man came to pick him up and left him, saying he could call him whenever he needed a favour. He suggested he could call in the favour and maybe get Dawson to call at HMP Northwood again to pick up a friend. That friend, he suggested, could be a cop who could then possibly infiltrate the gang. It sounded like a crazy idea but one worth looking at.

The Head of Security at HMP Northwood was Chris Harker, or should I say, Mr Harker. He was a very pleasant man, very upright and you could tell he was very disciplined, probably ex-forces. He listened carefully to our plan and said it was feasible. The usual release time was between seven and eight in the morning, so if someone was to come inside the prison, it would have to be very early. The problem with that was shift changeover at seven o'clock. He suggested that it may be better if whoever came into prison came the night before and spent the night in a segregation cell, or seg, as they called it. Then the morning shift would have the correct release details and it would all seem very natural and legitimate. He said whoever came would have to research the prison and be allocated the same release items as a prisoner. The plan was coming together and when I ran the idea past the boss, he seemed ambivalent. All we needed now was a volunteer to go into the prison.

I arrived at HMP Northwood around five o'clock that evening and asked for Mr Harker. He duly attended and apologised that he was in a rush as he was going out that night, but everything had been attended to. I was to be released at seven thirty in the morning and would be placed in a segregation cell overnight. I had made a couple of visits to the prison to get to know the layout of the place, which I found intimidating. It wasn't something I was used to and that was the start of my problems. I was going to be caught in a big lie.

After working with Dylan, the informant, the plan was 'that someone' would pick me up on release. It could be Dawson or Tanner or someone close to them. I was told there was the possibility of a 'run' to Glasgow, which to me meant a drugs run. I had been allocated a prison holdall, black shoes, three shirts, underwear and socks. I was to be issued with thirty-six pounds, which incidentally was money I gave Mr Harker from the police pot for him to give back to me the next morning upon release. I had to be in my cell before lockdown. Everything was going to plan. Mr. Harker said his goodbye and hoped to see me in the morning. Clunk! The door closed.

The cell was sparse, bar the bed, mattress, pillow and blanket. There was a small desk and chair, but that was it. It was half past six, and everyone had to be in their cell for lockdown at seven o'clock. They wouldn't open up until six the next morning, or so I thought. I had been told to dress in tracksuit bottoms, sweatshirt and trainers. No money, no belts, no ID, no nothing. That is exactly how I presented when the cell door opened in the evening and a prison officer stood there.

'Who the fuck are you?' he asked.

'Erm erm, Jim Bentley,' I nervously replied as I got to my feet.

'What you in for? I don't understand this. Why are you here?' he enquired.

'Mr. Harker put me in here. I'm being released in the morning,' I said.

'Released? According to my paperwork, you're not. Why are you in Seg? It would be best if you went back up on the wing. Which wing are you off,' he asked.

It was realisation time. The plan that sounded so good was now falling apart and there was a possibility that I would be transferred to one of the wings with all the other prisoners. I had messed up big time. The officer asked me many more questions, and I replied that he needed to see Mr. Harker as he had all the answers. Eventually, he shut the cell door, shaking his head as he did so. I now realised I had made a big mistake.

With the banging, clanging and shouting, I never slept a wink. The prison officer never came back during the night and it was a different face that opened the door in the morning.

'You say you're going out today,' enquired another prison officer.

'Yeah, you'd best see Mr. Harker, he knows everything,' I said.

'Harker doesn't start until half eight in the morning and I don't see how he would know,' the officer added.

'Trust me, he does know,' I replied.

'Trust you, trust you, like fuck I would. You having a wash or what?'

'No, I'm good thanks. I'll wait for release.'

As the officer started to close the cell door, he peeked inside and said, 'Your release might be a long time off yet, mate.'
The cell door slammed shut.

The lights were on inside now, and I could hear voices and music. The prison was waking up, but I had no idea of the time. It wasn't long before the door opened and the original officer came inside. 'Come on, get your gear and you can go in a holding cell until we sort all this out.'

I was escorted down corridors and through doors and by this time other inmates were also on the move. The officer took a large bunch of keys from his pocket and stretched the chain up to a big black door. In went the key and with one move, the door opened. He swung his head back and motioned for me to enter the room, which I did. It wasn't empty.

On the far side, a wooden bench ran the whole length of the room. It came out from the wall and I first saw the legs swinging underneath. Three figures, all dressed in black, stopped messing around and looked directly at me. It went very quiet as the door clicked and closed behind me. One of them, tall, thin, and with a shaved head, was continually spitting on the floor. He rested his elbows on his legs and put his hands on either side of his head.

'Look who we've got here then. Pablo fucking Escobar,' he said as the spitting continued. The other two characters burst out laughing and when I went and sat on the bench at the far end of the room, they slid up beside me.

'You got a ciggy?' one asked as the other started patting me down around my pockets.

'What you in for mate?' one asked as the skinny one projected his spit further into the room.

'Lost your fucking tongue, mate?' said the other one.
This was my worst nightmare and I was in at the deep end.

'What time is it?' I asked, and all three burst into laughter. They were like hyenas as they laughed and circled me.

'You a nonce mate, eh? You a fucking nonce? You just come off Seg?' the smaller one growled in my face. I just stared at him and realised it was fight or flight time, but sadly, there was nowhere to fly. The tall, skinny one started to spit at me and he, too, started to slide up towards me.

'Nice trainers, mate. How do you get them in here?' he asked as he began to spit on my trainers. 'Hey, how do you get them in here. You a nonce mate or a grass. I fucking hate grasses, mate. Do you know what I do to nonces, mate? I fucking shank 'em, alright.'
Shank is prison slang for a homemade knife or weapon. Usually, a razor blade melted into the shaft of a toothbrush.

The click of the door made all three of them bolt for the bench at the far end of the room. They continued to mess about between the three of them as they were when I came in.

'You called Bentley,' the officer asked me.
I nodded, and once again, he beckoned me out of the cell area using his head. I didn't look back at the three hyenas as I was just so relieved to get out of that room. I was led down a corridor and into another room where an officer behind a large, tall desk placed a black holdall in front of me.

'Shoes, three shirts, pants, underpants, socks,' he said as he placed the items in the bag. 'Ten, twenty, thirty, thirty five and one makes thirty six pounds,' and he placed the money on the top next to the holdall.

'Just sign here, here and here,' as he pointed to where I should sign.

'Mr. Harker in yet, please?' I asked.

'Please pretty please eh. Aren't we posh,' said the officer as he dragged the signed paper off the top of the desk. 'He's in at half past eight,' and with that, pointed towards another door, which immediately started to buzz.

The fresh air hit me as I walked outside. It was another holding area where another older inmate was waiting. The big wooden doors were too my left and the iron gates leading back into the prison were on my right.

"Here you are," I heard a voice to my left. I saw that a smaller door in the big wooden one had been opened. Another officer kept the door open and his key chain stretched from his belt across it.

'Mind how you go now,' he said in a Scottish accent as I ducked under his arm, avoiding the chain and stepping outside into the big wide world. Oh, what a night indeed!

The tatty old BMW flashed its lights, and I saw the driver's door open. I recognised the head that popped up as Dylan, the informant who knew Malky Dawson. He had kept his word and turned up. No doubt Gary from the Drug Squad would be rewarding Dylan afterwards. I walked across the square to the far side, where the car was parked, and Dylan came to meet me. He took my holdall and then went to the rear of the BMW and opened the tailgate. He asked how things were and my facial expressions painted the picture for him. I didn't know who was with Dylan in the car. It could be Tanner or Dawson.

'Get in behind Sully,' Gary said as I looked at which door to get in. The name Sully didn't mean anything to me.

I saw a figure in the front passenger seat and got in the car behind the driver's seat. Dylan closed the tailgate and got in the driver's seat.

'Jim, this is Sully. Sully, this is Jim a mate of mine I met inside a while ago,' Dylan said as he started the car.
I nodded, said, 'Alright, mate?' and collapsed back in my seat. I'm not sure if Sully said anything.

I could see Dylan's eyes in the car mirror.

'You had a rough time by the looks of things, Jim,' he said.

'Just a couple of pillocks trying it on at the end, but nothing much,' I replied.

'I asked Sully to come for some backup as I didn't know if anyone else would be waiting for you,' Dylan added.

'Cheers, pal,' I added as Sully sat in silence.

We drove around the back streets and soon were on the dual carriageway and motorway. Despite the many prompts to engage in conversation, Sully remained quiet throughout. He either knew something was amiss or didn't trust Dylan. As we hit the outskirts of Blackton, the car pulled into a country lane and then layby. Sully opened the passenger door, said goodbye to Dylan, and said he'd call him. The door closed and Sully walked across to a Ford Fiesta and got in.

'Well, that didn't go to plan, either,' I said as I slumped back in my seat.

***

As we considered the next plan of action, Gary from the local Drug Squad rang me the week after to say that Dylan had been in touch and that he couldn't arrange for Malky Dawson to come to prison to collect me. He got someone who worked on the doors with Malky called Barry Sullivan. It didn't take us any further other than Sully could vouch for me in the future. There was now also another added problem as Dylan had been arrested with a large quantity of amphetamine on his way to Scotland. He'd been arrested out of the Northshire Police area, but Gary had been to see him and try to interview him. Gary had to misrepresent the reason for seeing Dylan to the custody staff, as he knew Dylan would want to trade information for his liberty. People would ask questions about why Gary had been to interview Dylan, which could easily identify him as a police informer. It was a tricky situation, but Gary had to protect Dylan's identity for his safety.

Regarding my pick-up from prison, Malky Dawson was tired that morning and was not interested in making friends with Dylan's mates. He wasn't interested, so he sent Sully along to help. He knew that Dylan was going to do a Glasgow run later that day, apparently with a boot laden with amphetamine sulphate.

Dylan, who was now facing serious charges, was represented by a solicitor hired by Tanner and Dawson, so it was a complicated situation. When the solicitor arrived and asked to see the custody record, there would be an entry along the lines of 'interview by DC Gary Lawton, Blackton Drug Squad'. The solicitor would want to know the reason for the interview from both the Custody Officer and Dylan and why he wasn't informed. To the curious, cynical and criminal ones, it would show that if Dylan was speaking to cops about other issues and not what he was arrested for, he was a grass. Tanner and Dawson would then be waiting to see if there were any police raids or search warrants executed shortly after Gary's visit to Dylan. The solicitor who Tanner was paying the bill for, would also report back to Tanner with his observations. There could be no slip-ups in order to protect Dylan.

The custody record read, 'declined to be interviewed,' which is what happened. However, in the interview request process, Dylan had requested to see officer Gary to see if he recognised him. It was all part of the plan. In this process, somehow, Dylan passed the address 107 Park Rd, Blackton, to Gary with the wink of an eye.

The custody officer or anyone else was none the wiser. When the solicitor arrived, all would be revealed. Dylan would say he refused to be interviewed and deny knowing DC Gary Lawton. If the address that Dylan gave, proved useful, Gary would later submit a secret letter to the Judge, called a 'text', which I explained in a previous chapter. No one would ever know that Dylan ever assisted the police. Only the Judge may reflect that assistance in the sentence Dylan received. Again, that had to be handled sensitively as it still could identify Dylan as the informant. Five people were arrested who all received ten years imprisonment and another defendant got a conditional discharge. Doesn't it take a lot of working out who the grass was?

The energy in the office was on Operation Empathy and the impending arrest phase, so although the boss and team were kept in the picture about Tanner and Dawson, it was carry on and 'sort it out' myself. Gary apologised and said he would help where he could, but his own office had key performance indicators that had to be met. He was, therefore, being pulled away from the Tanner and Dawson investigation. It didn't matter too much as Danny and I were now involved. However, before he was pulled away Gary did some background work on the address 107 Park Rd. It was a terraced house in the south of Blackton and near the big amusement park, Leisureland. It was a deprived area and one where the residents didn't tolerate the police. The occupant of 107 was a Glaswegian man, Terence Bell and although he had a bit of form, he wasn't well known by the authorities.

Danny and I parked the car on some wasteland at the amusement park and crossed over the railway bridge. We both looked like a pair of scruffy lads, so we soon blended in with our surroundings. It was indeed a deprived area with rows of terraced houses with the usual mattresses in the front gardens and kiddies toys piled high. One garden contained an old toilet and bath and broken down cars with flat tyres were dotted all around the streets. Park Road was at the entrance to the small park at the bottom, which led to the wasteland, the railway bridge and the theme park. We weren't too far away and had found a great place to park should we ever want to conduct enquiries or observations.

After a quick walk around the area, we'd noticed some nicer houses amongst the untidy ones and wondered if any of the occupants were 'good, spirited citizens' or 'homewatch co-ordinators'. Gary laughed at us when we suggested the same to him and he clarified that there would be no help from anyone from that particular estate. It was head-scratching time.

Danny suggested we contact another office to see if they had an observation van. We could park it on the street and watch the address to see if anything happened. We could also get the office together and mount a surveillance should the occupants of 107 make an appearance, so we could see where they went. The plan was moving forward and after speaking with our friends at the Burnton RCS Office, I pulled onto the waste ground near Leisureland in their plumber's van. It was ideal. Gary from the local drug squad joined us for a short while to help and suggested that he would speak to his supervisors and see if he could get a plain clothes constable, who knew the area and residents, to sit in the back of the van and carry out the observations. With the local cop in the back, I could drive the van onto Park Road and leave it in a position that gave a good view of the house. Problem solved.

With the cop in the back, with an empty bottle should he need the toilet, I slowly started moving forward in the plumber's van and manoeuvred slowly towards the exit.

'Help, help, get me out. Get me out of here. Help me please, help anyone, please get me out of here.' Then came loud banging from the back of the van.

It was obvious someone was in distress and it was the cop who was locked in the back. The banging started on the doors and got louder and louder before the screaming started again. What on earth was happening? I stopped the van and started to unlock the rear doors. As soon as the key made its final turn, both doors burst open and the young man's boots followed shortly after. Screaming loudly, he jumped from the back of the van and ran across the wasteland. I watched as he disappeared into the distance. I stood there a little perplexed when Gary came on the radio and asked how it was going.

It would appear that our young, keen volunteer didn't realise he had claustrophobia. He got himself all worked up and into a panic before eventually, all apologetic, returned to the van. It
was obvious he couldn't help us. There was only one thing left for it.

Danny pulled the van into the kerbside and shouted through to the back to me, 'How's that?'

I looked through the cardboard boxes packed up near the rear windows, giving an excellent view of the plain front door of 107 Park Road. Between 107 and 109 was an entry that led through to the back doors. A bedroom was above the entry, the same for all the houses. They were terraced but had passageways leading through to the back. One of the houses had the bedroom over the entry. Danny had now locked the van and he was long gone. We had enough of the Priestown crew with us to follow anyone should they come out of the address. They didn't! I sat in the darkness and silence for four hours, looking at the front door. Once the driver had parked the van, you were stuck all alone in the back. A wooden panel separated the driver's cab from the back, so although there were peepholes in the panels, you couldn't get from the back into the front and vice versa. You needed someone to drive you into the area you were carrying out the observations and someone to drive you back out. To get out of the back of the observation van, when it was parked, was virtually impossible.

The next day, it was the same as the day after. The rest of the team helping Danny and I were getting frustrated, and so was I, spending so much time in the back of an observation van. On day three, things changed. A Ford Sierra pulled up outside the address and who should get out but Malachy Dawson. He went to the rear of the car, opened the tailgate and removed a cardboard box, which he carried as he disappeared down the entry between 107 and 109 Park Road. My Canon camera was ready and took as many snaps as possible, albeit they contained little evidence. What was in the box? Dawson was presumably inside 107 for around ten minutes before leaving without the box. A gaunt, thin man came from the passageway as the Sierra pulled away. He turned right out of his address and headed for the railway bridge and the wasteland on the other side, where I presumed all the Priestown team were parked. There was a mad scramble as the man headed towards the wasteland and Leisureland. He looked older than he was. He had a bald head and wore a shabby beige coat. The team followed him on foot through the theme park and into the street, running parallel to the promenade. He entered a bookmaker's shop and Mark Smithies followed him in. All we heard from Mark for the next two hours was that there was no change. The bald man was spending his money on the horses and by all accounts, a lot of it. As the light faded, the bald man left the bookies and Mark Smithies followed him for a while, but it seemed he was doing a return route to 107 Park Road. Indeed, he was and soon disappeared down the small garden path and into the entry between the houses. I continued the commentary on the police 'in car radio' as he disappeared. I was then aware of voices at the side of the van.

'I'm telling you, I saw a red light come on,' said a voice to the side of the van. Faces then started to appear at the back windows, and they began to cup their hands as they looked in through the cardboard boxes.

'There was a red light come on in the back. It's a cop car, I'm telling you. It's cops they're watching someone.'
Then, the bang on the side of the van. Then, there was a bang on the other side of the van. Faces then started to appear at the front windscreen and I could make at least three of them out. I whispered into the radio,

'Preacher to any team, I have three, maybe four persons at the van. They think it's a police vehicle and they are banging on the side.'

The camera and bag then started to slide toward me as the far side of the van seemed to lift in the air. It went back level again and then rose once more. I couldn't see anything from the rear windows, and luckily, the cardboard boxes were stuck in place.

'Right, come on then, after three. One, two, three,' and the other side of the van lifted again. They were trying to turn the van over.

'Preacher to any of the teams,' I whispered, 'they are trying to turn the van over. They are trying to turn the van over.'
I sat motionless as the faces came to the back windows again.

'Set the fucking thing on fire,' one of the voices said as I heard the petrol cap being unscrewed. This was getting uncomfortable now.

'Preacher to the teams, they are talking about setting the van on fire now. Anyone receiving?'
There was silence. Then I got the whiff of petrol.

The light was fading as another figure appeared at the bottom of Park Road and started walking up towards the van. This was getting scary. The figure started walking to the back doors and windows of the van. He had long dark hair and I could see he was carrying a plank of wood or a bat. Voices were raised and the figure with the long hair swung the plank above his head and shouted,

'Now fuck off and leave my van alone,' as the figures scattered around him.

The driver's door opened and Frank got in. I saw Danny running up from the bottom of Park Rd, so he jumped in the passenger seat, and off we went. Phew! It was another close call, and I was beginning to think I was a jinx. It was back to the office, so I had to brush myself down and start all over again. I was still smarting from the comments about me, so I felt I had to prove myself. It wasn't a particularly nice feeling.

The observations continued using different vehicles and surprise, surprise but whose fancy BMW should also park outside the address on Park Road, Tanner's. Diagonally across the street from the entrances of 107 and 109, a sign had been placed in the garden: 'Flat to Let.' It was an unfurnished upstairs flat that gave a great view of the street, particularly the comings and goings at 107.

After some negotiations with the letting agency, I got the keys to the flat, but there was a big BUT! No one must ever know that the flat was used for police observations, particularly the people who lived below. They weren't the sort of people who embraced the police and I could see it from the agency's point of view. It was agreed that we would use a back entrance to the flat when the people downstairs were out or in bed. This meant once you were inside, you stayed inside until it was clear to come out.

I parked the car on the waste ground over the railway track, which was way out of sight, but on those first visits, I had to enter the flat in the early morning hours to get the camera equipment and seats inside. We couldn't flush the toilet or run any water until we knew for sure the flat underneath was empty. It was challenging, to say the least. The front room that overlooked the street gave a great view and to mask the camera, a thin curtain was placed across the room to hide the camera lenses. My emergency garden chairs proved uncomfortable, so I visited the garden centre to get a low-relaxing chair and a sleeping bag. It was winter and freezing cold and I had to sit and watch for hours and hours on end.

The weeks went by, and in turn, Danny and I carried out observations and took photographs of the comings and goings at 107. It was a lonely place in that front room as you couldn't walk around for fear of downstairs hearing you. So, you had to tip-toe everywhere and climb into the sleeping bag and wrap up warm. The camera and tripod were strategically placed so that if anyone attended the address, it would be captured on film. Today, of course, a tiny covert camera would be fitted somewhere, but not back in the day. The long, lonely days and evenings started to get to me and getting inside so early and coming out late meant there was no time for running or other physical activity. Danny and I would take turns to sit for hours on end. One day Frank came to collect me and I knew the family downstairs were out so we chatted and watched for a while.

'I've been to one of them meetings,' Frank said, 'you know about those drugs from Phlegmland.'

'You mean Belgium, Frank,' I replied.

'That's what I said, Snotland. Think they're all clever, don't they all the bosses and Customs? They think they're all upper class, don't they? Well, I bet none of em, none of em can name one painting by Mozart, can they?'

Frank was indeed correct. He was a lovely character who didn't shy away from work. He laughed with us and ran with the pack. He knew of the divisiveness in the office. He reached into his jacket pocket and pulled out a crispy white plastic bag. I recognised the bag instantly, as with a young family, one is always looking for bargains. It was an Asda bag of chicken, and the bargain was six drumsticks or six thighs for a pound or similar.

'Here, do you want one?' he said, offering me the open bag. I was half tempted, but Frank then killed my appetite, 'Sister-in-law brought them around last night as they're way past their sell-by date. She said they'd be okay for the cats. Well, they smell alright to me so fuck the cats, I'm having em.' I laughed. Although he had been the subject of many a prank and I had been on the end of his tongue more than once, I liked Frank.

A pattern had emerged on Park Road. Either Dawson or Tanner would arrive and shortly after the bald, gaunt looking man would come out and walk over the railway bridge to the betting shop. He would spend the afternoon there and spend a couple of hundred quid. It was apparent he was getting paid for something by Tanner and Dawson. We could only assume that the boxes going into the premises contained drugs. What we didn't see were boxes coming out.

It was afternoon and Park Road was very quiet. The family downstairs were making a noise. I was cold and nodding off to sleep at times. I was wearing my best bobble hat and gloves and had my sleeping bag pulled to my chin. The flask of coffee and the sandwiches were by my side. The fancy BMW pulled up and this time, both Tanner and Dawson got out. They went to the rear of the BMW and opened the boot. Click, click as I pressed the camera. Then bingo. As he held out his hands, Tanner started to pass Dawson bags of white powder and pile them up like loaves of bread. Tanner then took hold of some bags and closed the boot before they both disappeared down the passageway of 107. Again, back in the day, photographs were not digital, so it was twelve, twenty-four or thirty-six exposures, and you had to have the right speed film, or they would turn out too grainy and blurred. All films were black and white, and I had to renew an authority to use them each month. This seemed too good to be true. If these photographs came out as I hoped, they would be excellent evidence.

When I picked up the processed films at the photography unit in Northshire Police HQ, the results were fantastic. It couldn't be any clearer. The presumption was that the bags I had captured Tanner and Dawson carrying were drugs. Both Tanner and Dawson, hands-on. It couldn't get any better.

Danny and I went for a briefing with the boss, and he said he now wanted the operation brought to an end. The arrest phase of Operation Empathy was about to begin and all staff had to concentrate on that. We also had some financial evidence showing Tanner and Dawson were living beyond their means. There was other evidence and links that, when all pulled together, painted a perfect picture of what Tanner, Dawson and the betting man were doing. One unfortunate spin-off from the investigation was that he parked in a company car park near the seafront when the team surveyed Tanner, as he drove away from Park Road. A very smart blonde lady joined him in his BMW and off they drove to a small bed and breakfast further up the coast. We had by this time worked out that it wasn't Tanner's wife, but we didn't expect it to be the wife of a serving Police Inspector in Blackton. Oh, what a tangled web we weave.

It was agreed that the optimum time to execute the search warrant at 107 was when either Tanner or Dawson were there. It would be fantastic if both of them were there at the same time. With local detective Gary's help and those from Priestown, Danny and I gathered a team to bring the operation to a close. The boss gave us four days to hopefully get them all together at the address, but whatever happened, the operation had to conclude by Thursday of that week. We hadn't as yet recovered any drugs.

The arrest team was led by another local officer who knew the area. Five other detectives sat in a police personnel carrier nearby in Blackton, ready for the call to move in. They had the search warrant, battering rams, etc.

Monday came and went with Danny and me, carrying out the observations from the flat. Nothing happened. No one moved. I was working the early shift on Tuesday morning, and Tanner's BMW pulled up. He then went down the passageway with a carrier bag. He wasn't in long before leaving in his car. Shortly after, the bald man came out on foot and made his usual trip to the betting office. Wednesday was quiet, nobody moved, and tomorrow, Thursday, was our last day. I went to see the boss and asked for more time but it was a definite 'No'. We had to execute the search warrant at some stage tomorrow, Thursday, then take it from there.

Danny worked the early shift on Thursday, and nothing was moving at the address. We had agreed to go in if nothing happened by eight o'clock. The afternoon was long and tedious, and the family downstairs was shouting and screaming again. The light started to fade and we analysed when Tanner and Dawson had been turning up at the address. There was no set pattern. It was going to be down to luck.

Around six thirty, Lady Luck landed in the form of a BMW and two occupants, Tanner and Dawson. This was it. My senses were on full alert. I sat up and started to take the photos again and then whispered into the police radio,

'Preacher to all the teams, subject vehicle stop, stop, stop outside the subject address. Subjects are out, out, out of the vehicle and walking towards the subject premises. Alpha One (arrest team), are you in position?'

'Alpha One, yes, yes,' came the reply.

'Preacher to Alpha One, strike, strike, strike,' I said nervously into the handheld radio. When those three words came across the radio they did focus your attention. This is it. We're going in. Anything could happen.

I entered the time of thirty one minutes past six o'clock for both Tanner and Dawson going down the alleyway of 107. I sat, watched and waited for the police personnel carrier and arrest team to arrive. Two minutes later, it still hadn't arrived. We didn't have too much time to play with as these two wouldn't stay that long in 107.

'Preacher to Alpha One, what is your position, please?' I demanded over the radio.

'Alpha One to Preacher, making ground, stuck in traffic,' came the reply. Stuck in traffic, stuck in traffic, I thought to myself. I couldn't believe my ears and again my mistake. I had trusted the efficacy of my fellow staff. Wherever the local officer had parked was not close enough. This was a nightmare. I looked down at my watch. They had now been inside for four minutes. Come on, Alpha One, hurry up, I thought to myself.

'Preacher to Alpha One, your position,' again I demanded.
I watched the seconds tick down on my watch. I kept looking at the passageway and pleading, 'Please, please don't come out.'

'Alpha One, still held in traffic.'
I closed my eyes and breathed heavily. The arrest team was not going to make it. I kept watching the passageway, then the watch, and waiting and waiting. 'Come on, come on,' I thought to myself, willing the personnel carrier to appear.

I looked down at my watch. It was six-thirty nine and then the inevitable.

'Preacher to the teams, subjects out, out, out of the premises and in, in, in to the subject vehicle. Vehicle manoeuvring and it's off, off, off in the general direction of Blackton town centre. Alpha One, did you receive the last?' I said into the transmitter.

'Yes, yes, making ground,' came the reply.

Tanner and Dawson had been inside the premises for eight minutes, which was about the average. The arrest team had parked somewhere more than eight minutes away. Travelling at thirty miles per hour, one could park four miles away and still get there in time. To say I was angry was an understatement. We had them both there, in the safe house, hopefully with the drugs. It was a devastating blow.

The personnel carrier then drove by and I agreed to meet them at the bottom of Park Road near the railway and wasteland. I was angry and cursing at myself. We had both of them together in the house with the bald man. There was no getting away with it. But no, due to someone's incompetence, they had gone. I tip-toed out of the flat, down the back stairs and ran across to the railway line and the wasteland.

The driver's door of the personnel carrier opened, and before I could speak or shout, the driver held his hands up, 'I'm sorry, I'm sorry, I parked at the cricket ground and couldn't get across the traffic.' I wanted to hit him! He was unaware of the stress and aggravation this would cause.

Danny and I got together and planned the next course of action. We had to go now. The boss had told us Thursday was the last day. So, at seven o'clock and hoping to make amends, the local officer and others walked down the passageway of 107 Park Rd and calmly knocked on the back door. The thin, bald Glaswegian opened the door and was pushed back instantly as the officer charged inside. Danny, two others and I headed for downtown as we knew Tanner and Dawson worked the doors at the Aladdin nightclub on Thursday. As we parked the car in the centre of Blackton, reports were coming in that several kilos of powders had been recovered from 107 with bags, weighing scales, books, including workings out, telephone numbers and everything connected with selling drugs. Dawson's and Tanner's telephone numbers were included in the book, as were the names of other dealers in the town. There was also a small holdall with £10,000 cash inside.

All four of us stood waiting for the pelican crossing to change. Aladdin's was in the background. The club was in darkness as it was still early, but we thought it would be our first port of call to find the pair. I looked on the opposite footpath at the pedestrians waiting to cross to our side and there stood two men. I thought it was Tanner and Dawson, but I wasn't sure. I had been watching them for months, and although I was not one hundred per cent sure, they looked like them. I couldn't believe it. As the pelican lights changed to green and the beeping started, we began to cross. I didn't have the time to communicate with Danny or the other two, but as Tanner got near me, I realised it was him. He looked directly at me and saw the recognition in my eyes. I pictured receiving that rugby ball many years ago as a youngster in the Chief Constables semi-final. I put my head down and charged towards the opposition. Bang! I hit Tanner full-on and heard all the wind coming out of him. It knocked him straight back and onto the floor. His car keys fell to the side and I jumped on top of him.

'You're under arrest for supplying drugs. You do not have to say anything unless you wish to do so, but anything you do say will be taken down and given in evidence.'

Tanner was still dazed and confused, as I think Danny and the other two team members were. Immediately, Dawson squared up to the three and started to attack Danny. Tanner, seeing this, shouted in a very Scottish accent, 'Polis Malky, Polis, Polis.' These were the last words that either of them would speak. Dawson stopped fighting and Tanner started to get to his feet. The handcuffs were placed on both of them and one of the team summoned the local officers from Blackton, who arrived shortly afterwards in a police van. Incidentally, the van arrived much quicker than Alpha One did with the arrest team for Park Road. Both suspects were searched and off they went to the custody office at Blackton.

The work was only beginning, as we had to determine which officers had been at what locations to avoid cross-contaminating the evidence. If Tanner and Dawson didn't speak, we may have to examine 107 Park Rd forensically. It was all very complicated, but in the end, we got there. We searched all the home addresses, their vehicles, Aladdin's and 107. We recovered about 5 kilos of what we thought was amphetamine sulphate or 'speed', a half kilo of cocaine and a few kilos of glucose. This is what they had been using as a cutting agent. Tanner and Dawson had no drugs on them when searched. Nothing was found at either of their home addresses.

Danny and I sat back in the chairs and looked at the office clock. It was three in the morning and we were still at Blackton. Tanner and Dawson had yet to be interviewed and the drugs to be analysed. It would be another full day again tomorrow, but I had an hour's drive back to Priestown and another hour back home to Sandford. Then up at six o'clock and an hour's drive back to the office. It wasn't worth going home. Also, I was still in a very 'hyper state' after the roller coaster events of the evening. There had been some ups and downs in the day and it had been an experience. We both drove back to Priestown and I slept on some chairs in the office. I say sleep but my mind was racing. I maybe got an hour's nap.

It didn't seem that long when Danny arrived back in the office. After a quick shower, we collected all the observation logs and photographs and both headed off for Blackton Police Station. It would be another busy day as we had the interviews of Tanner and Dawson. The evidence wasn't damning, but I thought there was sufficient to put before a jury. I'm not sure that would happen today, as I think the benchmark is now a lot higher for the chance of a conviction. As stated, Tanner and Dawson answered 'no comment' to all the questions, allegations and photographs shown to them. I did notice Tanner's solicitor's eyebrows raise when the photo of the pair carrying the bags of white powder came out. That one photograph was a game changer.

After a long, hard day, Danny and I returned to base at Priestown, and Julie said the boss wanted to see us both. As I climbed the stairs to his office, I could smell the alcohol. DS Ray Ingham and the boss were there with an open bottle of Johnny Walker whisky on the table. They both had a glass each then the boss poured one each for Danny and me. Congratulations and compliments were the order of the afternoon, but it was all disingenuous to me. I knew what I knew.

There was also the very sensitive issue of the Police Inspector's wife, who regularly visited a bed and breakfast with Tanner. I'm told he was devastated when he found out.

***

Several months later, I was called back to give evidence at the Crown Court in the case of Tanner, Dawson and Bell. They had all been charged with conspiring with each other to supply Class A and Class B drugs. The cocaine being Class A. I gave evidence for two days as the defence tried to discredit me and the evidence Danny and I had amassed. There are several sayings in the world of investigation, for instance, 'the evidence iceberg,' 'trial agenda', and the like, which describe the defence tactic of trying to discredit the process in which the evidence was collected. The evidence will speak for itself. The defence will attack the process in which I got the evidence. This was their only defence.

The bundle of surveillance photographs were passed to the jury as I went through my evidence and the surveillance logs.

The prosecution barrister led me through each days observations and invited the jury to look at the photographs as he did so. He started with what I thought was a peculiar request when he said, 'Officer, in your own words, tell the court what happened on this particular day.'

As you know, I have a weird sense of humour, but when he said to use my own words, I actually considered asking him whose words did he think I was going to use? Shakespeare's, Wordsworth's? So, I thought of giving my evidence something along the lines of,

'At this address, I did observe,
The hour of each event and thus declare,
Within this document, I did relate,
The happenings are detailed and accurate'

Alas, the angel grabbed hold of me by the lapels, and I saw the devil scampering over my shoulder and away out of view. Now was the time to be sensible, so I quickly regained my emotional discipline.

'Officer, you are saying that just before midday that Wednesday, you were carrying out observations when the BMW arrived outside 107 Park Road. Is that correct?'

'Yes, that is correct, counsel,' I replied. 'I made an entry on the surveillance log at that time that describes what happened and I took a photograph at the same time,' I replied.

'Your Honour, could I invite the jury to look at page nine of their bundle, the surveillance log exhibit reference JG17 and also photograph number seven in their bundle, exhibit reference JG92,' prosecuting counsel asked the Judge.

The barrister highlighted, one by one, the log entries and descriptions of what happened, and then we came to *the* photograph. The one of Tanner and Dawson carrying the bags of white powder. It was damning. The powder could have well been glucose, but the picture it painted was that of two drug dealers. They could not get away from that. If nothing else had been found, no drugs, no scales, no workings out, the jury may have been persuaded to think it was washing powder or kiddies milk formula. But there was no getting away from it. That photograph painted a thousand words.

Each had a separate counsel and they attacked everything they could. I had to go through the evidence three times as they all had a go at me in different ways. They all said I was mistaken at best and a liar at worst. Questions were raised as to why Tanner and Dawson were not arrested at six thirty-one when they both entered 107 on the arrest day.

'I will tell you why they weren't arrested at the address, officer, shall I? They weren't there. You've added an entry to the log, haven't you, and included a previous photograph?' one of the defence barristers added.

So, it went on for two days. When completed, all the surveillance logs were signed and date-stamped. The photographs taken by the Canon camera were state-of-the-art. You could time and date stamp when the photograph was taken. This was groundbreaking technology, and the time and date would be printed on the photograph. According to the defence, none of this was tamper-proof.

On day three of the trial, the prosecution case ended and rather surprisingly, the defence did not want to put the defendants in the witness box. They merely suggested to the court that the prosecution did not come up to proof. It wasn't for the defence to prove their innocence. The prosecution had to prove the case beyond all reasonable doubt. There had been several legal arguments behind closed doors and not for the jury's ears, about discrediting the evidence and questioning the lawfulness of it. In particular, *the* photograph. That one photograph was the case in itself and the Judge allowed the jury to see it.

The jury found all three men guilty of the offences in less than an hour. Tanner and Dawson were sentenced to ten years and Bell to seven years imprisonment. Tanner and Dawson were also subject to some financial scrutiny and were both served with orders under the Proceeds of Crime legislation. If they didn't pay £100,000 to the Treasury, a further three years would be added to their sentences.

Danny and I travelled back to Priestown, and I was pleased with the outcome, but I had more of a sense of vindication after what I had been told in the back channel by Macintosh. No one mentioned anything when we got back and the whole office was preparing for the arrest phase for Operation Empathy. What had raised its head, however, and caused some trouble in the office was it was 'alleged' that someone had very intricately cut the whole of the last chapter out of the back of the boss's Ken Follet novel. Someone had lent it to him on recommendation and later asked him about the twist at the end of the book. When the boss said it was boring and he didn't understand the ending, a close inspection of the book revealed an impeccable job of removing the final chapter.

Angels and demons again.

CHAPTER TWELVE

UNDERCOVER

When I joined the unit, I became aware of the different 'specialist' roles. There was a key role for the camera operative, so I volunteered to attend a training course and become skilled in surveillance photography. The next skill area I was introduced to was that of the CROP officer. Covert Rural Observation Post. I have covered this in a previous chapter, but basically, this involved digging holes in the ground and hiding in order to carry out observations. Volunteers attended the training course and were exposed to the elements at night, having to capture evidence in the most trying of circumstances. This wasn't for me.

Another skill area was that of the Financial Crimes Officer. As it says on the tin, their job was to financially investigate the subjects of the operations both proactively and reactively, hopefully recovering financial assets and disrupting the drug gangs. The final area in which one could develop oneself on the Regional Crime Squad was in an undercover role. This sounded more interesting.

My first real taste of undercover work was when I was asked if I could go into a biker's pub, as there were numerous reports of customers smoking marijuana and possibly taking stronger substances. I agreed, as I had previously had numerous motorcycles and had been motorcycle racing at Brands Hatch. So, I had a lot of knowledge. What I didn't have was a motorbike. Frank soon came to the rescue with that and we visited a local police pound and I picked a Suzuki 250 and off I went. Was I insured? Probably not.

My partner in crime in The Grey Horse was Beano. He, too, was a biker and worked in a different Regional Office. Every Wednesday, we would meet at Priestown Office and he would jump on the back of a stolen 250 Suzuki and off we went to The Grey Horse. I still had my leather jacket but had to borrow a helmet from….. yes, you've guessed it, the police pound.

The pub was packed and you could hardly see across the bar with the smoke and fumes. They were indeed smoking marijuana inside and there were a noticeable number of the West Indian community in attendance. I still had my red, green and gold 'One Love' tee shirt that Tony Hill bought me. Blending in a pub full of bikers wasn't a problem for me or Beano. The first night, we kept ourselves to ourselves and got more involved in talking to people as the weeks passed. This is when I realised this role wasn't just about blending in. It was about having a back story of who you were, where you were from, etc. It's called a legend. You had to be somebody from somewhere. It had to be a grey story, vague but believable. Never get caught in a lie, is the saying. So I could tell the truth when someone asked what motorbikes I had previously had. When someone asked about my education, I could tell the truth with a few tweaks. It was definitely a skill and I was learning fast. However, I had already had some uncomfortable rides.

As a youngster, I learnt the hard way about telling the truth. To this day, people still comment on how I can hold a poker face and no one knows when I'm telling the truth or not. It started with getting into mischief. I wasn't a naughty kid, but I was a boy. I was inquisitive and perhaps did things I shouldn't have done.

'Now you tell me the truth, have you been in that cupboard?' came the yell from my Mum. I did what I was told and told the truth. Then I got belted and it damn well hurt. The next time I got into mischief, again, my Mum asked me to tell the truth, so I did, then got belted again. It hurt. This happened maybe half a dozen times, as I was a slow learner in my early days.

'Have you eaten that sausage roll from the cupboard, which was your Dad's tea,' my Mum yelled at me.

'No, I haven't', I replied.

'Now you tell me the truth, or you will be in big trouble,' she added.

'I haven't eaten it,' I said as defiantly as possible for a six-year-old.

'William, William, have you eaten your Dad's tea from the cupboard? The sausage roll,' my Mum screamed at my brother. Obviously, he denied it, so we played another game. We both had to stand there until one of us owned up. I had associated owning up or telling the truth with pain. I found it easy to ride it out and associated telling lies, or not the truth, should we say, with no pain. It was a no brainer for a youngster. I mastered my facial expression and my non-verbal communication (NVCs) and could sense the chink in Mum's armour. Once there was an element of doubt, deny, deny, deny. No pain. Mum interrogated me often, but I learnt not to flinch and soon mastered the poker face. Incidentally, the sausage roll wasn't as good as today's are from Greggs.

Back in the pub with Beano, by the fourth week, we had identified the key players and who were selling the drugs. We were offered spliffs, reefers, smokes and weed, but we were told not to buy anything, just observe and paint the picture to assist officers when they raided the pub. Beano and I never attended any formal briefings and unknown to us, the police managers had just informed the raiding party that they had received intelligence reports. No one except our boss and the local managers knew that Beano and I were inside the pub.

On the night of the police raid, we were given instructions for one of us to come outside and show ourselves around nine o'clock, if we thought the raid should take place. We could have gone outside every hour or half hour and it would still have been the right time. The place was awash with drugs, mostly marijuana, but some powders and pills were floating around.

At nine o'clock, Beano went outside the front door to show himself to the team and shortly afterwards came back to the pool room where we were sat. It was busy and smoky. I remember Beano was wearing his biker's leather jacket with the tassels on the sleeves. Loud music was playing in the pub when suddenly a tremendous loud crash drowned it out. It was the sound of shattering glass. The thick, frosted side window in the pool room shattered, sending splinters of glass across the pool table and everyone sat around. People ducked and turned their backs, some falling on the floor. Immediately noticeable was the glistening of the silver helmet badges as officers put thick blankets over the broken window and started to climb in. In a state of shock, Beano and I just sat and watched as people started scrambling to their feet and trying to get out of the small room. At the same time, the screams of 'Police Police' could be heard in a very chaotic scene.

As we both sat there picking the glass out of our hair and clothing, the expression on Beano's face changed somewhat as the regulars were running past him to evade the incoming police officers and placing their contraband in Beano's top pocket. By the time a uniformed officer grabbed him by the lapels, Beano had quite a stash of drugs in his top pocket. We were both manhandled out of the back door of the pub by several officers and pinned up against a wall in a small courtyard with other regulars. They seemed content after depositing their drugs in Beano's top pocket. I looked to my right at Beano and saw an officer reach in the pocket and pull out some rolled-up 'spliffs'. The officer then gave Beano a dig in the ribs. I loudly protested and received the same treatment. We both received a couple more digs each from the uniformed officers as people were searched. When the officer declared to a Sergent what he'd found in Beano's pocket, we were both unceremoniously dragged away. This was hardly the place to declare that we were police officers, was it?

Beano and I were led away to a police van and placed inside by our uniformed colleagues. When we arrived at the Police Station, we weren't escorted to the custody office as the others were but met by a Police Inspector and taken to a private office. This certainly turned some heads with the uniform staff on the raid. We completed our evidence books and bagged and tagged all the reefers, spliffs and other illegal substances that had been placed in Beano's top pocket. I was a little perturbed about our manhandling but was advised by the Inspector to 'pipe down' and accept it as one of the 'perks' of the job. I laughed.

Several people were charged with possession of drugs, but more importantly, the licensee was charged with managing premises where drugs were being taken, which ultimately led to him losing his licence. Apparently, he had been advised and then told in the strongest terms to get his house in order by the licensing authorities. Sadly, he had ignored the advice and had been rather blatant in allowing his premises to be used in such a way. Beano and I were never called to give evidence and I'm not sure if it was declared to the prosecution team that we had ever been in the pub. That is how it happened in the day.

My next role was buying chemicals from a crime gang in Nottingham. The background story was complicated, but the gang had been manufacturing amphetamine sulphate and had surplus chemicals to sell. I think the chemical was called BMK, or, to give it a proper title, Benzyl Methyl Ketone or Phenylacetone. It is a precursor for amphetamine, which possibly gave it a cat pee smell. Former drug squad officers reading this book will nod in agreement now.

Other regional officers saw the purchase as an opportunity and a way of identifying the gang members and maybe a way to infiltrate them. I'm not sure if undercover officers had already been deployed in Nottingham, but my job was to turn up, test the chemicals and buy them with cash if the test was positive. The deal was to take place at the car park of Nottingham Racecourse by the River Trent.

The deployment of undercover operatives was not yet professionally managed. This would come later and not without controversy. The deployment of operatives was very ad hoc at the time and on an office to office basis. But the police in Nottingham didn't want to get involved in the planning of the deployment, or what the operative looked like or how they would arrive. That was left to the individual operative and their local management. At this stage, in the late 1980s, there wasn't even a training course for operatives; it was all word of mouth and passing on experiences. The Metropolitan Police had begun to put together a two-week training course and up in Manchester, the officers in Operation Omega had not even been thought of. You either sank or swam and I had already nearly had a couple of drowning issues.

With the help of Frank, again we visited the police pound and this time, picked up another either stolen or seized motorcycle. It was a water cooled, triple cylinder Suzuki GT750. I was at home on the machine, having possessed one. Frank had now a contact at the police pound and told me it wasn't exactly rocket fuel getting the bikes. I thought about correcting him but just left it. I still had my helmet and motorcycle clothing and would have borrowed Beano's leather jacket, but it was far too small. I was given £2000 in cash, the testing kit and just briefly told that if I dropped a little of the BMK liquid into a vile of clear liquid, the reagent and it turned pink, it was BMK and to make the purchase.

I also had to consider being scammed myself. as a colleague of mine was, shortly before this operation. Let me briefly tell you what happened. I don't know how the drug deal had been arranged, but a colleague, Colin or 'Col' from another RCS unit, had also embarked down the undercover path. Three, maybe four units all came together as a drugs deal was going to take place at Sandford railway station. Local drug dealer and gang member Kenny Bishop was going to be on the other end of the deal. Kenny was a tasty criminal and could well be armed. He had previous convictions for firearms offences. At the briefing, we were all given our observation positions inside the station. The deal Col was making was for a kilo of heroin, at a price of £18,000, from Kenny at six o'clock, inside a burger bar.

Just before six, Col and his minder, who had a bag of show money, entered the burger bar and Col walked across and shook the hand of a mixed race lad, who we believed was the drug dealer Kenny. Sat with Kenny was an elderly Asian man who looked like he should be attending to goats rather than selling heroin in Sandford railway station. The show money appeared and before Col purchased the drugs, they had to be tested, of course, for heroin. Any drug dealer worth their salt would have a testing kit containing a reagent. Usually, in liquid form, you would spoon a small amount of the powder into a small bottle with the reagent and shake. Depending on what reagent you used, the liquid would change colour, usually purple.

The agreed testing place was the burger bar toilets. If the sample tested positive, i.e. the liquid turned purple, then Col would take off his jacket, which was the arrest signal. This is where Kenny was very crafty. He ripped a corner off the page from a magazine he was carrying, explaining that the shiny paper would not absorb the heroin. He was indeed correct and the majority of dealers used magazine paper to sell their drug wraps. With paper in hand, Kenny then said that in order to prove it was the same piece of paper, he would write his telephone number across the top of the page. This he did and all present witnessed it. He then spooned a small amount of brown powder out of the larger bag that the goat herder was holding. He tipped the powder into the paper, with the telephone number written across the top and neatly folded it. Kenny placed it in his pocket and both he and Col went off to the toilet, where Col was going to test it. Kenny put his foot against the door to stop anyone coming in. He then removed the folded wrap he had emptied the powder into at the table from his pocket and unwrapped it to reveal the powder. To prove it was the same wrap and powder, the same telephone number Kenny had written was there, across the top. It had to be the same piece of magazine paper. All good so far? Col, the undercover officer, emptied a small amount of the brown powder into the bottle of reagent and it instantly turned purple. We have ourselves a kilo of heroin, thought Col.

The observation and arrest teams sat in the burger bar, focused intently on that toilet door. It opened after a couple of minutes, and Kenny walked out first. Col was behind him and immediately took his jacket off, which was the signal that the test had proved positive for heroin and to arrest Kenny and the goat herder.

'Strike, strike, strike,' came the call over the radio as officers leapt from their tables and rugby tackled Kenny and the goat herder to the ground. The kilo of heroin was recovered in an Asda bag under the table and the show money was safe and sound. What an excellent job!

Well, before we move on, let's just slow things down and do a slow motion, action replay shall we? When Kenny was sat at the table with Col, he emptied the powder into the paper and then wrote his telephone number on it etc. He then placed that paper wrap in his *right* hand pocket. The powder is from the bag of 'heroin' he wishes to sell to Col. However, when he gets into the toilet, he reaches into his *left* pocket and takes out a very similar wrap, again with his telephone number written across the top. In Blue Peter language, one that he'd prepared earlier. The only difference was that the one he had already prepared did, in fact, contain heroin. So, the paper wrap Col tested was, in fact, out of the left pocket and did contain heroin, hence the positive test. The powder in the right pocket and the kilo bag being looked after by the goat herder contained Bisto gravy powder. Col was about to pay £18,000 for a kilo of Bisto gravy.

Initially, there was euphoria and some back-slapping about the arrest, but when a dog in the burger bar started licking the Asda bag, it was apparent that all was not well. The next clue was when Kenny was booked into the custody office, he called himself Kenny 'Bisto' Bishop. It was an easy mistake to make, and if you weren't street-wise to the scams and tricks of the trade, you could easily get caught out.

Col retired gracefully from any further undercover work and Kenny, the goat herder and the gravy were sent packing. As they say, every day is a school day.

So, back to the Nottingham connection, the motorbike and the purchase of the chemical BMK. I had taken Eddie from the office along with me as a pillion and backup. Parked nearby was a surveillance team and someone with a camera would have been watching and maybe taking photographs near to the car park. The meeting was scheduled for eleven o'clock and just before that, the trusty stolen Suzuki motorcycle pulled onto the gravel car park. I knew the bike had a two-stroke engine and there was lots of smoke billowing out of the exhaust. It wasn't very clandestine. It was pouring with rain, so I parked the bike under a tree for shelter. A silver Skoda then drove into the car park and stopped a distance away. There were at least three or four in the car and the driver got out. He was tall, dark hair and bearded. What stood out was his red Hawaiian shirt, in complete contrast to the British weather. Eddie had the £2000 in notes tucked away somewhere. The driver started to wave at me and beckoned me over. I kept the helmet on and walked towards the Skoda and the red shirt. It was pouring down, and the poor man was getting wet.

'Shame about the weather,' I said when I reached him. 'Why not park as far away as you could from me?'

'Don't be a cock. You,' he shouted and pointed at Eddie, 'you stay put. Where's the money?' he asked.

I nodded at Eddie, who wasn't going anywhere in any case and indicated he was holding onto the money. I was to test the BMK and give Eddie the nod to release the money should the test be positive. I was very aware of the recent scam on Col, but when the Hawaiian man opened the tailgate of the car, there was a brown five-litre bottle of liquid. If there was going to be a switch with the bottle, like with the Bisto gravy, then Derren Brown had nothing on this guy. I was aware of two other heads in the back of the car who both turned around when the tailgate opened. They were white men but turned away as soon as they had their glance out of the back.

I started to screw the top off the rather large bottle and the front passenger came around at my side. I was a little cautious, but I didn't have any money, so I couldn't see him doing anything to me, hopefully.

'Go up to him on the bike and when I give the signal, get the money off him,' Hawaiian shirt said to his passenger. Sure enough, the passenger walked across the deserted car park to Eddie in the pouring rain. He too, was wearing a shirt and jeans and was getting soaked.

With the liquid in my testing bottle, a shake here and there produced a rather pink liquid. If my briefing team were correct, I had a five-litre bottle of the chemical BMK, which was a precursor for amphetamine sulphate or 'speed'. I turned and gave the thumbs up to Eddie, who handed over the envelope to the Skoda passenger. After a quick look inside, he too gave the thumbs up and the Hawaiian guy invited me to take the bottle. As I picked it up, I suddenly realised how heavy it was and that I had nowhere to carry it on the bike. How was I going to hold it whilst riding?

Like a dual at dawn, I started walking back to the motorbike and Eddie. The car passenger walked towards me and the Skoda. We met in the middle and I couldn't resist. Please don't think I'm being flippant about the role I was playing. I was as nervous as hell, but I couldn't resist.

'Will you do us a favour, mate, when you get back to the car?' I asked the passenger as we met in the middle.

'Yes mate, what is it? He replied.

'Tell your friend he looks a right tit in that shirt, will you,' I said as I made my way back to Eddie and the bike. The car passenger laughed and walked on.

I could see the same question going through Eddie's mind as I lifted up the bottle. Where on earth was it going to go? Well, it went inside the front of Eddie's small jacket, which we zipped up as far as we could, which was not very far. I started the 750 and in a haze of blue smoke, headed for the exit and West Bridgford. This is where we were to be debriefed and make our evidential notes. We looked a right pair riding off with a five-litre bottle between us on the bike. What do they say about planning and preparing?

I was halfway through the notes when the door opened and a man in a collar and tie walked in. I presumed he was a local boss and he asked how the notes were going. Then, he asked a very stupid but serious question.

'Which one of you has got the gun, the shooter?'

I looked at Eddie and looked at this man standing before us and asked him to repeat himself, which he did.

'We've had an informant just ring in about the deal and he said he was in the Skoda and that the rider of the motorbike was a big fella and tooled up. He said the rider had a gun inside his jacket, which was seen when he bent down to test the drugs.'

I know what you're all thinking, angels and demons and all that, but I will hold my hands up here and admit to things. Yes, it was me that ate my dad's sausage roll. Yes, it was me who put Vim scouring powder in my Mum's talcum powder holder. Yes, it was me that injected ink into Frank's banana but take a gun out on an operation like that. I really don't think so. Where would I get a gun from in the first place? Well, apart from a homemade banger gun. You may recall my experiences of shooting Fez in my initial training in Sandford. I don't like guns and made the boss in front of me very aware of that. He left the office before asking another rather stupid question, 'Are you sure you didn't have a gun?' Actually, I thought, now you come to mention it, I've said I wasn't carrying a gun, haven't I? But you know, I actually might have been now you have just mentioned it. I just forgot. How ridiculous of the man.

The purchase of the BMK was a small piece of the evidential puzzle. Eddie and I were later informed of the arrest of an East Midlands team that had hired some industrial premises to make amphetamine sulphate. The tell-tale sign that alerted all their neighbours and police to their illegal activity was the smell of cat pee and, of course, stupid Hawaiian shirts.

***

Margaret Borland was in her thirties and lived in an inner city council estate. She looked hard and someone not to mess with. It was a poor and deprived area where she lived and the local pub was called the Magpie. The brewery had a sense of humour as if anything was left unlocked or not tied down, it was gone. Burglaries were rife and it really was the animal kingdom way of survival in the area.

One night in the Magpie, Maggie, who incidentally was no angel, confided in a friend that her husband was having an affair with a younger girl on the same estate. Maggie had done her investigations and the evidence was strong. Her fat and lazy Barry was seeing a younger woman. She had confronted Barry, but he had batted away the allegation as pure nonsense, even in the face of all the evidence. Seems that fat Baz was also quizzed by his Mum and asked to tell the truth! He told Maggie that if she didn't want to stay in the relationship, the door would always be open. Sadly, Maggie had nowhere to go and no one to help. She did have a solution to keep Barry and hopefully end the relationship he was having with his younger friend. Maggie was going to kill her.

Shocked at Maggie's intention and knowing the younger girl, the friend was tormented as to what to do. She tried to talk Maggie out of doing anything stupid, but Maggie was adamant that she was going to murder the lover and had started to plot how to do it.

The friend chatted it through with her partner and seeing that Maggie was intent on carrying out her threat, they both decided to visit the local police station. 'Nightmare Lane' nick was positioned in the centre of about four estates in the area. The station derived its name from the lane it was on, but for cops who were sent there, it was a 'nightmare'. You were surrounded on all sides by deprivation, poor people and crime. It was an extremely busy BCU to work on. Some hated it, some loved it. The officers had very few friends on the estate, so there was only one style of policing. Firm but firm.

'Sarge, there's a woman at the desk saying her friend on the estate is going to kill someone. What should I do?' asked the young officer on station duties.

'Tell her to get in the queue with the rest of em,' came the reply.

After listening to the friend's torment of what to do, the young officer told her there was probably nothing in Maggie's threats and she was probably only saying she was going to kill the lover as a natural reaction to finding out that fat Barry was having his leg over somewhere else. The couple left the police station unhappy but took the officer's advice to 'see how it went' and to call back if anything developed. The next day, they were back.

Maggie had started to come up with all sorts of plans to kill the lover. Some of them easily achievable. She had also given thought to evading arrest and this was in the days before the internet. Today, she would probably have left a digital evidence trail in her browser's history. The difference this time, though, was that Maggie wanted her friend's partner to carry out the murder. Although he liked

Maggie, killing someone on her behalf was just crossing the line of where their friendship was. So, after another visit to Nightmare Lane police station, an idea was raised that the friend's partner could introduce someone who was capable of killing the lover and also capturing evidence. e.g. a police officer. As I pointed out to my supervisors, the only snag with this was when Maggie was arrested. She would then know her best mate sold her out to the cops and it could have severe consequences for her friend and partner on the estate. In the animal kingdom, the grass, the snitch, the rat or whatever you want to call them are not well thought of and there could be serious repercussions for Maggie's friend and her partner.

As the bosses scratched their heads, I suggested the bus queue approach. This is whereby the friend and partner introduce someone, a police officer, to carry out the killing. That officer meets with Maggie and gets the plot and then just before they carry it out, they say they can't go through with it for whatever reason, but they know a man who can. That officer then introduces the next officer in the queue and the same process is repeated until that officer backs out and introduces the next officer. Eventually, after introducing three or more officers, the 'evidential' officer is finally introduced, who captures all the evidence and Maggie is arrested. When Maggie turns round to her friend and partner and accuses them of introducing a cop, they could say, 'Not us'! It was someone else in that queue. None of the others would be traceable and should the matter go to court, there is a process that would allow the information about the undercover officers in the queue to be kept private and not disclosed to Maggie. The idea was that, hopefully, Maggie would think the next to last person in the queue was the one who introduced the cop. This hopefully would take the spotlight away from her friend and partner and identifying them as the source of the information.

After the issue was passed down the queue a couple of times it landed in my lap and would I meet Maggie and listen to how she was going to kill her husband's young lover? As I have said, work in this covert and undercover area hadn't been professionalised as yet, which meant that I had to borrow motorcycles from police pounds and, on this occasion, had to borrow Danny's car.

'What do you want to borrow my car for,' was the question he asked.

'To help a woman called Maggie kill her husband's lover, that's all,' I laughed back at him.

Firstly, I had to be kitted out with all the modern-day equipment to capture the conversation with Maggie so that it could be later assessed as evidence. I visited our technical unit and was shown the state-of-the-art Nagra reel-to-reel bodywork covert tape recorder. It was the size of an encyclopaedia! The contraption had to be strapped and taped down on my chest, away from my heart. Learning from experience, those tape recorders positioned over the heart captured the 'whoosh' of the muscle pumping blood around the body and not the conversation it was supposed to do. The technical unit were also testing out something very new. Microwave. Don't ask me how it worked, but I had to wear another pack on my back. It was an encyclopaedia type mechanism strapped on with sticky tape. It beamed the conversation to a relay pack, which allowed the bosses to listen in on headphones in a nearby car. It was all very state-of-the-art. I walked out of the technical unit looking like my legs were too thin and disproportionate to the top half of my body. Give me a pair of green tights and I would have looked like the toad in Toad Hall.

The meeting was scheduled in a side street near the Magpie pub at one o'clock. I'd been given my instructions on how to power everything up, which I would do about five minutes before Maggie arrived. Danny's car was a Nissan. Originally, it was white, but now, with age, it had turned brown with rust. It did a job and it got him to work and back. It was an old car and Danny told me to take it easy. Maggie had been told to look out for me and the car by the undercover officer, the one before me in the queue. It was all stations go!

I arrived on Grundy St at around ten minutes to one and tried to remember the instructions of how to turn everything on. I am told what happened next was extremely funny. Detective Superintendent Macintosh was overseeing this part of the operation from the back seat of the 'Command Car'. Apparently, he sat there with his contraption on his knee and a technical officer by his side, trying to tune it into the different frequencies. He kept asking Macintosh if he could hear anything, but Macintosh couldn't tell what he was saying as he was wearing the very modern and noise reduction headphones. Suddenly, Macintosh grabbed the headphones and ripped them off his head, throwing them at the technical officer. He loudly cursed and accused him of trying to burst his eardrums with the noise of loud music.

'But boss, that can't have happened as we're not on commercial radio airwaves. You can't have heard music,' the techy pleaded as the boss tore into him.

'I'm telling you that was the radio coming through them headphones and too bloody loud. Nearly burst my ear drums for goodness sake,' Macintosh shouted at him.

Well, it had happened exactly as I'd imagined it would do. In my mind's eye, I pictured Macintosh with his headphones on and twiddling with all the dials. So, just before I fired up the microwave super booster, I got as close as possible to the car radio and turned it up full blast. Then I switched on the microwave and what I pictured might happen with Macintosh, actually happened. I know it's childish, but I thought I'd try it to release the pressure.

'What the fuck is this,' shouted a tall, thin woman who was standing at the side of the car. I had the driver's window open a little and she continued, 'turn that music down you daft c***, you'll have everyone looking at us.'

I hadn't timed and dated the recording, which I should have done at the beginning with a brief introduction. It was too late now, so I assumed this was Maggie.

'You'll get pulled by the filth in this, you know, around here,' she said as she pointed to the car. I had been prior warned she was a little aggressive and 'in your face' by the others in the queue before me.

'Is it Maggie?' I asked.

'Well, who the fuck do you think it is?' she answered.

I leaned across and opened the front passenger seat door and beckoned her to get in.

'Are you going to sort me out or what? It's been a mare trying to get someone. I'm only asking you to murder someone. It's not like I'm asking for anything big, is it, for fucks sake,' she added as she sat down and closed the door.

This may be an appropriate juncture to explain, in simplistic terms, the law about *entrapment* and *agent provocateur*, etc. Picture the scene in Paris in 1789, the peasants were hungry and the ruling elite were resistant to reform, leading to the storming of the Bastille and the beginning of the French Revolution. Robespierre and his secret police were attempting to flush out the elite and the way to survive was to provide information and accuse others. This led to people creating crimes themselves, inviting people along to participate in the crime and then informing the secret police of their wrong doings. Off to the guillotine they would go, and one's survival was only guaranteed until the next time. Bring that concept forward to modern times and the defence would argue that it was indeed the state that created the crime and then invited the poor defendant along to partake in it, before informing the police. In 1929, a Royal Commission on Police Powers and Procedure defined agent provocateur as follows,

*'A person who entices another to commit an express breach of the law which he would **not** otherwise have committed, and then proceeds or informs against him in respect of such an offence'*

So, if I had never met Maggie and then listened to her account and then encouraged, enticed or coaxed Maggie into killing the lover, then I would have played the role of the *agent provocateur*. Another way of explaining this is to imagine a bus journey and who is driving the bus. In this case, Maggie is driving the bus. It's her idea, her plans, her methodology. Maggie is in control in that driver's seat. My role is merely to wait at the bus stop and wait for the bus to come along and jump on board. Maggie still has to drive it and my job is to play as little a role as possible in order that Maggie continues to drive. I can't encourage, entice, etc., as that would be her defence should the case go to court. She could claim it was a crazy idea and one she had no intention of carrying it out until she met this man in a Nissan rust box, who encouraged her to do it.

The law is open to interpretation and there are many cases where the comments and rulings of the Judges have set precedents for future cases. To give an example of how fine a point it is, consider these two statements should an undercover operative ask them of a drug dealer.

'Can you get me two bags of cocaine?' versus *'I need two bags of cocaine?'*

Now, which statement could a clever barrister use as a defence to say their client would not have committed this offence if it wasn't for the undercover operative asking them to do it. The interpretations are complex and there have been many court rulings over the last century regarding the issue.

Back to Maggie and me sat in the rust box of a car. I have my recording devices all working and from now on in, what Maggie says will be used against her in court. Sadly, Maggie doesn't know that. Let me take you back to the 1990s when a young man called Bryce was part of a car stealing gang. He was stealing at least two a week and when an undercover police officer rang him to buy one, Mr. Bryce duly obliged. He was selling a £28,000 Saab convertible to the officer for £2,800. After conversations between them were partly recorded, Bryce was arrested and convicted of the offences. He appealed on the grounds that although the officer was in an undercover role, when he asked questions of Bryce about the car, this amounted to a 'police interview' and should have been undertaken within the bounds of the law. The Judge in the case, Lord Chief Justice Taylor, commented that the undercover officer asked questions that went to the 'heart of the matter' when they need not. 'The questions were not necessary to the undercover operation,' the Judge added. The inference being that the police could interview suspects when in an undercover role outside the law (Police and Criminal Evidence Act). This meant that suspects had no protection and even though the officer was undercover, if he was going to ask questions that went to the heart of the matter, he should have given Mr. Bryce the police caution. Yes, you are reading this correctly. Even in an undercover role, the officer should have cautioned Mr. Bryce and blown his own cover. That is what was now being asked. The Court of Appeal quashed Bryce's conviction and the case caused real issues for the undercover policing tactic.

Back to Maggie and I sat in the Nissan rust box. I have to make sure that Maggie is driving the bus. i.e. it's her idea to kill her husband's lover, that she has planned it all and I'm merely stood at the bus when I get on for a ride. I also have to make sure that I don't ask her questions that go 'direct to the heart of the matter' or if they do, I should give her the police caution. This obviously would then alert Maggie to the fact that I am perhaps not a trained assassin but, in fact, a police officer. I knew from this point forward that what I said or did would be subject to legal scrutiny. I was already literally walking on eggshells.

'What's the craic then,' I asked and Maggie then went into her plan of how I should go about killing fat Barry's lover. It involved waiting outside the Magpie pub after the Spiders Web disco on a Sunday night and following 'Chanel' back to her house near the gas works. Maggie knew what time she left and what route she took home as she had followed her a couple of times. When she got to a quiet passageway near the canal, I had to knock her out and then inject her with insulin. Fat Baz was a diabetic and she had lots of syringes of insulin. Once I had completed that part of the plan, I then had to throw Chanel in the canal. As Maggie commented herself, it was easy. I asked her how much she was going to pay me and she said she'd saved £500.

It was a very sad situation. A woman so desperate not to lose her partner, who she hated, but was willing to kill another person to keep him. After listening to her for twenty minutes or so, Maggie was adamant she was going to do it and if I couldn't help her then she would get someone else. She said I could always contact her through Tracey at the Magpie pub. I said I would do at some stage. What I really meant to say was that someone else was going to contact her and they probably would be wearing a uniform.

Maggie was subsequently arrested and the whole desperate saga was captured on two C90 police interview tapes. The local police had a duty of care for the lover as well and when she was warned that someone may try to kill her, she packed her bags and off she went to try and lure someone else. Fat Barry probably wasn't that bothered about all the fuss, so long as he got his social money and went down the Magpie on Friday night. At her court appearance Maggie pleaded guilty and received a community order and was now at peace as she had fat Barry all to herself. Maggie blamed the previous undercover officer to me for introducing me and capturing the evidence. She had no idea her friends had instigated the whole process.

Sadly, the Nissan rust box blew a head gasket on the way back to Priestown and had to visit the scrapyard in the sky. Danny was not impressed, but I think I did him a favour.

CHAPTER THIRTEEN

EMPATHY ARRESTS

The evidence gathering phase of Operation Empathy was now coming to a close and the idea was to line all the ducks up in a row and arrest all suspects at the same time. The Mooney family were obviously top of the list and then the different players in the hierarchy would be picked off accordingly. Moored just off the coast of Morocco, the trawler Lady Lily was yet to be loaded with tons of cannabis resin and there had been a serious hiccup when the Moroccan authorities arrested the crew for having a gun on board the trawler. It had also sprung a leak which was waiting to be fixed. Clive Makinson, Carl Tulip and others could be picked off at any time and the authorities out there would merely put them on a plane back to the UK.

The Mooney family were all in residence, as were the majority of lieutenants in the family's drug and money laundering trade. Mick Maybell was the only leading player who couldn't be tracked down. Enquiries with our colleagues at Customs revealed that he had sailed on the night ferry from Hull to Rotterdam two days ago. Intelligence had been received that he was in the Amsterdam area driving his BMW estate to collect a consignment of drugs. UK police officers were at the time not allowed to work on foreign soil and a request from the powers that be for a team of us to go over to Amsterdam and arrest Maybell was flatly rejected by the Dutch. Once we located Maybell, then, it was all systems go and arrest the Mooney team, which consisted of roughly twenty-five middle tier drug dealers and importers.

Early the next morning, Danny and I were told to make our way to Hull docks and await further instructions. There had been a suggestion that Maybell was heading back in that direction and they wanted us in position. We stayed around the docks area for a while before being stood down to a local police station to await further information. We were told to find some accommodation in the early evening and be ready again for the ferry docking early in the morning. This we did and it so happened that the police station had a training facility and some dormitories, which we reserved for the grand price of six pounds a night. We had to find our own breakfast, though.

We asked the local officers if any local hostelries were worthy of a visit and they pointed us in various directions. I was given strict instructions not to go to the Stones Inn on a nearby run down estate. Totally unaware of the conversation I had just had with the local officer, Danny led the way as we trudged around Hull until we came to the Stones Inn on a rather run down estate. Danny went in first, and it was a definite re-take of the scene in the film American Werewolf in London when the two young lads walked into the pub called the Slaughtered Lamb. The whole pub seemed to look at us for what seemed an age, until I went to the bar and ordered a couple of hand pumped pints of bitter, or Thomas Titter if you were with Frank. It was one of the best pints I'd tasted and I let the punters know at the bar. Before I had finished the first pint, the barman had pulled the second and nodded to an older bald headed man at the bar. One of the locals bought me a drink, so I bought him one. Then, the dominos came out and then the pack of cards. What a night it was. We were quizzed as to what we were doing in that part of Hull by the locals but came up with a credible story about meeting our two mates who had been up in Amsterdam who had a car full of cannabis resin to offload. I honestly think we could have taken some orders. We had a great night and after a lock in with the locals, sadly were a little worse for wear as we tried to find our way back to the police station. When we got back, it was locked up and in darkness. A few phone calls later and after closely inspecting our IDs, a patrol officer did the honourable thing.

After a few hours of sleep, we pulled into a small car park on the docks and waited for information from the boss or Ray Ingham. It wasn't long before we were both fast asleep, only to be rudely woken by the rat-a-tat-tat on the driver's window.

'May I ask what you are doing here?' came the voice from the head that peered in through the driver's side window.

I rubbed my eyes and tried to come to my senses, but I saw a warrant card being pushed towards my face.

'Her Majesties Customs Investigation Branch. What are you doing here?' he said once again.

Reaching into my wallet, I pulled out my police warrant card, thinking I would trump his Customs card.

'Regional Crime Squad from Priestown, we are just waiting for further instructions from our boss,' I told him.

'About what? Are you waiting for someone to come off the ferry with drugs? If you are, you are conspiring with them to import them into the UK. I want to know what you are doing here?' he demanded.

'I'm not waiting for any drugs coming off the ferry and I'm not at liberty to tell you what we are doing here,' I replied.

'Right, you are both under arrest. You do not have to say anything……' he continued.

Flippantly, I held my wrists out of the car window so he could put handcuffs on them, should he have any. I knew he wouldn't and I wondered if this was payback time for putting all those drinks on Customs Mike's room bill in Dover. Another car arrived and some more plain-clothed, presumably Customs officers, got out. They were all in conversation and another shorter one wandered over to the driver's side of the Cavalier.

'Alright, lads. We're not trying to be difficult, but you must tell us what you are doing here,' he said nicely.

'Seeing that I'm under arrest and have been told that I need not say anything, I am exercising that right and wish to see a solicitor as soon as possible,' I replied with the best poker face.

'Under arrest, under arrest. Who's arrested you?' he asked.

I pointed at his colleague, who had now removed the battery pack off a new mobile phone from his car. It was huge and he was on the phone with someone. Danny wanted me to get them to ring DI Roberts or Ray Ingham, but I was a little vexed by how the Customs Chief Investigator, Columbo himself, had spoken to me.

As the officers had a group huddle, the force to force radio in the car crackled into life and the operator asked us to contact Priestown office as soon as possible. The Customs officers had other things in mind. They wouldn't let us go until we supplied the boss's details and spoke to him. To make matters worse, when the Customs officers asked our boss what we were doing, he wouldn't tell them either for fear of prejudicing the arrests. It was a stand-off situation and by now, the clock was ticking. We soon learnt that our boys from Operation Empathy were not on the morning ferry. Problem solved. Well kind of.

Eventually, Customs let us go after I had some fun teasing Customs Columbo himself. I wanted him to de-arrest me, but he denied that he'd ever said he was arresting us both. As I was driving slowly off the car park, I shouted that I was going to sue him for false arrest.

'Oh, just fuck off,' he shouted as he flicked a couple of V's at me. Both Danny and I burst out laughing as we made our way back to Priestown.

Ray Ingham had been busy ringing around the hotels in Amsterdam. The Mooney gang had used the Renaissance and Ambassador hotel chains in the past and each of their security departments had been contacted in a desperate attempt to locate Maybell and one other in the black BMW estate. Search warrants had now been obtained for fourteen UK addresses and the number of arrests to be made was twenty-five. There were hundreds of photographs, surveillance logs, financial enquiries and other evidence linking all the team who had conspired with each other to import drugs into the UK on specified dates.

Late that afternoon, the direct line in the office rang. This phone was only used by informants and the like and was always answered blandly, 'Hello, can I help you?' This call was for Ray and it was the security manager from the Renaissance in Amsterdam. Maybell and another foot soldier were resident in the hotel and were checking out the next morning. The security manager was a former Dutch drugs squad officer and Maybell had foolishly asked for the BMW to be valet parked. From the smell alone, the security manager knew it was packed with cannabis resin. This was it. This was the call that everyone had been waiting for. Four years of preparation. All that needed to happen now was for us to contact our law enforcement colleagues in Amsterdam, get Maybell and the other lad arrested and get the car searched and impounded. Once that happened, the domino effect would kick in and all the other drug search and arrest warrants would be executed. There was one big problem. The Dutch authorities would not search the car nor arrest Maybell and the other foot soldier.

We had all been called into the office that Sunday afternoon for a briefing. Once again, family life had to stop and be put to one side whilst the bosses contemplated what to do next. Ray Ingham was continually on the phone with his police contacts in Amsterdam, but their liberal attitude was that the drugs in the car was only cannabis, a Class B drug. Albeit, there was a lot of it. Maybell was also leaving the country, possibly the next day in any case. So, why should the Dutch get involved as it wasn't their problem? It was a UK problem, heading back to the UK. Their attitude was deal with it when it arrives in the UK.

There were several issues with letting Maybell 'run' and come back to the UK. One of them was the legal side involving the importation as it may have been an abuse of process. The State knew about the crime and did nothing to prevent it. It wasn't entrapment as such, but it would be a good argument for any barrister to make. The 'machine' was ready to go now. All the ducks were in line. Briefings were taking place in different offices regarding 'early morning turn out's' as we called them to go and arrest the Mooney gang. We couldn't wait for Maybell to choose when he was coming home if indeed he ever was. If he got wind of the arrests, he would probably head for the Costa del Crime. The gang was also known to leave cars all over the continent and return to them later. Also, if he was arrested in one of the ports, he would have to remain in custody there and not back at Priestown. This wasn't a good situation. Everything depended on the arrest of Maybell and the unknown foot soldier. We needed them arrested now in Amsterdam!

Roermond, in southern Holland, was the location of an IRA attack on a UK serviceman some twelve months earlier. The soldier had travelled to Holland from his nearby base and was assassinated when a number of bullets were pumped into his car. The IRA were still active on the continent and a threat to military personnel. It would appear the Dutch received some good intelligence on that Sunday afternoon. They received a tip-off that two active service members of the IRA, possibly driving a BMW estate on UK plates, had decided to spend the night at the Renaissance Hotel in Amsterdam. Intelligence reports then started to hit the Dutch authorities that late afternoon, suggesting that the said BMW was parked underneath the Renaissance Hotel and contained weapons and explosives. The Dutch authorities could no longer ignore this threat and made covert enquiries with the hotel and were pleased when they spoke with their former colleague, the security manager. He confirmed the details of a BMW estate and that it had just been valet parked in the car park. This was a red alert for the Dutch and the area was immediately sealed off.

A jubilant security manager rang our office to talk us through the events. It appeared that Maybell and another Northshire lad, Jordan Bolton were dragged screaming in handcuffs, after armed police had stormed the hotel and arrested the pair of them in their room at gunpoint. The BMW in the basement car park was sealed off and bomb disposal experts were en route to examine the vehicle. Although it was not good publicity for the hotel, the security manager said it was a pleasurable watch as the armed stormtroopers dragged the squealing pair across the marble floor in handcuffs.

There were smiles in the office and the arrest phase of Operation Empathy was now to commence first thing in the morning. What a stroke of luck it was, particularly that afternoon as well, that the authorities received that intelligence and information about the IRA. Luckily for us it was wrong and Maybell and Jordan weren't IRA active service members but we weren't bothered as it got them both arrested. The Dutch searched the vehicle and only found a quarter of a ton of cannabis, three kilos of cocaine and over a thousand sheets of LSD tabs in false bottom spray cans. The car was full of secret compartments but no weapons or explosives. The authorities in Holland merely confiscated the drugs and escorted Maybell and Bolton to Rotterdam, in the BMW. They were placed on the night ferry back to the UK. On that ferry were four RCS Officers waiting for the ferry to dock and arrest Maybell and Bolton in the UK the next morning.

The office briefing that Sunday afternoon back in Priestown was dispersing and DI Roberts had allocated which house Danny and I were to visit early morning. We had been chatting about the IRA connection when the boss became inquisitive about our conversation. I told him of our night out in Westkapelle and the driver of the car who gave us a lift in the early hours. I explained how he had warned us of an IRA presence in the area and how relevant it was. The boss's facial expression said it all really as his eyebrows met in the middle. It looked like one of those sherbet sweets had just burst in his mouth. He rubbed his chin a couple of times, pointed at me and asked,

'Has this IRA tip-off got anything to do with you?'

Angels, demons and sausage rolls.

***

The 'early morning knock' came for Vince Graham and many other of the Mooney gang that following morning. It was six o'clock as I walked down the path of Graham's house in north Blackton. It was a nice, semi-detached house and would have been expensive. Graham was a lieutenant of sorts for the Mooney family, although he had not really featured in the 'hands-on' evidence. He was a 'behind the scenes' player and the financial investigators had been working hard to chase his movements. He was, I suppose, a 'Mr Fix-It' and being an entrepreneur, he would know how to 'wash' the cash and the ill-gotten gains of the drugs gang.

I looked down at the doorstep and there was a full pint of gold top jersey milk. Some of you reading this won't know what that means, but others will remember the cream on the top and those cheeky little blue tits used to beat you to it. Behind me, there were cops in crash helmets with the odd riot shield in view. A couple of officers had already climbed the fence to the back and I decided to wait another couple of minutes for them to get in position. Dawn had broken and although it was a fresh morning, the sky was blue and I only needed the trusted Levi jacket to keep me warm. Instinctively, I bent down and picked up the milk bottle. I hadn't knocked but I heard the door being unlocked from the other side. It slowly opened and there stood Vince with a large suitcase in his hand. He was casually dressed and looked at me, holding the milk.

'You have my milk bottle in your hand,' he said.

'I do, Vince. Indeed, I do,' I replied.

'Why do you have my milk bottle in your hand?' he asked.

'I'm hoping, Vince, that you will put the kettle on and make us all a cup of tea whilst we search your house with this search warrant,' I answered. He looked at me studiously and considered his reply.

'You'll want this suitcase then, there's another one upstairs,' he said as he put the suitcase down and turned back into his house.

'Please do come in,' he added, 'how many for tea?'

We did a count up and sure enough Vince put the kettle on and took the bottle of milk from me, giving it a good shake before pouring it into the half or dozen beakers on the sink.

'Jim, Jim,' came a shout from an officer upstairs, 'another suitcase in the back room crammed with notes.'

I looked at Vince and raised my eyebrows. Then I looked at the officer with the suitcase that Vince was holding when we came in. The officer had opened it and that too was full of bundled bank notes, probably a thousand pounds in each bundle and folded the drug dealer's way. That was four twenty pound notes all wrapped together and folded neatly inside another twenty note, making a hundred in each wrap. Ten wraps in each bundle meant a thousand pounds.

I raised my eyebrows higher and looked at Vince.

'I'm an entrepreneur. Cash is king. I know it's early but I am on my way to the bank to pay it in officer. Honest,' he smiled.

'Mr Graham, you are under arrest for conspiring with others to import drugs into the UK. You do not have to say anything.......'

Vince smiled and drank his tea. Whilst his house was being searched, he was taken to Blackton custody office where the Mooney family were being taken after their arrest. It was all planned so that the Mooneys could see that some of the key players of their organisation were in the cells with them. No drugs were found at Vince's but a large number of financial documents were seized which hopefully would show that Vince was one of the outlets where the Mooney family could launder their drugs money.

As we all settled around a table in the canteen with our bacon sandwiches, the news was filtering through that Maybell and Jordan had been arrested at Harwich. The Dutch police had put them on the ferry in Holland and made sure they made their way back to the UK. On board and waiting were the RCS officers who bided their time and waited for the disembark call when the ferry arrived in Harwich.

As the two dealers returned to their BMW, the officers moved in and arrested them.

The authorities in Morocco had done exactly the same and after the trawler Lady Lily sprung a leak just off the coast near Essaouira, the crew were sitting ducks. Some of them didn't have passports and all were arrested and put on a plane for London Heathrow. An arrest team were dispatched to Heathrow in what was now a large operation. News was also filtering through that some of the gang were caught throwing kilo bars of cannabis resin out of windows when arrested at their homes and other searches had proved fruitful with drugs found in garden sheds and in specially made compartments. Luckily, there was no more barbed wire in the middle of a farmer's field.

Some twenty people in all had been arrested and after breakfast, it was time to allocate the interviewing teams with the suspects they would be interviewing. I teamed up with Danny once more and we had been allocated the boxer himself, David Mooney. I had seen this man on numerous occasions whilst standing at bus stops, phone boxes and through the eye of a lens. Now, I was going to meet him face to face over an interviewing table.

I went to the cell area and requested that Mooney be removed from his cell for an interview. A rather rotund gentleman stood up and introduced himself as the family solicitor, Mr. Shaw. We shook hands and awaited the appearance of the boxer from the cell corridor. We didn't wait long and David Mooney walked from the dark corridor into the bright lights of the custody area. Unfortunately for him, this wasn't a fight I suppose he wanted. He walked with an arrogance and looked straight ahead. He completely ignored me and greeted his solicitor. He reminded me of Don Johnstone from Miami Vice. He was wearing a light, cotton, beige-coloured jacket with his sleeves pulled up his forearms as Crockett used to do. He wore a light blue Armani polo shirt and expensive looking jeans. His shoes were dark brown suede and highlighted his pale skin with his no socks approach. The shoes looked like they cost a lot. His face had been punched a few times but I thought he would be a lot bigger when he was close up. I tried to introduce myself but he ignored me and we all walked off to the interview room.

After the introductions and legal formalities, we started the interview. I had a plan as such but in today's world, that plan would have been given more thought and been more thorough. Also back in the day, we didn't have to give the suspect or his legal advisor an insight into what the evidence was against them before the police interview. As a result, Mooney and his solicitor were blind as to what was going to come out in the interview. The usual practice in this case was to reply to every question 'no comment' and assess the evidence later when the prosecution team had a duty to disclose all the relevant evidence prior to the trial. My anticipation therefore was Mooney would reply 'no comment' to every question. I wasn't wrong.

The critical evidence I had were photographs of Mooney onboard the trawler, Lady Lily, in various harbours, Girvan, Port Ryan and Fleetworth. He could deny it was himself, but his car was on the quayside and the financial and telephone enquiries had revealed he was in the area and staying at local hotels, paying with his credit card. I had some photographs which I had taken of him loading up the trawler with provisions. It was damning evidence of him associated with the trawler, now stuck in Morocco.

After forty minutes of 'no comment' replies, the C90 tape beeped to say it was coming to an end. Tape recorded interviews with suspects were new and introduced as a result of PACE, the Police and Criminal Evidence Act 1984. That law had also allowed the suspects the right to consult with solicitors prior to a police interview and have them present throughout, as was the case with David Mooney.

'Mr. Mooney, have you ever been to Girvan?' I asked.

'No comment,' came the reply.

'Have you ever been on the quayside at Port Ryan near Stranraer?'

'No comment.'

'What about the quayside at Fleetworth?'

'No comment.'

'Have you ever loaded up a trawler called Lady Lily with provisions?'

This time there was silence and Mooney looked straight at me. He was contemplating something and paused a while. Then, I could see the rage building inside him. Here came the boxer.

'Look, I have never been…..'

His solicitor, Mr. Shaw intervened and told him he shouldn't answer. Mooney turned towards the solicitor and shouted, 'When I want your advice, I will ask for it. Do you understand? You are here to represent and defend me and not to fucking interfere. That understood Mr. Shaw, eh? That understood?'

Shaw sat back in his chair and was probably thinking it didn't matter as he was on the pay roll in any case. He probably got well rewarded. Mooney turned to me, he stared at me and I could see the anger and rage in his eyes. In a very slow and determined response, he said through his teeth, 'I have not been to Girvan, I have not been to Port Ryan and I have never been on the quayside at Fleetworth and never ever loaded a trawler up with anything. Do I make myself fucking clear, you prick?' His eyes never left mine and I could see the scars on his face and where someone had re-arranged his nose. He had a smile on his face but I don't think he found this funny. It was more of a grimace. He was cornered and he didn't like it. He came out of his corner fighting.

'For the purpose of the recording, I am now producing a photograph taken on the sixth of April last year, exhibit number JG47. This photograph shows a white BMW convertible registered number DM10 on the harbour side at Girvan in Scotland. The photograph also shows the trawler Lady Lily in the foreground and you, Mr Mooney, standing on the deck carrying a tray of bread. Is there any explanation you would like to offer Mr. Mooney?'

He stared at me defiantly. He was angry. I think this was realisation time for him. He thought this may have been a quick arrest and maybe a short interview where he would deny everything and be released as the police had no evidence. On this occasion, he was wrong. I went through each photograph, painting the picture for the recording of Mooney in each of the locations, either by the side of Lady Lily or on board. He stared at me intently throughout the process. He didn't speak again.

After a busy couple of days, all arrests and interviews concluded. A prosecuting barrister had been assigned to the Empathy team and after advice, it was decided to lay charges that the gang had conspired with each other to import controlled drugs into the United Kingdom. All the key players in the gang were charged. Father

Anthony Mooney and sons Michael and David were further interviewed about their financial assets. The financial wizards in the investigation team had placed restraining orders on all their belongings and property. They said 'no comment' to every question. Clive Makinson, Carl Tulip, Mick Maybell, Jordan Bolton, Vince Graham and many more foot soldiers refused to answer questions and were all remanded in custody pending their trial. It was the start of another phase of the investigation. Trial preparation.

***

The trial at Northshire Crown Court was set to run for twelve weeks. It had now been over twelve months since the arrest of all the key players in Operation Empathy. There had been a number of legal battles in the meantime, with the Mooney family being granted bail. Father Mooney, Anthony, had become unwell and there was some debate as to whether he should actually face a trial. A number of the foot soldiers had already pleaded guilty and were awaiting the result of this bigger not-guilty trial for their sentences. We were also made aware that the Mooney family hadn't been frugal when hiring their silks. They had the best legal team from London on their case.

There were hundreds of witnesses and it was a very complex situation with some international witnesses being flown in and then either not being required to give evidence or sent away to come back another day. Around the fourth week of the trial, a jury member was stood on the platform of the local railway station on their way home. Two men approached her and said they recognised her from the jury and the trial and asked her if she was frightened of any repercussions from sitting on a jury deciding a case on international drug trafficking. The next morning the jury member reported what had happened to her colleagues on the jury and to the clerk of the court. After a meeting with counsel, sadly, the Judge had no alternative but to dismiss the jury and order a retrial. I think the street term for what happened is called 'jury nobbling'. The Mooneys had got to members of the jury.

Six months later, the second trial started amid tighter security and in a different location. The whole process started again until a jury member received a phone call at home advising her to be extra careful travelling to and from the courthouse, as there were some bad people around. They had obviously followed her home and, again, in their attempt to derail justice, threatened a member of the jury. There was no alternative to abandoning trial number two.

Nearly two years after the arrests, the third trial started at Southshire Crown Court and the Judge made it very clear that the trial would continue whatever happened. All bar the Mooney family had now pleaded guilty to conspiring to import drugs into the UK. They were all waiting for the Mooney trial to conclude so they could be sentenced.

After eleven weeks, the defence barristers closed their arguments, and the matter went to the jury for deliberation. The jury were staying in a local hotel under police guard. After nearly ten days of considering their verdict, excitement was raised when a note was passed to the clerk of the court saying that the jury had reached a majority verdict.

'Would the foreman of the jury please stand,' said the clerk in the packed courtroom. A small man with glasses sat in the far corner of the jury box got to his feet.

'Have you reached a verdict on which a majority of you are agreed?' the clerk asked.

'We have,' the bespectacled man answered.

'Dealing with the indictment against Anthony Mooney (Father) of conspiring to import controlled drugs, do you find the defendant guilty or not guilty?

'Not Guilty,' came the reply.

'Dealing with the indictment against Michael Mooney of conspiring to import controlled drugs, do you find the defendant guilty or not guilty?

'Not Guilty,' came the reply.

'Dealing with the indictment against David Mooney of conspiring to import controlled drugs, do you find the defendant guilty or not guilty?

'Not Guilty,' came the reply.

***

The key lieutenants in the conspiracy, including Makinson, Maybell, Tulip etc. were all sentenced to ten years' imprisonment or more. Seeing that there is an automatic reduction of 50% off their sentence, that meant five years in prison. They had already served nearly two and a half years in custody on remand awaiting their trial, which meant they would be free in two and a half years.

By the time of the trial, many of the investigation team, including me, had moved on. I don't think fingers were pointed or a blame game ensued as to why the main men walked free and only the underlings went to prison. Perhaps it's a fact of life, that's how it happens. Was there sufficient evidence? Yes, of course. Was the jury 'nobbled' again? Who knows. Maybe on the day, the jury weren't convinced, or maybe after eleven weeks or so couped up in a hotel, they'd had enough.

What happened to the Mooney family? Sadly, the father passed away shortly after the trial and the police got the blame for putting an innocent and respectable business and family man through the ordeal. Brothers Michael and David started to rebuild their empire, learning lessons on how to do it better next time. Three years later. Operation Kraken commenced with several specialist officers looking into the criminal affairs of two Blackton brothers called Mooney.

They say crime doesn't pay. I suppose you get the justice you can afford.

CHAPTER FOURTEEN

TIME TO GO

'That Jim Graham?' asked the voice as I picked up the telephone.

'Yes, this is Jim Graham; how can I help you?' I asked.

'You live at 35 Beech Close in Sandford, don't you?' the voice added. I was now listening intently. The caller had my full attention.

I asked, 'Whom am I speaking to?' The caller was indeed correct about my home address.

'I'll be honest, mate, I'm not your biggest fan, but I don't like what's happening behind your back. I've been to your house today with one of your supervisors and they measured your mileage and then checked what you are claiming on expenses. We set the mile counter outside your house, mate and measured the miles to your office. I hope what you claim is correct because if it's not, you're in deep shit.', The line went dead.

I sat there in silence and attempted to take in what I had just been told. Behind my back, a supervisor in the office where I worked had been to my home address, measured the mileage to the office and then compared it to what I was claiming. Each day I had a ninety-mile round trip to get back and forth to work and that is exactly what I claimed. If it was true what the caller said, I could no longer work in such an environment at Priestown. Relationships are a two way thing and built on the pillars of trust and confidence. Both those had just been shattered. I may have done some crazy things in my time and I know I must have been a challenging character to supervise but I am not a thief. It was an attack on my integrity. I worked extremely hard and I admit I played hard. I got the job done and done well. I had a sense of pride in my work and learnt from the time in my uniform days and as a young detective at the hands of the bullies.

I had a very good idea who the supervisor was as he had done similar things to other members of the office in the past. I decided not to challenge him but just bide my time and watch my step. Sometimes you have to pick your fights or get even another way. This was an area I was a specialist in.

I was leaving for work at six thirty every morning and getting home at the very earliest and if I was lucky with the traffic, at six thirty at night. A normal day was a long day. The long days and the weeks away had meant family life had to be sacrificed. After all the years have passed, I still look back and feel guilty about the times the children went to bed with Daddy still at work. I made sure that particular night, I set off for home very early to beat the traffic. I made sure I bathed the kids and put them to bed with their usual story of Meg and Mog. They were growing up quickly.

Elaine and I discussed the future and the situation at Priestown and I knew I couldn't work there any longer. For whatever reason, I was being targeted and I would rather jump than be pushed. The overtime was good and it paid the bills and we would miss the money, but little Andrew was nearly school age, which meant that Elaine could soon return to work. After some reflection, we both decided that in the morning, instead of travelling to Priestown, I would travel to the RCS Headquarters in Southshire and speak with Det. Supt. Macintosh. I would tell him what I had been told and ask to be returned to CID duties in Sandford forthwith.

***

'You are going where I say you are going, young man, and that is to Burnton RCS Office as Acting Sergeant. You have passed your promotion exam, haven't you?' asked Macintosh. Indeed, I had passed the promotion exam but I was waiting for a promotion board interview. 'You will start a week on Monday at Burnton. The DS there has had to fill the vacant Detective Inspector's post. You will fill his post,' Macintosh added.

I travelled back to Priestown and acted as if nothing had happened. I had rung Julie in the office and said that I had been summoned to see Macintosh. The supervisors in the office knew where I was. Nothing was said when I got back but it didn't take long before DI Roberts called me in his office. He had received a call from Macintosh who had told him about my impending departure to Burnton RCS Office. He didn't add much and neither did I. It seemed he'd got his way.

That week I made sure that all my belongings were packed up and I had a quiet drink with those who I was close to in the office, Danny, Frank, Shaun, Mark and the others. It was a great ride and I was sad to leave but it was the right decision. I said my goodbyes and without looking back, drove off the car park and for the final time drove exactly forty five miles home. I wasn't coming back. I had been very privileged to work with some special people and made some wonderful memories in my time at Priestown, but every end has a beginning.

***

'Right lad, you come here with a good reputation,' said Ken Barry, an old-school cop and my new Detective Chief Inspector at Burnton RCS Office. 'All I ask for is loyalty and hard work, Jim,' he added. I assured him of both and spent the next few weeks settling in. There was a new team of officers to get to know and I could just tell from the outset that I would enjoy my time at Burnton, however brief it was. Burnton Office focused on regional and organised crime and not just drugs and it wasn't long before I had a job to 'bring to the table'.

At Priestown, instead of travelling all the way home in the early hours only to return shortly afterwards, I negotiated a cheap rate at a local hotel. I got to know the manager and when I was summoned to the phone at Burnton, I was told it was Keith from the hotel. He explained that one of his receptionists had, in confidence, been telling the other receptionist about her current boyfriend. It appeared that the lovely Simon in his Peugeot sports car was living beyond his means and trying to buy her love by showering her with gifts. Unfortunately, the gifts were stolen, but at least he meant well.

Our Simon had become an expert in empty house frauds. He would visit an area, locate all the empty houses, offices and the like, and then visit the estate agents to get some keys to look around the property, as a potential customer. The older and more abandoned properties were his favourite, and if nine estate agents said he couldn't have the keys to look around on his own, there was always one who said he could. He would inspect the property and when he got the right one, would take all the mail from behind the door and immediately get a new key cut before returning the original key to the estate agents. He would apologise for not renting the property and then go to work researching the mail and the previous occupants. He would build up a profile and each week collect any replies by mail to the premises when he visited in his own time, using his new key. Eventually, when he had enough information, and in the days before money laundering legislation, he would visit the local bank and open up an account using all his fake IDs. Then, he would apply for credit cards and have a carousel system going by paying monthly credit card bills with cheques from other fraudulent bank accounts and pushing his overdrafts to the limit. When the bank or credit card company started to chase him for non-repayment, he merely ditched the cards and the address and found some new premises. Quite ingenious really.

    Anyway, our Simon was travelling far and wide so that if caught on camera, local people wouldn't recognise him. The information from the receptionist at the hotel, via, of course, the other receptionist, was that he was planning a weekend away whereby he would visit exclusive golf clubs in the country and purchase as much of the top quality clothing, golf clubs and the like, as he could. Wentworth, Sunningdale, Royal St. George's and the Belfry were on his list to visit. He never brought the stolen goodies home but had a lock-up near Priestown, which was apparently like Aladdin's Cave. The only thing I didn't know was when our Simon was planning to go on his spree.

    New to the office and wishing to set an example, I worked on the research side of things and mainly corroborated what the receptionist said. Simon was a clean slate and had no previous convictions, but he had a fancy sports car and a nice house and seemed to be out of work. I tried to find his storage location but couldn't locate it. The only thing to do was to follow Simon on his jaunts and catch him in the act. This meant travelling a good distance with overnight accommodation required for staff etc. From the information gathered so far, he would strip out the golf club shops of top-quality clothing and equipment worth thousands.

    There was a buzz around the office as news spread amongst the staff. There was a 'job on' which meant travelling, overnight stays and more importantly, overtime. We could claim a maximum of twenty-four hours authorised overtime in a month. It wasn't a free give away, there had to be a good reason and the boss had to give the nod of approval. Some months, I worked double the hours but only claimed the 24 hours as that is what we did in the day. All I needed now was the weekend that our fraudster Simon was to make the journey and we were good to go.

I received the phone call. The news was in. The golf trip would go ahead that coming Friday, in three days' time. Excellent, I thought, as I shared the news with the office. However, the looks on people's faces when I told them was incongruent with their previous excitement. Ashy stood there as I told him about the weekend job, and the look on his face was like he'd just won two football season tickets for a team in Turkey. He was thankful for the information but looked disappointed at the same time. There was a hush across the room and Ashy disappeared into the DCI's office. It wasn't long before Ken Barry stood at his door and waved me in.

'I believe you've had information that our friend is going to do the golf clubs this Friday then,' he said with a very serious face.

'That's right, boss. I don't know exactly where he's travelling to, but he is aiming to do all the big clubs and wipe them out of stock using the credit cards he's obtained in the frauds,' I replied.

'I think we are going to struggle with staffing it, Jim, that's the only problem,' he added.

'It's not going to be a problem, boss, as I have already 'sorted it out' and I have planned the teams, vehicles and operational order. Everything is done and I think everyone is keen to go,' I said.

'The problem is Jim, and you wouldn't know this as you're new, but Friday is golf day in the office. This particular Friday is extra special as we have drawn Bellchester CID in the Chief Constables Cup. If you can get staff from another office, then fantastic, but we won't be able to cover it,' he said as I tried to comprehend what he was saying. 'It's a shame that because it sounds a great job but any other day except this Friday, Jim,' he added as he stood up and opened the door for me to leave.

The office was empty and there was a deadly hush about the place. One of the team, Lorraine, came in unaware of what had happened,

'You look like you've seen a ghost,' she said as she bit into a large salad sandwich, 'where is everyone?'

Jokingly I said they were all out playing golf to which she very quickly replied, 'No that's only on a Friday.'

***

I was soon distracted by a memo I received inviting me to Westshire Police HQ for my promotion interview to the rank of Sergeant. After passing the promotion exam, the next two hurdles were the 'assessment day' and 'promotion board'. The assessment day I had previously attended. It consisted of group exercises, where I was assessed and then had a 'one-on-one' with an assessor where they gave me a hypothetical situation. I then had to list all the force resources I could remember to assist me in solving the problem, which incidentally involved a missing child. I had horses, dogs, helicopter, fixed wing aircraft, underwater search teams all rolling off the tongue. In reality, none of the resources were ever available! I remember it being a very stressful and emotionally draining day but uneventful. A couple of days later, I was told that I'd passed the assessment day and should prepare for the interview board.

All kinds of rumours were circulating about what questions they would ask you during the promotion interview. Some involved discipline, others involved motivating staff and other general leadership-type questions. I thought I was well prepared as I entered that old board room and looked around at the old carvings and mahogany woodwork. My interview panel consisted of an Assistant Chief Constable, Barry Bannister. An out and out bastard. Next was a Chief Superintendent of an inner city station, Clive Peters, another bastard and finally, an independent person who was part of a new department called Human Resources or HR as it was to be known.

The interview was going well and I was fielding the questions.

'As a shift supervisor on a busy inner city BCU, how will you manage your workload? How will you prioritise your tasks?' asked Bannister.

'Do you mean like spinning plates? How will I spin plates?' I enquired.

'If you want to put it that way, yes, how will you spin your plates?' said Bannister.

'I won't have any problems with spinning plates as my Dad was in the circus, and he taught me how to do it,' I added with a poker face, sitting back inwardly smirking.

I can't really describe the facial expressions of speak no evil, hear no evil and see no evil but all three of them flinched not one bit. They didn't blink. They didn't move, their eyes all trained on me. Humour and alcohol had been great shields for me during my service. Alas, both of them had flaws and this was one of them. I very soon realised that this was not the time nor place to introduce humour. It was like I had just farted and they had all heard it but no one knew what to do or say. We sat there for a good ten seconds before Bannister opened his mouth again. I had an idea what he was thinking.

'You are the custody Sergeant in Sandford Central police station, tell me what are the most important sections of Code C of the Police and Criminal Evidence Act 1984, regarding the detention of suspects,' he asked as he ran his sabre right through me.

I sat there and felt the pins and needles in my head as all three of them glared at me. Quite simply, I didn't know and to make matters worse, he knew that I didn't know. Next move.

'I must apologise for my sense of humour, which I admit was totally inappropriate in something as serious as this. I was trying to break the ice. I'm sorry. As for the question on PACE, again, I apologise as I don't know the answer,' I said with the realisation I was now going to be slaughtered.

Bannister looked directly at me with anger in his eyes, 'Have you prepared for this interview, Constable?' he asked.

'I have, Sir, but I now see I have not prepared as thoroughly as I should have done,' I replied.

'What have you learnt from this for your next promotion interview?' he asked. By now, I was well and truly on the spike and I pulled the best puppy dog face I could as I faced my executioners. He was telling me I had failed and to prepare for next time. Was he?

'I have learnt that I need to learn Code C of PACE because, as a custody officer, that will be my lifeline and I have to be more aware when to use humour, if at all Sir,' I sorrowfully replied.

'I'll give you credit lad for your honesty because if you had tried to bullshit me, you would have failed this interview. Thank you, Sergeant, that's all.'

With that, I got to my feet and surprised them all by shaking all of their hands and thanking them before leaving.

Did he call me Sergeant?

***

I was back in the Burnton office, a little bruised and feeling sorry for myself, when I was contacted by my old office at Priestown, who asked if I would be prepared to go back to Holland to speak with the solicitor in Amsterdam regarding the sale of his yacht to the Mooney gang in Operation Empathy. Obviously, I wasn't going to refuse that little jaunt, was I? I wasn't travelling alone as some financial investigators were also going to Holland to further their enquiries and trace the tentacles of the Mooney money laundering operation.

Once more, I visited the Magistrates Court in Amsterdam to obtain the necessary authority. Then, I traced and interviewed the solicitor about the missing details of the boat purchase. The financial team were trying to close down the Mooney empire. This was, incidentally, before their trial, which I explained in a previous chapter. The trial of the Mooneys et al. took place two years after their arrests.

After travelling around Amsterdam all day and interviewing the solicitor and his colleagues, I had a clear plan for the next couple of days to collect further evidence of the transactions. I had sorted all my flights, accommodations and travel expenses myself. Was it fish for dinner? Who knows, but that life lesson has stayed with me, and far from criticising DI Roberts for leaving me in the lurch that day with Jason Saunders, he taught me a valuable lesson. I am very grateful to him for that. He could have sugar-coated it better with me, but the principle is still the same. Nothing is insurmountable. I am a great believer now that we all possess sufficient intelligence to 'sort it out'. However, when you allow people to sort things out, and they do, then praise must follow. Not criticism! If they don't sort it out, brush them down and start over again.

It was early evening in late August 1991. The sun was going down and it was still very warm in Amsterdam. Right said Fred was blasting out of the bars, telling us he was too sexy. I was sitting with some of the financial investigators enjoying a glass of strong Heineken or two when big Keith walked in.

'I've just rung the office; Macintosh wants to speak with you urgently,' he said as he wafted away the plumes of marijuana smoke. No, I wasn't smoking the stuff, but it appeared that everyone else was. I crossed the canal and went to a quiet phone box on the other side of the walkway.

'Yes, boss, it's Jim Graham, you wanted to speak to me?' I said as soon as I heard his voice on the line.

'Where are you now?' he asked.

'Old Sailor bar in Amsterdam,' I told him.

'What,' he screamed down the phone, 'well, you better get your arse back here and quick. You are being promoted on Friday morning at Headquarters. You are on D shift at Oldtown, and I think you will be on nights on Monday.'

I thanked him and replaced the receiver. Wow! I tried to take everything in as I walked back to the bar and Right said Fred. Here I was relaxed and enjoying a beer in a foreign country whilst gathering evidence and in a few days, I would be wearing a 'big hat' on nights in Oldtown. I had to arrange my uniform and Macintosh had already reminded me of my haircut. There was a lot on my plate before Monday, but don't forget my Dad was in the circus and told me how to spin them.

The KLM flight touched down on Thursday afternoon at Sandford. Operation Empathy, Simon the fraudster were now in the past for me. I now had to visit the clothing stores, have a haircut and re-arrange all my diary. I arrived home to the excited children who had baked Daddy a nice cake with candles on it. Obviously, the candles weren't for me, as the children had to blow them out time and time again. It was a mixed feeling in the family. Elaine was happy that I was nearer home, but I was back wearing a uniform and the dreaded shift pattern of afternoons, nights and earlies. I was a fish well and truly out of water again being a uniformed Sergeant. The other matter at hand was that I was now a supervisor, responsible for a shift of fifteen or so officers.

'Don't worry, Sarge,' said the clothing assistant as he plonked an oversized Sergeants tunic on me, 'everyone is in the same boat. It's like riding a pedal cycle. You will get the hang of it.'

After the swearing in ceremony that Friday morning at HQ, it was confirmed that I was going to D shift at the very busy Oldtown police station, and yes, I was supposed to start nights on Monday. From Amsterdam to Oldtown. What a journey.

I stood in a line of newly promoted staff in the headquarters restaurant, all beaming with smiles about their promotions, but I am sure as anxious as I was about the next steps. The server looked at me inquisitively and I asked her,

'Is it fish for dinner?'

QUEBEC ONE

My Time in Yesterday's Police Force

PART III

James Graham

CHAPTER ONE

INDUCTION PHASE

Oldtown police division, BCU (basic command unit), had a good reputation. There was a saying that most police customers were from the 'bottom block', the psychiatric unit of the local Oldtown and District General Hospital. Indeed, it was the farthest block away from the hospital's entrance, hence its name. I was also told to look out for people wearing white training shoes, which was apparently the 'bottom block' uniform.

'People will present themselves in suits and ties and come across as highly intelligent. My advice to you is to check what they have on their feet before deciding what they are saying. If they have white trainers on, ring the bottom block, as they'll probably be missing from there,' said one advisor.

I was told which bosses to look out for, the ones that would 'do your legs' and the bosses that were 'alright'. The other Sergeant on the shift was Dave Beesley. He had around twenty-five years' service, so he had been around the block a few times. I was told he stood no nonsense. He was a man of few words. Firm but fair. He was liked and disliked. Incidentally, his sister, Amber Beesley, was mentioned in my first book when, sadly, she mixed with the wrong crowd and ended up being another victim of the drug trade. We had some common ground but it wasn't the best topic to open up our first meeting with.

I left home at ten o'clock that Monday night, wearing my potato sack like uniform. Itchy trousers, Van Heusen shirts that rubbed around the collar and some new Doc Marten boots. I had already spoken with Dave Beesley on the telephone and he said he usually got in the office just before eleven to prepare the duties and then brief the shift. I had a lot to take in.

After the thirty minute journey from home, I parked the car on the small police staff car park and noticed a small restaurant overlooking the car park called 'The Blue Lamp'. It was an Italian but closed on Monday. I explained who I was to the staff at the police station public enquiry counter and they opened the electronic door to let me through. It was an anxious time as I found the Sergeant's office on the ground floor. There were some rumours that the police station had been built back to front as it was extremely difficult to get suspects into the custody office. They had to enter the building at the rear and had to climb two flights of stairs. Whereby, at the front of the police station, members of the public walked directly into reception on the same level and the door behind reception led to the custody office. Indeed, it was a weird setup, and it would have been so easy to bring suspects in at the front. My guess is that the chief engineer probably wore white trainers. The station, for some reason, had been nicknamed Quebec One.

I walked into the locker room and I had been allocated a locker with a broken lock. I nodded to some officers who walked past and then put on the tunic with the three stripes. The nods changed to, 'Alright Sarge.' As I entered the Sergeant's office, a female police officer turned to greet me.

'Hiya Sarge, are you Sergeant Graham?' she asked.

'I am indeed Sergeant Graham,' I replied.

'Well, what it is Sarge, I know it's your first night and all that but my boyfriend has been using my car to bring me to work. Anyway, he got stopped for speeding in it over the weekend and he has to produce the insurance. I've checked the insurance and I'm not sure he's actually covered. Can I produce it on his behalf, Sarge?' she asked as I tried to comprehend her request.

'Any Patrol Sergeant available, any Patrol Sergeant please at Oldtown,' came the crackle from the officer's radio. She answered, '2234, I'm with Sergeant Graham now, over.'

'Yes, Oldtown to Sergeant Graham, we have an arson just reported on the St. Margaret estate where the boyfriend has set fire to the flat. His partner has jumped from the window and is injured on the floor. Ambulance en route Sarge, but we have no patrols to send.

There is also a large scale fight at Ali's Kebab house on Queen Street, reports of machetes being used, again Sarge, no patrols available. Sergeant Graham informed at 10.38pm, Oldtown out.'

Before I got a chance to speak to the female officer or tell the communications or 'Comms' what to do about the arson, another Sergeant walked into the room. I knew it wasn't Dave Beesley, but it was one of the Sergeants on the afternoon shift who was about to finish.

'Hiya, is it Jim?' he asked as he held out his hand to shake mine. 'Yeah,' I replied, 'Jim Graham.'

'Right Jim, just a quick run-down but we've got two vehicles off the road. One is in a PVA where a clown has T-boned Geoff as he was on his way to a job, and the other one has seized up, I think. No one has put any oil in, I don't think. You've also got 1589 Doug Wilson gone sick on you mate and I think they're one down in Comms as well.'

I could hardly catch my breath when Dave Beesley walked in, pipe in mouth with a blue trail of smoke following on behind. He held out his hand, 'Alright Jim, fun started already.'

'Sorry to bother you, Sarge, but what do you think about my boyfriend and that insurance thing?' asked the female officer.

'Assistance required patrol, assistance required, Ali's Kebab shop, Queen Street. Any patrol to attend, please? Officer requires assistance,' came the message from now a number of police personal radios that officers were carrying. Footsteps could be heard running down corridors, sirens started in the police station yard, voices were yelling instructions. The afternoon Sergeant that was finishing threw Dave Beesley a set of car keys,

'Come on Jim, grab a radio, let's go. Welcome to Oldtown.'

Printed in Great Britain
by Amazon